GHOST BOG

A JAKE CAINE ARCHAEOLOGY MYSTERY BOOK TWO

STEVEN KUEHN

CAMEL
PRESS
KENMORE, WA

CAMEL
PRESS

A Camel Press book published by Epicenter Press

Epicenter Press
6524 NE 181st St.
Suite 2
Kenmore, WA 98028

For more information go to:
www.Camelpress.com
www.Coffeetownpress.com
www.Epicenterpress.com
www.stevenkuehn.com

Cover design by Scott Book
Design by Melissa Vail Coffman

Ghost Bog
Copyright © 2025 by Steven Kuehn

Library of Congress Control Number: 2024952556

ISBN: 978-1-68492-254-3 (Trade Paper)
ISBN: 978-1-68492-255-0 (eBook)

This book is dedicated to a very special beagle, Piper, who helped me clear the cobwebs on long walks and let me tag along as she labored to clear the yard of rabbits. I still miss you every day, and you will always have a place in my heart.

ACKNOWLEDGMENTS

M Y THANKS TO ERIN WESCOTT AND Jolene Kuehn for their feedback and suggestions on early drafts of this novel. Thanks also to my favorite beta-reader, Dick Daly, for his input and assistance when a fresh set of eyes was needed. I would also like to thank my editor, Jennifer McCord, and the fine folks at Camel Press, for all their help shepherding my novel through the publishing process.

CHAPTER 1

A MUFFLED RUMBLE LIKE THUNDER ECHOED ACROSS the clear sky—but it was not thunder. Death was approaching.

Motionless, ignoring the biting flies and gnats, he stood alone, peering into the brush, keen eyes searching for movement, and watching for any sign of their approach.

He relaxed his grip on his weapon, for just a moment, and then corrected himself as the noise rose again. Or had it? It was hard to be certain, here among the branches and brush.

It was not supposed to be this way. This was not where they were meant to be. His eyes flickered, briefly, in the direction of his brother, also lost among the brambles and leaves and thorns. They should be standing near to one another amidst the vast, rolling grasslands in the lands of the setting sun—not here, in this stinking, wet sea of scrubby trees, clinging vines, and soft ground.

But there was nothing to be done of it, not now. The leaders had brought them here to start anew, far from their old homes. The thunder grew louder again, but less clear. It seemed to fill the land in front of him. On the open landscape, there, there one could see the prey, see your companions, and see when to strike. This was madness; to hunt in this foul place was to invite doom.

A sharp cry cut the air, coming from the north— or was it the west? The rumbling thunder grew in intensity, drumming the very air in front of him. Another shout, louder and clearer, on the opposite side. A massive form crashed through the vegetation a few yards to his right and then another farther off to his left. He raised his arm to strike, uncertain of the nearest target, when another massive phantom burst through the vegetation immediately before him, striking him down before he had a chance to cry out.

The echoing thunder rumbled over him as he lost consciousness. Death had come.

SEVERAL THOUSAND YEARS LATER . . .

"Got some more bones over here, boss."

"Me, too. A whole bunch," another yelled. "I've never seen so many bones in one place!"

A distant rumble like thunder echoed across the clear sky. A few faces look skyward, puzzled, but most remained fixated on the damp earth strewn before them.

With an inward sigh, the boss leaned against her shovel handle and surveyed the meadow bog. "Why do the biggest discoveries always happen on Fridays?"

"Got some over here, too," another said, from a spot not too far away. "Want me to flag it?"

"Going to have to," the boss replied, swatting at a particularly pesky mosquito. A smear of wet black mud appeared on her cheek. "We'll need a good map to show where the remains were found, if we're ever going to figure out what happened here."

A few heads nodded in agreement, but most of the crew continued to work without comment. They knew their business, grim as it might be at times.

"Hey, make sure those bones are tightly wrapped with foil," the boss said, checking on the progress of a nearby digger. "Don't worry about the soil, we'll get everything clean back in the lab."

"This isn't going to make the chief too happy," another person offered, pulling off his mud-stained gloves. He dropped an item into a paper sack and began scribbling notes on the outside of the bag.

"Why not? All the evidence, all these bones, shows that something big happened here."

"Going to take a lot of work to figure it out, though."

"So?" the boss replied. "A little effort isn't much with a case like this. Besides, you know how much Jake likes a good mystery."

CHAPTER 2

Late autumn, one year later . . .

"SORRY WE'RE LATE. THERE ARE CONSTRUCTION zones every twenty miles on the interstate, and it took us forever to get packed up last night. Tough getting going this morning."

"No problem, Sam," Professor Jake Caine called back, smiling. "The Ghost Bog site has been here for 7,000 years. I don't think a few extra hours will make a difference."

"That's what you think," Sam Noggle said, running a calloused hand through his thin gray hair. "Me, I've been waiting my whole career for a site like this one."

"Let me introduce you to the crew," Jake said. "You know Heather, and this is Michelle Fraser, one of my recent grads. She's working in my lab until she starts grad school next semester. Rob Pratt and Curt Shaw are part of the Wisconsin State University contract archaeology crew."

Michelle was in her early twenties, with reddish-brown hair and large brown eyes. Rob and Curt were in their late twenties, each having worked for the Wisconsin State University contract program for the last five years. Rob was thin, about six feet tall, with thinning black hair sticking out from beneath the Cubs cap he wore religiously. Curt was a bit shorter and stockier, with curly dark brown hair and a shaggy beard.

"Rob and Curt were part of the contract crew I had up at the Nushka Lake site a few years back, when we got socked in by that early blizzard," Jake remarked. "So, they're used to harsh working conditions in the frozen north. But hopefully we can finish up here before the snow falls and the ground freezes."

"We damn well better," Sam replied, kicking aside some red and orange leaves that littered the ground outside the dig area. "Ain't like we can come back and finish in spring." The archaeological excavation was part of a property transfer project with the state, and the Department of Natural Resources planned to establish Ghost Bog as a State Natural Area. The official transfer and construction were scheduled to begin on March 1st of the upcoming year.

Sam shook hands with each of them and paused when he reached Heather. "So, you're back at it, huh? Knew you wouldn't stay out of grad school for long."

"Well, the Wisconsin State University archaeology department was falling apart without me, to be honest," Heather said. She was a senior graduate assistant at WSU and would soon be defending her dissertation proposal. Heather had taken some time off from her studies following the Waconah field school the year before, but had returned in time to join the Ghost Bog dig. "Just needed a little time to clear my head. Besides, Michelle will be sure to need my guidance next year."

Sam grinned, then scanned the excavation area with an experienced eye. "Looks like you got a fair amount of the site opened up."

"Yes," Jake said. "We had good weather last week, and the soil over the bone bed is pretty thin. Once the grid was in place, we were able to move a lot of dirt."

The young woman standing behind Sam cleared her throat, getting his attention.

"Oh, right. Everyone, this is Al Lambert, one of the archaeology lab techs at the Lewis and Clark Natural History Museum. Susan Baxter," he said, pointing to the middle-aged woman standing a bit off to the side, "is my assistant, a zooarchaeologist at the LC."

Susan nodded with a polite smile, but she looked warily at her surroundings as she brushed away some curious late-season mosquitoes. Even dressed in jeans, flannel shirt, and hiking shoes, she looked noticeably out of place in the wooded bog.

"Al?" Heather asked.

"Short for Alyssa. Either one's fine." Al had short brown hair with a dyed purple streak on one side. Several tattoos were visible on each forearm, peeking out from her faded and stained sweatshirt.

"What's the 'el-cee' mean?" Curt asked, as Rob nodded in agreement.

"That's just shorthand for Lewis and Clark Natural History Museum," Al replied, pointing to the faded decal on the door of their van. "LC is just a lot easier to say."

"Alright, that's enough chit chat for one day," Sam said. "Too much work to do, never enough time or money. Let's get at it!"

Working together, the archaeologists soon had all the equipment unloaded from the Lewis and Clark Museum van and stowed in a large metal shed at the edge of the parking area. The WSU crew walked back to the dig while Jake took the new arrivals to the far end of the clearing.

"I had Susan and Al read the technical report and the grant proposal on the ride up, so we should be up to speed," Sam said.

"We drove up from the University a week ago, just before Halloween, and spent the first full day clearing the brush and small trees out of the bog. We set up a grid across the site and marked off one-meter squares," Jake said. "Curt and Rob opened up four units at the west end, and Heather and Michelle are excavating those units in the south-central area."

"How far does the site go into the woods?" Al said, pointing toward the tangled mass of brambles, poison ivy, and scraggly trees that bordered the north edge of the clearing.

"Actually, the area inside the lathe and flagging tape is pretty much the whole site. Covers about half an acre, maybe a bit more."

"I thought bison kills were much larger," Susan said, frowning. "What about the big drives and jumps out on the Plains?"

"You do see larger sites like that out there, but in the East the herds tended to be smaller," Jake said. "In Minnesota and Illinois, for example, most of the bison kills may only have a dozen animals represented."

"Bison herds east of the Mississippi were probably isolated groups, eking out a living in whatever grassland habitats they could find. And herd size varies seasonally, too, Susan," Sam said. "Didn't you read those articles on bison ecology I told you about?"

"Well, I meant to, but I hardly had a chance with all the time spent packing," Susan snapped. "And you insisted that I had to identify all the bones from the Nolan site before we left, too."

Al reddened a bit, with the air of a child embarrassed when their parents argue in public. Sam shook his head but didn't reply. Jake was a bit surprised by their rancor, but assumed they were both simply tired and stressed out from packing and the long drive.

"So, Jake. Where should we get started?" Al asked, breaking the awkward silence.

"Susan and I can start a block of units in the middle," Sam said, ducking under the flagging tape. "Should be plenty of bones right dead center."

"Uh, okay. Sounds good," Jake replied as Sam hurried off, Susan trailing behind him. He turned to Al. "I guess you're stuck with me, then. I've got some units started on the east edge of the clearing. Might not get as much bone as Sam and Susan, but at least we're close to the screens and backdirt pile."

Jake led Al across the uneven ground to their dig spot. She pulled a floppy brimmed hat and worn gloves from her backpack while Jake explained their excavation methods.

"This 2 by 2 meter square overlaps the east edge of the site. I've already shoveled off the top 30 centimeters; it's all sterile soil, no artifacts at all. The bone bed shows up about 35 or 40 centimeters down, so from this point we'll trowel down by hand."

"Leaving all the bones in place, right?"

"Right. Once we've exposed the bones and any artifacts that turn up, we'll map everything and take a bunch of photos. Collect all of the soil in these buckets, and then screen it over there in case we miss anything."

Al nodded. "How far down does the bone bed go?"

"Maybe 15 or 20 centimeters. Nothing has been found below 60 centimeters, so that's where we stop. There's a distinct yellow clay at that depth so you can't miss it."

"Cool." Al stood on one side of the excavation block and glanced at the clipboard with the unit paperwork. She scanned it for a moment. "Looks pretty simple. I've used forms like this before."

Jake pulled his trowel from his back pocket, took up position on the opposite side of the unit, and they began carefully scraping away the moist, black soil. They worked in silence for a few minutes, and soon bits of reddish-brown bone appeared from beneath the ground. More dirt was removed and additional fragments emerged, along with some large specimens and complete elements.

"Looks like the edge of a metatarsus there," Jake said, pointing to a large bone on Al's side of the unit. "Trace it back along the edge and see if there are any ankle or toe bones present."

"It's wild to think that 7,000-year-old bones are still preserved here, just a few feet below the surface," Al said, pulling a paintbrush and sharpened wood dowel from her dig kit. She gently scraped away more soil and soon several cylindrical toe bones were exposed.

"Yeah, I guess so," Jake said as he brushed some loose soil from a series of flat bison ribs. "It was pretty dry in the bog when the survey crew went through last year, otherwise they may not have been able to test out here. Hate to think that they might have missed one of the oldest bison kills east of the Mississippi River."

A few sluggish mosquitoes drifted down, seemingly to inspect the bones for themselves. Jake topped off the soil in one bucket and pulled an empty one in as a replacement.

Al shifted position to reach another large piece of bone. "I've got a little more space in this bucket, then I'm going to screen. Okay?"

"Sure. I'll clean up this quarter and do the same. There's some foil in the toolbox if you need to wrap up any small, fragile bits of bone." Jake stretched his back and looked across the clearing. Heather and Michelle were busy mapping the bones in their unit, and Curt and Rob were screening. Sam was troweling furiously while Susan sat on an overturned bucket, fanning herself with a plastic dustpan. Jake had known Sam for years but had rarely seen him so excited. Obviously, his idea to include Sam and the Lewis and Clark Museum in a joint excavation was a wise move.

It hadn't been entirely selfless, however. Excavation of a site like Ghost Bog, almost unique east of the Mississippi River, represented an amazing achievement for the Wisconsin State University Archaeology Department. Involving the highly regarded Lewis and Clark Natural History Museum ensured the site's prominence in the scientific community. Jake's role as site director would undoubtedly help his chances for tenure and advancement.

"Hey, I have to ask," Al said. "Why did they name the site 'Ghost Bog'?"

"That's the name the locals have for this spot. It's right on the edge of a larger wetland, sort of a timber swamp and marsh habitat. It floods some years, but still fits the ecological definition for a bog." Jake paused to pour another scoopful of soil into the bucket. "But this particular location," he continued, in a low voice, "...has a special reputation. Eerie lights dancing among the trees, ghostly voices carried on the wind. Not a safe place to be after dark. Supposedly."

"Oh, sweet. We definitely have to camp out here one night!"

"You're braver than I am," Jake said, grinning. "But it's starting to get pretty cold at night. To say nothing of roaming bears, looking to fatten themselves up before hibernating."

"It would be worth it," she replied, laughing. "I grew up on scary movies. What could be cooler than a mystery at an archaeological site? Besides, it's not like there was a murder here or something."

A stray cloud blocked out the sun for a moment, and a shiver ran down Jake's back, despite the warmth of the autumn afternoon. Murder at an archaeological site was not something he would have thought possible, either, until Waconah. Returning his attention to the loose soil and bone in his unit, he was thankful that lightning rarely struck twice in the same spot.

CHAPTER 3

THE ARCHAEOLOGISTS WORKED STEADILY FOR THE remainder of the day, stopping only as darkness began to engulf the clearing. Sam wanted to stay longer, arguing that if they purchased construction floodlights, they could extend their excavations at the site for a few additional hours each evening. Not surprisingly, there was little enthusiasm for his suggestion.

The crew arrived at Ghost Bog early the next morning, although some of them moved a bit sluggishly in the cold morning air. Sam was not among them, however, as he had rambled incessantly since they left the hotel.

"I just think it's weird, that's all," Sam said, pulling his battered backpack from the back of the Lewis and Clark Museum van. "I mean, what kind of slogan is *The Littlest County with the Biggest Heart*?"

"It's too cutesy," Heather agreed, as she checked the supplies in her dig kit. "They're really reaching to find something interesting about this town."

"It's not that odd," Jake said, setting a cooler on the ground. "Kohl County is the smallest county in Wisconsin, and Scenic is the only big town in the county. They're right on the edge of the northern vacation area, so they put out the welcome mat for visitors. Peter said tourism pretty much runs the economy in the community."

"Who's Peter?"

"Peter Holcombe. He's one of the county officials, and I think their unofficial local historian," Jake said, walking over to Sam's van to assist with the unloading. "He helped us out with some maps and legal documents, back when the survey started. Really interested in archaeology. Been out here a couple of times since we started."

"I hope that's not going to be a problem," Sam said, spraying some bug repellant on his exposed skin. Despite the waning summer temperatures, the mosquitoes and flies were still active in the bog. Heather coughed loudly and walked away quickly to avoid the fumes.

"What's that?"

"Visitors, at the site. We're never going to get all our work done if we have to stop every half hour to entertain a bunch of gawkers."

"It won't be that bad. Besides, we want to stay on good terms with the locals," Jake said, reaching for a long leather case. "Hey, what about this?"

"Hmm? Oh, that's just the museum's shotgun."

"What do you have this along for?"

"Oh, I always have it in the van when I'm out in the field," Sam said, unzipping the case and pulling out the gun. "It's just a little .410, with bird shot for collecting specimens for the zoology comparative collection."

"Do you think it's a good idea to have it banging around in the back of the vehicle? It's not loaded, is it?"

"Course not. Shells are in this little box here." He slid the gun back into the case. "We're in northern Wisconsin with hunting season right around the corner. I bet every truck in the county has a gun in it."

Jake shrugged. "Still, I'm not sure . . ."

"Look, if you're gonna get all fussy on me, I'll lock it in the shed, okay? I don't expect I'll have time to do any collecting on this trip anyway."

"Fine, I didn't mean to start anything," Jake said, and tossed the padlock key to Sam.

"Susan, go ahead and uncover our units," Sam said, his stern voice echoing across the clearing. "I'll pull the paperwork from the site notebook after I put the shotgun in the shed."

Susan nodded but didn't show any particular enthusiasm for the upcoming work. Jake started off to join Al at their excavation spot when Heather and Michelle intercepted him.

"Hey boss," Heather said, glancing at her sketch map. "You want us to keep exposing the big bison at the north edge of our unit, right?"

"Yeah," Jake said. "Looks like most of the rib cage is there, so they may have only butchered part of the carcass. I want to see how much they left behind."

"I think I have part of the pelvis, too, near the wall," Michelle added.

"Good. After you map the north wall, open another 1-by-2 in that spot and bring it down to the bone level. Then we'll map the whole animal and take it out."

"Okay, but it'll probably take most of the day to move all that soil," Heather said. Both girls looked dubious.

"Has to be done. Why? Is that a problem?"

"Sam said we have to hustle on this project. You know, get out as much bone as we can before we close down for the season."

"When was this?"

"He was really adamant about it last night at the diner," Michelle said.

Heather nodded. "And this morning, on the ride over in the LC van."

"There's plenty of time and money in the budget to excavate twice as much as we proposed in the research plan," Jake said, frowning. "Sam's probably just . . . overly excited about the bison kill. It is a unique find for Wisconsin. Look, keep working like usual. No rushing and no short cuts. Okay?"

Both women agreed and went back to their units. Jake made a mental note to remind Sam that quality work was more important than speed, particularly here. With a site this significant, they couldn't afford any mistakes.

His reverie was interrupted by Al. "Jake, do you want a photo of these articulated elements?" She had uncovered their unit and was brushing away some loose soil from a series of closely packed bones. "It was starting to get dark when we took those photos last night, so I thought you might want some with better lighting."

"Yeah, let's do it. They look pretty good on the map we drew, but you can never have enough detailed field photos."

Al cleared away some more dirt while Jake set up a small dry-erase board, photo scale, and north arrow on the far side of the exposed elements. The site name, unit number, and other provenience info were written on the board. Al took the photos, and Jake recorded the exposure numbers on the unit paperwork. With that task accomplished, they began to carefully remove each bone, placing it into a bag with a number corresponding to its designation on the map.

Throughout the morning, the scraping of trowels against soil and muted conversation were the only sounds arising from the group, while birds sang amidst the remaining red and gold leaves rustling in the nearby trees. Shortly before noon, the muffled crunch of tires on gravel broke the quiet solitude.

"Got some visitors," Al said, glancing up.

"Oh, yeah." Jake looked over as two vehicles pulled to a stop, and then checked his watch. "Right on time. I thought Peter might stop by today. Excuse me a second."

Jake walked to the edge of the site and ducked under the flagging tape surrounding the excavation area. The visitors were milling around their cars as Jake approached, smiling, and gave a wave to Peter.

"Hello, Peter. I thought you might stop by this morning."

"Hope we're not intruding, Professor," Peter said, adjusting his glasses. He was slim and slightly built, with thinning hair and a pronounced comb over, and dressed in his usual gray slacks, pale blue dress shirt, and Town of Scenic windbreaker. A tall, heavy-set man with reddish-brown hair stood at Peter's side, sharply dressed in a dark blue suit. Both men appeared to be in their early fifties. Another six men and women assembled behind them, some of whom also wore Town of Scenic attire. One or two had cameras at the ready, and most were looking about expectantly.

"Not at all. Always happy to show guests around the site."

"May I present Mayor Michael Greene?" Peter said, nodding to the man standing to his left. "He's been quite anxious to see what you've been finding out here."

The mayor shook Jake's hand enthusiastically. "Pleasure to meet you, Professor Caine. Lucky Mike Greene, that's what my friends call me! Peter's been raving about the great things you've been finding out here. Imagine, 10,000-year-old buffalo bones, right here in our county!"

"Well, not quite that old, but thank you," Jake said. "At 7,000 years old, it still represents the oldest bison kill east of the Mississippi."

"Ten, seven, what's the difference? Can't get bogged down in details. It's my job to run the whole county! Petey here, he's the bean counter down at city hall."

Mayor Greene roared with laughter at his own cleverness, and most of the new visitors joined right in, at least half-heartedly. Jake caught, ever so briefly, a scowl on Peter's face, but it vanished as quickly as it had appeared. Maybe he imagined it.

"I thought you were in charge of zoning and maps?"

"I am," Peter said, smiling again. "But I'm also the town financial officer, county tax assessor, registrar of deeds, and a few other things. It doesn't make sense to have overlapping jobs, so Scenic and Kohl County all work under one management system."

"It's a pretty small county, Professor, so nearly everyone serves in more than one position," Mayor Greene added. "None of the departments warrant a full-time position, 'cept the mayor's office, of course." More laughter followed, weakly echoed by his impromptu chorus.

"Let me introduce you to the rest of our little group," Peter said, as the noise died down. He introduced each person in turn, describing the multiple duties each person was responsible for in the Scenic County or city government.

Jake greeted each one, shook their hand, and hoped he wouldn't be quizzed on their identities later. He then led them on a brief tour of the dig, keeping them outside the active excavation area. Heather and Michelle's unit, densely packed with bison bones, was of particular interest and became the preferred photo-op for the group. Curt and Rob scored a few fans with a small scatter of lithic chipping debris and the tip of a large spearpoint. Jake even cajoled Sam into showing the visitors a rather large humerus, complete with cut marks. The guests were genuinely impressed. Sam answered their many questions with good humor, but Jake could see he was impatient to return to his digging.

"Val, come up here and get a shot of me with this leg bone thing," Mayor Greene announced, waving over a short, brown-haired woman with a massive camera bag over her shoulder. She had been standing a few yards away, taking photos of the entire excavation area, but rushed over in response to the mayor's shout.

"Valerie Lamont runs the *Scenic Sentinel*," Peter said, noticing Jake's bemused expression. "She's also head of the Tourism Board, and her husband is the school superintendent."

Valerie took a few photos of the mayor at different angles, and then paused to change lenses. "This is wonderful, Professor. Would you be willing to give a presentation on your dig to the students this fall? I'm sure they would be thrilled."

"Fantastic idea, Val," Mayor Greene said, before Jake could reply. Sam stood a few feet away, cradling the returned humerus, and glared as the mayor continued. "A couple of public lectures at the community center would be a big draw, too. But long term, that's what we need to be thinking about. How about some display cases, with artifacts from the site? Throw in some photos of the dig, a little background text, and we could scatter them all over town."

Sam let out an angry, garbled response, loud enough that everyone could hear but not clear enough to be understood. Jake spoke up to curtail any trouble.

"Once the excavations are finished, we'll be busy with the analysis and report preparation for quite some time. After that, it might be possible to send a few items up here on a temporary loan. Or we could create some replica items for a display and donate those to the county." Jake turned to Valerie and handed her his business card. "And of course, I'd be happy to come back this fall and talk to the students."

"Great, great! Larry, be sure to coordinate with Val and get some of the photos up on the Scenic website, right away," Mayor Greene said. "And we'll need some details on what they're finding out here."

"We have some information sheets on the dig that might help," Jake said. "They summarize the age and nature of the site, images of some of the bones and stone points that we've found, and a little bit on bison ecology and just how important this site is."

Peter nodded in agreement. "I still have some of the copies you gave me when you started." He turned to Mayor Greene. "It should have all the info we need."

"Good. Pete, make sure you write it all up real public friendly. No offense, Professor, but we can't use anything too technical or it'll bore everyone to death."

"Not a problem, I understand."

Out of the corner of his eye, Jake caught sight of Sam, handing the humerus to Susan before throwing his hands up in the air in frustration. He stomped off toward the equipment shed, where he stayed hidden until the mayor and his entourage had left.

CHAPTER 4

T HE REST OF THE DAY PASSED without incident. Sam was unusu-
ally subdued during the lunch break but by midafternoon was
back to his usual self. The absence of further visitors to the site
may have made a small contribution to his improved mood. Jake
decided to let the morning pass without comment but resolved to
discuss it that evening if the opportunity arose.

At the end of the day, the crew returned to their hotel and
cleaned up before heading over to a Chinese restaurant for dinner. Susan declined, blaming it on a migraine, and Curt and Rob
went off to a nearby sports bar to watch a game. After eating, Jake
and Sam returned to their room and started reviewing the day's
paperwork.

Before Sam had arrived, Jake moved his luggage and assorted
boxes off the second bed and stashed these and other items in the
corner. Although space was limited, doubling up saved money for
the dig and upcoming analysis. Even so, there was barely room to
maneuver.

This evening, stacks of field forms and related paperwork were
strewn across one of the beds, and the desk was buried beneath a
large hand-drawn map of the site, showing each excavation unit
along with notes on the bones and artifacts recovered from each

location. Jake and Sam sat nearby, checking forms and recopying significant information in the site notebooks. Two bottles of beer sat on top of the mini fridge, like little soldiers awaiting orders.

"Bone count is dropping in Curt and Rob's west units," Sam said, tapping a pencil against his clipboard. "Maybe we should move them down here, toward the center."

Jake peered at the artifact count listed on the map. "They're still getting lots of lithic debitage, though, and they had that spearpoint fragment from the east half. How about if they open another set of units to the east? We can see if the artifact concentration continues, and in any event, they should find more bones."

Sam nodded and penciled in some small squares on the map.

"Al and I will be done with our units soon," Jake said, before pointing to another location on the map. "After that, I thought we'd start digging over here, maybe work along the edge and then start pushing toward the center."

Sam studied the map with a critical eye. "That should be good, as long as it doesn't take too long. If Susan and I open these units next, we can join up this whole area as one big excavation block."

"I don't anticipate any problems. Al knows her stuff and works fast."

"Yeah, she's got a couple of years under her belt, workin' digs in Missouri and Iowa, mostly." Sam paused, studied the map, and then drew in another set of units in the untouched area between his units and those to the north and west. "Your crew is doing good work. Moving a fair amount of dirt, and their notes and paperwork are good and thorough."

"Curt and Rob each have about ten years field experience, and Heather's been working with the contract program on-and-off since she was an undergrad," Jake said. "They all know the pressure we're under to finish this project on time, and under budget."

"Must be tough on you, teaching full time and running the contract archaeology program," Sam observed. "Me, I never cared much for the logistics side of field work."

"Someone had to take over when the former director left. No one else in the Archaeology Department was interested, or willing. If I hadn't agreed, there's a chance they'd have shut the whole thing down."

"That would have been a damn shame. But still . . ."

"It'll be alright. I'm only the *acting* director anyway," Jake said. "If this project is successful, I'm sure the Department will hire a full-time director next spring."

Jake was keenly aware of the value the contract archaeology program brought to the Archaeology Department, in terms of outside funding, student opportunities for field and lab work, and research prospects. Despite the added workload, he was excited to continue as the director. The recognition from the Ghost Bog dig would serve as a strong argument in his favor, to say nothing of added job security and helping with his push for tenure.

"What about Michelle?" Sam asked, shifting topics. "She's a bit younger than the others," Sam said, scratching at a mosquito bite on his forearm.

Jake shrugged. "Michelle's a little green, but she has a strong work ethic and a good attitude. And she's interested in zooarchaeology, so she was pretty excited for a chance to work on a kill site. Besides, I needed another female to balance out the room assignments."

"That tight budget is gonna hurt us down the line, Jake," Sam said, voice raised. "Wish we could have just camped out at the site, like we did in the old days."

Jake forced himself to not roll his eyes, having addressed this same argument months earlier during the planning process. "Northern Wisconsin weather in November is too unpredictable. Crawl into your tent at night and wake up buried in snow. Besides, you have to add in the costs of a camp kitchen, bathroom facilities, all of that. Rough days are easier to handle knowing you have a warm room and hot shower waiting for you back in town."

"At least the weather is decent, for now at least," Sam said.

"How is Susan doing?" Jake asked. "Not to pry, but she's not a field person, is she?"

"That obvious, huh?" Sam chuckled, and then took a sip of his beer. "No, she's been a lab tech her whole career. Knows her bones, though, and since she'll be working with me on the analysis, I figured it would be good experience for her. You know, see how the bones are distributed, get a better understanding of element articulation, that stuff."

Jake nodded. "Makes sense. It'll probably take her a few days to pick up the ins and outs of fieldwork."

"She'll be fine. Actually, Susan almost insisted on coming along, back when you first called me about the project."

"Hmm. Guess she thought it was something so unique that she didn't want to miss out."

"Definitely. Who could pass up the opportunity to work on a bison kill, this old, and in northern Wisconsin, of all places? It's the archaeological find of a lifetime! Hell, the data we pull out of Ghost Bog could rewrite our understanding of early Archaic life across the Midwest."

Jake took a sip of his beer. "You're right, Sam. But . . ."

"Here we go."

"You're going to have to relax, let up a bit. The crew is doing a fantastic job and we're already ahead of schedule. And we are going to see more visitors." Jake raised his hand before Sam could respond. "I'll take care of the public relations stuff, okay? This is a WSU project anyway, so it falls on my shoulders. You just focus on the excavation."

Sam stared at Jake for a few seconds, eyes sullen under his bushy, furrowed brows.

"Fine," he said finally. "I know I'm comin' across kinda intense, but you can't blame me. This is *the* site, Jake, the kind of site I've been looking for all my life. It can be the biggest, most important thing I've ever worked on. The most significant project of my career! And maybe the last chance I'll have to make my mark in zooarchaeology!"

"What are you talking about? You've worked on dozens of important projects. And you've got lots of good years ahead of you yet."

"Maybe," Sam said. "But I'm not going to let anything interfere with this excavation. Anything. And that's the truth."

CHAPTER 5

"HEY, WHERE THE HECK DID THESE dogs come from?"
Sam's outcry got everyone's attention, but only Susan looked alarmed. She attempted to shoo the larger dog away from the edge of her unit, but the dog simply wagged her tail and dashed over to Al. Al knelt to pet the dog, who immediately rolled onto her back.

"Relax, Sam," Jake said, removing a glove to pet the smaller, gray-colored dog. "This is Shadow, and the rambunctious one over there is Gypsy. They belong to the landowners, the Emersons."

"Speaking of which, here they come," Heather said, pointing in the direction of the house on the opposite side of the meadow.

Jake caught Sam muttering under his breath. "Behave yourself, Sam," Jake said in a quiet but firm voice. "This is private land, and we're only here thanks to their good graces. After we found the site last year, we explained its significance and they were thrilled. In fact, they insisted that the archaeology had to be done *before* they'd sell the property to the government."

"Huh. Guess that makes them unlike every other owner I've had the misfortune to deal with. Most of 'em can't sell fast enough. All they see are dollar signs."

"Harold and Vera aren't like that at all," Jake said, shaking his head. "He improved the access road and used his tractor to haul the shed over for us to use."

"I see the pups made it here afore us," Harold called out, waving, as he and his wife reached the site. "Course, they're a few decades younger than us, well, younger than her, at least!"

"Oh, Harold, you hush now," Vera said, holding up an old wicker basket. "I've brought some snacks. You children need to keep your strength up."

"Mmm, I smell cookies!" Heather, Curt, and Rob crowded around Vera. Michelle and Al soon joined them, and Vera beamed with pride as the diggers devoured and raved about her cookies.

"Shack working out for ya, then?"

"Yeah, thanks again, Harold," Jake said. "We're finding tons of bones. We'd never be able to fit all of them in our rooms back at the hotel."

Harold nodded, glancing at the open units and all the exposed bison remains. "Glad you could use it. We didn't have any use for this old shack anymore, and it weren't no big thing to drag it across the meadow." He squinted at Sam, seeming to notice him for the first time. "Got some more helpers?"

"Oh, right. Harold, this is Dr. Sam Noggle, a zooarchaeologist from the Lewis and Clark Museum in Missouri. He'll be analyzing all the bones we dig up."

"Nice to meet you," Sam said, shaking Harold's hand. "I, uh, really appreciate you letting us excavate this site. Nothing like it any place east of the Mississippi."

"So, you're the bone guy, huh? I got some old bones in a box up to the house. You're welcome to 'em, if you want."

"Well, thank you. That's mighty nice of you," Sam said. He reached down to pet Shadow, who was sniffing around at his ankle. "Never saw a beagle with so much dark gray hair before."

"Yeah, he's got some odd mix in his background, I think. Only one in the litter like him." He pointed to the tri-colored dog, now sniffing diligently along the edge of the clearing. "Gypsy, she's the hunter of the pair. Always bringing back squirrels, rabbits, and the like. Never eats 'em, but sure is proud to show off her catches. Even had a duck once. Not sure where she found that. I suppose the duck was flying over and decided the bog would be a good spot for a nap."

Both archaeologists laughed, and the conversation drifted into small talk about the recent spate of warm weather and various events in town. Jake took some extra time to point out some of their more interesting finds, including a heavily worn stone knife and the tip of a spearpoint, found lodged between two ribs. Sam added a few comments about the bones and the overall significance of the site. He was on his best behavior, but Jake could tell by his demeanor that he was anxious to return to work.

"This always has been an unusual area," Harold said, handing the artifacts back. "Not just the special bog plants, neither. Supposed to be haunted, of course, and all sorts of legends about this place. Most of 'em not so good."

Sam continued to fidget, obviously afraid that Harold would continue with an extended tale about the local spirits. Fortunately, Michelle came to the rescue.

"Professor Caine? When you have a moment, I have some questions about the bone group in my unit."

Jake nodded, and Harold seemed to take the hint. "Well, you folks are busy, so we'd best get out of your hair," he said with a smile. "C'mon, Vera. You're gonna fatten these kids up so much they won't get a lick of work done."

"They work hard and they've earned them, Harold. You had more than your share this morning before we left, and you haven't done a bit of work in the last two months!"

"You tell 'em, Mrs. Emerson," Heather said, popping the last bit of cookie into her mouth. "Mmm, mmm! Gotta keep my energy up for digging out these bones."

Harold chuckled and shook his head. "Well, I'll bring those bones over in a day or so. Might take a bit of digging of my own to find 'em all."

"Thanks," Sam said, already returning to his unit, where Susan had begun to scrape more dirt into a pail. "I do appreciate, um, everything you folks have done."

"Happy to help out." Harold turned to Jake, and fixed him with an odd, knowing stare. "You do be careful, though. Never can tell with legends."

SAM'S MOOD WAS NOTABLY IMPROVED FOLLOWING the Emerson's visit, aided by his discovery of two more nearly complete juvenile bison skeletons in the 2-by-2 meter excavation block he and Susan had recently opened. He was digging even faster than before, and Jake sent Al over to help Susan screen from time to time. As the workday drew to a close, Jake went to the water cooler to refill his canteen and bumped into Susan, taking some bandages from the first-aid kit. The cover of the kit was spattered with fresh droplets of blood.

"Are you okay?"

"Oh, yes, I'm fine," Susan said, attempting to staunch the seeping cuts with a tissue. "Just a few nicks from the screen."

Jake frowned, seeing multiple small cuts and deep scrapes on both hands, as if she had been rubbing them with sandpaper. Her flowered gardening gloves, tossed nearby, were shredded.

"Those gloves really aren't tough enough for fieldwork," Jake offered. "We've got some heavy leather gloves in the shed. Want me to grab a pair for you?"

Susan nodded, wincing as she cleaned her hands with an alcohol wipe.

"I could have Al help Sam screen for a while tomorrow, give you a chance to rest up. Michelle and Heather could use some help mapping their finds . . ."

"No. No, that's not necessary," Susan snapped. "I can handle the work, you know."

"Okay. No offense meant. This is a group effort, that's all. Don't be afraid to ask for a little help now and then if you need it."

She didn't reply, so Jake went to the shed and after a few minutes searching, found two small pairs of gloves. He brought them back to Susan, who took them with a mumbled thank you. She brushed a hand across her cheek, and Jake thought she might have been crying. Before he could say anything, he spotted the wicker basket, a few feet away.

"Whoops. Looks like Mrs. Emerson left her basket behind again." He walked over to retrieve it. When he turned back around, Susan had risen and was halfway back to her unit. Jake sighed, uncertain if he should pursue the matter, but decided against it for the time being. He told Al that he was going to return the basket and would return shortly.

Jake followed the well-worn if somewhat circuitous dog path across the meadow to the Emerson's home. As he stepped onto the porch, Mrs. Emerson met him at the door.

"Oh, so that's where my basket had disappeared to! Thank you, Professor."

"My pleasure, Mrs. Emerson," Jake said, smiling. "You know, you're spoiling us with all these treats. I think my crew would like it if I hired you on full-time as our camp cook."

"You flatterer, you," Mrs. Emerson said. "Would you like some cranberry pie? I could bring you a piece, out here. I'd ask you in but Harold is napping in his chair."

"Sounds delicious, but I need to get back to the dig. Besides, I wouldn't want the crew to find out you're giving me special treatment over here." Jake gave her a wink, and she laughed.

"Oh, you are a devil, young man. Well, off you go then. Wait. Did Harold tell you about Keith?"

"Keith? No, I don't think so."

"That man! I don't know how I put up with him. Our nephew, Keith, is a lawyer who works part-time for the county. He's very interested in archaeology and promised to stop by your dig one of these days."

"I'll be sure to give him the grand tour. I can even let him help out with some screening and digging, if he wants."

"That would be just perfect," Mrs. Emerson said. "Keith is such a darling boy, and pretty much the only family we have left. Always stopping by to check on us. Well, as much as he can. So busy, all the time! But he was ever so excited when he heard about your finds in the bog. It's all he could ask about, every time he called."

"He sounds like a great guy. Tell him he's welcome any time."

"You'd best hurry along now, dear. There's a cold front moving in, so you'd all best bundle up tomorrow."

Another ten minutes passed, while Mrs. Emerson described how quickly the local weather could change, and then insisted he take a tray of brownies so his crew wouldn't get hungry driving back into Scenic. As he escaped back across the meadow, Jake began to worry that his crew would soon grow too large to fit comfortably in their excavation units.

CHAPTER 6

As Mrs. Emerson had predicted, the November winds shifted during the night, bring in a cool blast of arctic air. It was noticeably colder the next morning, with a sheen of frost visible on the tarps covering the Ghost Bog excavation. The archaeologists stamped their feet and blew on their hands to keep warm. Someone made an offhand remark about fall giving way to winter, and Sam had a minor fit in response, arguing for longer work hours, the purchase of a barn heater, and working over the weekends. So much for learning to relax.

The crew started out slowly but was back up to speed by mid-morning, aided by the increasing warmth of the rising sun. Even Sam had mellowed, but it didn't last.

"What, another one? Dammit, Jake, did you sell tickets to this excavation?"

Jake's broad shoulders sagged as he stood up, only to see a fancy white SUV with out-of-state plates pull to a stop at the far edge of the parking area. Rather than attempt to placate Sam, once again, Jake slipped past him and set out to greet the new visitors. By the time he ducked under the flagging tape, Sam had stopped grousing and was back scraping soil away from a bison spinal column.

Three people stood expectantly by the side of the SUV. An older gentleman, about Sam's age, appeared to be in charge. His beige slacks, tweed jacket, and shiny loafers were decidedly out of place in the forest; he obviously wasn't there to offer his services as a volunteer. A bearded man in his late twenties was leaning against the vehicle, looking somewhat bored, while a smiling young woman with short reddish-brown hair stood next to the leader.

Jake brushed his hand off against his jeans and reached out to greet them.

"Professor Caine? I don't think we've been formally introduced, although undoubtedly my reputation precedes me. I'm Dr. Matthew Walker. Of Snelling College," he added, when Jake did not respond.

"Uh, hello. Nice to meet you."

"Let me introduce my assistants. This is Ryan, a lab tech in the Zoology Department on campus, and Laura is a graduate student in the Vertebrate Paleontology program. They're here to help me out with our project."

Ryan was shorter than Walker by several inches, with black hair and horn-rimmed glasses. He nodded curtly when introduced. Laura was short with pale skin and freckles, and big, bright eyes. She almost gushed as she shook Jake's hand.

"Follow me," Jake said. "I'll give you a tour of the site. Now, you said something about a project – "

"What the hell are you doing here, Walker?"

Sam's outburst echoed across the clearing, and every head swung around in shock as he stomped to the edge of the excavation area, fists clenched.

"Get out of here! Now! You've got five seconds to get back in . . ."

"Now, now, Doctor Noggle," Walker replied, wagging his finger as if disciplining a naughty pet. Jake didn't appreciate the snarky manner in which he employed the title doctor. "That's no way to speak to a professional colleague, especially one who outranks you, ha-ha, so to speak."

Sam's face was beet-red. "I don't know what you're playin' at, but it ain't happenin' here," Sam yelled, angrier than Jake had ever seen him. "You get in your car and out of here before I totally lose it!"

The entire crew, along with Walker's two assistants, stood in stunned silence. A leaf hitting the ground at that moment would have sounded like a thunderclap. Even the nearby birds were mute, but the new arrival didn't seem fazed in the least.

"But Doctor Noggle, come now. I'm merely here as an interested colleague. Where is your professional courtesy?"

Sam sputtered and clenched his fists, eyes wide. Jake worried that Sam was on the verge of a heart attack.

"Okay, whoa! Let's just ease back here," Jake said, stepping into the space between the two men. They were still a dozen yards apart, but he wasn't taking any chances. "Doctor . . . Walker, was it? I can give you a quick tour, but this might not be the best time . . ."

"Jake," Sam growled, hands shaking. "I do not want this SOB anywhere near this site. I ain't gonna get into this now, but you have no idea what he's like." He exhaled loudly, a focused effort to calm down. "You don't know what he's like . . ."

"Oh, Sammy, it's quite all right. I understand now," Walker said. "You're just embarrassed by the shoddy condition of your dig site."

Walker turned and addressed his two companions. "Ryan, Laura, let's see how many mistakes we can find. We'll make it a contest! I'll start."

The unwelcome visitor made a quick production out of reviewing the site, walking back and forth but never crossing the flagging tape barrier, and maintained a good distance from where Sam stood, fuming. He nodded several times, and even clapped his hands once and pointed at something that he apparently found particularly striking.

Jake stood stunned, trying to keep an eye on Walker while simultaneously trying to make sense of Sam's litany of complaints about their guest. Susan now stood behind Sam, futilely imploring him to calm down.

"To being with," Walker announced, "those units walls are definitely irregular. And I don't much care for this haphazard unit placement. A series of cross trenches would be much more efficient. Hard to see the stratigraphy the way it is now, wouldn't you agree?"

Ryan and Laura both nodded in agreement, but uncertainty clouded their faces. If not for Sam's explosive reaction, Jake would have thought for sure that this was all some absurd practical joke.

Unchallenged, Walker was building up steam. "I don't think the main gridline is even straight, now that I get a better look. Ryan, best check on that with your pocket transit when you have a chance. Hmm. Laura, the pedestals under those bones look a bit thin, too, or am I mistaken?"

The entire crew stood mutely staring at the outspoken stranger in the tweed jacket. Walker looked around, seeming to notice the individuals on the other side of the tape for the first time. Then he smiled.

"Wait, I think I've found the underlying problem. The crew, that's it! Can't expect perfection – or anything close to it – when you rely on poorly trained students and old contract shovel bums. Half the bones out here have probably crushed under their ham-fisted efforts."

Sam had gotten around the fencing and was advancing toward Walker, with Susan tugging at his arm. If Walker was concerned, he didn't show it. "Oh, hello Susan. Still toiling away in obscurity for this hack, I see. Pity. You could have had so much better."

"That's enough!" Jake snapped, stepping between Walker and the rapidly advancing Sam. "Dr. Walker, as much as I'd be thrilled to give you some instruction about this site, we're rather busy today and your unexpected intrusion doesn't fit our schedule."

Jake folded his arms across his chest and leaned menacingly toward their unwelcome guest. "I'm afraid I'll have to ask you to leave. Now."

Walker raised an eyebrow in mock surprise, the hint of a smirk visible at the corner of his mouth. Under Jake's withering glare,

Walker's response died in his throat. He swallowed hard and took a shuffling step backwards.

"Well, um, yes, I can see you have your hands full here. Another time, perhaps."

Jake didn't reply.

Walker nodded, before turning his attention to his wide-eyed staff and ordering them back into the SUV.

As he started the engine, Walker rolled down the window and leaned out. "Don't worry, I'll be back before too long. Oh, and take good care of *my site* in the meantime!"

CHAPTER 7

WITH MATT WALKER AND HIS ASSISTANTS gone, work at Ghost Bog returned to a semblance of normal. It was eerily quiet for the rest of the morning, with none of the normal chatter typically found at an archaeological excavation. Sam was the sole exception; he muttered loudly as he hacked at the soil with his trowel and barked at anyone who came within range.

Lunch was a subdued affair. Sam refused to stop working, and the others wandered off singly and in pairs, ate, and then returned to their units. After most of the crew had eaten, Jake decided to do the same, where he ran into Heather.

"Hey, boss," Heather said, as she pulled a sandwich and apple out of the cooler. "Some mood, huh? You could cut the tension here with a rusty trowel."

"Sure is," Jake said, as he paused to wash his hands with a splash of water from the jug. He took his lunch from the cooler and sat down on an overturned pail. Heather moved a camp chair closer and sat down next to him.

"Think that Walker guy will come back?"

"I don't know," Jake said, taking a bite and chewing slowly. "I sure hope not."

"What do you suppose he meant about 'his site'? He can't come out here and start digging, can he?"

"I don't think so. We have the only permit for the site, and the whole Emerson property is covered by our survey and testing contract." He paused to sip his soda. "The Emersons didn't say anything about him, and I can't believe they wouldn't have brought it up if he had approached them."

Heather nodded, and then popped a few chips into her mouth. They both ate in silence for a few minutes.

"I was, um, sorry to hear about you and Amanda," Heather said quietly.

"Yeah," Jake replied. "Thanks."

Amanda Rohm had been Jake's girlfriend, but the strain of their separate careers and trying to maintain a long-distance relationship had proven too difficult. They had hoped to resolve their issues during the Waconah field school, but a cold case crime that led to a modern-day murder thwarted their efforts. Amanda had ended their relationship during the pandemic lockdown.

"Any chance you guys might work things out?"

Jake didn't answer at once. He chewed his food deliberately, trying to process his response.

"No," he said finally. "Doesn't look like it."

Sensing Jake's discomfort, Heather changed the subject. "Too bad the second field school at Waconah got cancelled. The pandemic really threw everything for a loop."

"That's an understatement," Jake said. "And shifting to online instruction at the University was a real mess. But hopefully we'll get back out there next summer, or the year after, and finish what we started."

Two years prior, Jake had led a field school at Waconah, an Oneota village in east-central Wisconsin. Heather was one of his assistants. Building upon work done by another archaeologist years prior, Jake and his students uncovered numerous features and large quantities of ceramic pottery, stone tools, and animal remains. The potential significance of the finds warranted another season of excavation, as soon as it could be scheduled.

Heather finished the last of her lunch and lobbed an apple core into the nearby brush. "Do you think Sam will be okay?"

Jake glanced over at Sam, who was still down on his knees, troweling furiously and ignoring Susan's apparent attempts at conversation. "Not sure. He's wound pretty tight about this dig, and Walker showing up sure didn't make things any better."

"He might be happier if we had a bigger crew," Heather offered.

"Probably, but we just couldn't swing it with our budget," Jake said. "There was only so much funding available for crew salaries, housing, per diem, and all the other costs associated with running a field project. And half our funding is set aside for lab analysis, report prep, and curation costs. You know how quick those costs add up."

"I know," Heather replied. "But what about volunteers? I know you were asking around the Department for help . . ."

"I tried to sign up some volunteers, but it never worked out," Jake said. "Most of the students were busy with classes or outside jobs, and the few who weren't could only manage a few scattered days here and there."

"Hardly enough to make it worthwhile. I get it."

"And housing was an issue. Even for those willing to pitch in, having to cover their own hotel costs wasn't feasible," Jake said. "I did have one person who thought she might make it work, but last time I emailed her she was still trying to coordinate her vacation time."

"Well, one person wouldn't make much difference," Heather said, pulling her gloves from her back pocket.

"Probably not." Jake tossed his trash in the garbage bag and stood, ready to return to work. "I think Sam will be fine, provided we don't have any more surprises."

At that moment, the throaty roar of a powerful engine cut through the air, and an older Camaro rumbled to a stop in the parking area. Sam let loose with a lengthy stream of violent cursing, but Jake scarcely noticed. The car looked familiar, but he couldn't place it.

Heather, on the other hand, knew immediately who it was. "No. Oh, no! Not her."

"Hi, Jake," cried the shapely blonde woman who got out of the car. "Surprise!"

CHAPTER 8

"J AKE, THE LAST THING WE NEED is some untrained amateur mucking around," Sam said, his harsh whisper carrying across the site. "This site is too important."

"You've got it all wrong," Jake said, hands raised to cut off Sam's continued protest. "Pam joined the Northeast Wisconsin Archaeology Society—the group that helped out at our Waconah dig—and did an archaeology field course through a local college. She was all set to volunteer at our second Waconah dig . . ."

"Which got cancelled," Sam snapped. "Without any *real* excavation experience . . ."

"The Society president and her college instructor both gushed over Pam's field skills," Jake fired back. "She's a natural excavator with a great attitude, and willing to learn. I've been emailing Pam about Ghost Bog over the last few months, and she's really excited to help out. She's not going to cause any problems."

Brows furrowed, Sam glared back at Jake. "No offense to your field school, Jake, but there's a helluva difference between an Oneota village and an Archaic bison kill. Besides, somebody'll have to watch over her, check her paperwork, all that stuff. We'll end up short one person until she can get up to speed. If she ever does!"

Jake sighed, his exasperation with Sam rising. They were both still tense after the encounter with Dr. Walker that morning, and Jake had about reached his limit with Sam's continual badgering. Jake watched as Michelle gave Pam Hauser a tour of the site and introduced her to the crew. Heather, helping Susan screen dirt from her unit, had a sour look on her face and was whispering animatedly to Susan. He had a pretty good idea of the topic of their conversation.

"I'm certain Pam can handle the work. I'll review her paperwork myself, and there won't be any lost time," Jake said with finality. "And I'm not inclined to send her away, not after she drove across half the state, when we can use the help."

Sam started to respond, but Jake continued. "If she's willing to help out, I don't see any reason not to let her."

"I just don't want anything to slow us up any further."

"We're ahead of schedule already, Sam. We'll get even more done with Pam pitching in."

"What about Heather? She doesn't seem too thrilled to see her."

"Heather and Pam sort of butted heads when they first met, during the first Waconah field school. They don't have to work together, so it won't be an issue."

"Well . . ."

"And she's a deputy sheriff. She can probably arrest Walker if he comes back out here," Jake said, smiling.

"I'd prefer if she just shot him," Sam growled, but his resolve was weakening. "Somebody needs to shoot that bastard, that's for damn sure."

Jake didn't reply, hoping that Sam would come around. He could see Michelle and Pam at the far end of the dig, trying hard not to look in his direction.

"Okay, she can stay. But you're responsible for her work. One smashed bone, one mislabeled map, and she's outta here."

"I'm sure it'll be fine. Just think of all the extra ground we can open with an extra set of hands."

Sam mumbled something under his breath as he trudged back to his unit. Jake caught Michelle's attention and waved her and Pam over.

"Get the full tour?"

"Sure did," Pam said. "Michelle introduced me to the crew and showed me some of your latest finds. It's even more impressive than you described."

Jake met Deputy Pam Hauser during the Waconah field school, after trespassers visited the site after hours. Reciprocating Jake's growing interest in a cold-case death that occurred at Waconah years prior, Pam prompted him to investigate further, with her assistance. The two had struck up a friendship that flourished despite the distance and enforced isolation of the pandemic.

"Bison kill sites this old are uncommon," Michelle added, "especially this far east."

"It is pretty unique. People always picture bison out on the prairies, but they were found in the eastern forests, too," Jake said. "What's really significant is the age of the site and the bone preservation. A site like this is one in a million."

"So, do you have room for an enthusiastic volunteer?" Pam smiled, showing off her dimples. "Your friend Sam doesn't seem too keen on the idea."

"Sam's just worried about finishing the excavation before time runs out," Jake said, omitting Sam's other complaints. "He's fine with it, now that I've explained who you are."

"Sorry I didn't email you back about coming, but it took forever to finalize my vacation time," Pam said. "Once it was approved, I just hopped in the car and took off before the sheriff could change his mind."

"Don't worry about Sam," Michelle interjected. "He just has that kind of grumpy old man vibe. And this morning didn't go all that well."

"Yeah, our last visitor didn't exactly endear himself to anyone." Jake explained about Matt Walker's visit, his disparaging remarks about the site and the crew, and Sam's violent reaction.

"Wow. After that, I can see why he wouldn't welcome another

visitor with open arms," Pam said, as she tied her shoulder-length hair into a ponytail. "I didn't realize archaeological sites had such drama, like a bad reality show. 'Course, I should have picked up on that after Waconah."

"That's not really fair," Jake said, a bit defensively. "What happened there was just a fluke."

"Kidding! Just kidding, Jake. You guys *are* tense today."

"Sorry. So, you ready to pitch in and help?"

"That's what I'm here for." She held up her backpack. "Got my gloves and dig kit right here."

"Great. How about if I start you off with Michelle? She can show you the ropes. We're doing a few things differently than in the field school, but nothing too unusual."

"Mostly a lot more mapping," Michelle said, handing some finished paperwork to Pam. "Noting the location of the bones is the most important thing. It'll help later when we try to reconstruct the kill event, and what happened after that."

"Why don't you two work on Units 33 and 34, along the edge? We found some good-sized bone clusters in the test unit over there, and I'd like to open up that whole area. Most of the overlying soil has already been removed, so it won't take you long to reach the bone bed."

"Jake, um, what about Heather? She and I were still taking out the last of the bones from Unit 23 when Pam arrived."

"Al and I just finished up our unit, so she can help Heather with your old unit. Once it's done, they can pair up and start on the adjacent block."

With that settled, Jake told Al of the new arrangement and the two of them walked over and informed Heather. She nodded, answering in a short, clipped monotone, obviously not pleased with the situation. Al followed Jake back to the unit they had just finished, claiming that she needed to grab her gear.

"Did I do something? Heather seems pretty pissed about something."

Jake sighed. "It's not you. Heather doesn't care for Pam, for some reason. They, uh, had some personal issues back at the Waconah field school dig."

"That's where you solved that old murder mystery, right?"

"How did you hear about that?"

"Are you kidding? I think every archaeologist in the Midwest knows about that. It spread like wildfire at the regional archaeology conference that fall. Lots of folks were discussing it online after that."

Jake's shoulders slumped. This was not something he wanted to hear. He had gotten some good-natured ribbing from a few colleagues following the resolution of the Jacklyn Wardell case, but it had died down soon after. Jake was unable to attend the conference that year, but none of his friends who had gone made any mention of this. He felt betrayed.

Al picked up on his unease. "It didn't last all that long," she said. "You know how social media is. Something is all the rage for a few days, and then some new thing pops up to take its place."

"Yeah, sure. But that was a one-time thing. Not going to happen again."

Al nodded, grabbed her dig kit, and walked back to join Heather.

Jake watched her leave, and then gathered up his own gear. "Not going to have any more troubles like that."

CHAPTER 9

T HE CREW, NOW INCREASED BY ONE, worked steadily through the rest of the afternoon and into the early evening without incident. Pam dug and screened like a seasoned pro, and Michelle found only minor corrections were needed in her notes and maps. Jake noticed that Sam kept a watchful eye on Pam, ready to speak up should any problems occur.

Jake also found himself keeping a close eye on Pam, but for a much different reason. He was astounded by just how attractive she was—even more than he remembered from their brief time together during the Waconah field school. It wasn't just her blue eyes, wavy blonde hair, or her considerable . . . physical attributes. Pam's smile, the lilt in her voice, and her cheerful attitude all seemed like a refreshing tonic that Jake hadn't realized he needed.

It had been over a year since Jake and Pam had last seen each other, when he had given a lecture in Donovan on the preliminary results of the Waconah excavation. They had kept in contact via email and text after that, but despite their developing friendship, it had never grown into anything beyond that. Now with no romantic attachments, Jake wondered if that might change.

As they closed for the day, Pam invited them all to try out the pizza place not far from her hotel. Sam, Susan, and Heather declined, opting to call it an early night, but the others agreed. It was a bit crowded with late-season tourists, but the food was tasty. Buying the first pitcher endeared Pam to the crew, and everyone had a good time. Michelle and Al seemed particularly enthused with their new volunteer.

When the crew arrived at Ghost Bog the next morning, Pam was already there, uncovering her units and preparing to start. At the restaurant, Jake had cautioned Pam not to give Sam or Heather any ammunition for complaints. He had experienced first-hand the trouble created when childish cliques developed during an excavation, and he had no desire to see that happen here.

As if often does, the November weather shifted without warning and a warm front brought in unseasonably hot and humid weather. The mosquitoes and flies decided summer had returned and pestered the diggers without mercy.

"Jake, these were the last two mosquito coils in the shed."

"Okay, Curt. I'll pick up some more after work tonight."

"You shouldn't bother," Heather said, looking up from her screen. "They don't work at all unless you have them right down in the unit. The spray or lotion works the best."

"I'm not crazy about those sprays," Al said, joining the discussion. "If it can take the finish of a shovel handle, imagine what it does to your skin."

"Citronella candles work pretty well," Rob added, rolling up the sleeves of his shirt. "My girlfriend and I use them all the time when we go camping."

"According to the box, that's what is in these coils, but I guess it isn't as strong," Curt said, taking one coil and handing the other one to Al. "What about mosquito nets, you know, that fold over your hat?"

"Fine for your face and neck, but your arms are still exposed." Al set her coil on top of her dig kit, near their paperwork. "The Native Americans in the Northwest used cedar chips. Maybe we could try that?"

Jake shook his head. "I think cedar wood is pretty expensive. Besides, we'd need a ton of it to keep the whole area covered with smoke."

"How about bear oil? They used to do that, too."

"I can't imagine how much that would cost, if we could even find it." Jake agreed to purchase a variety of repellants, and let the crew decide which worked best. With luck, he thought, the temperature will fall again, and the argument will drop.

NOW WORKING ALONE, JAKE HAD OPENED a small unit along the south edge of the site yesterday afternoon, and dug down to the bone level. He mapped a cluster of foot elements and some scattered bones, took some photos, and removed them just before the day came to an end. Upon his return, Jake spent part of the next morning scraping through the rest of the level, marking additional bone fragments on his map, and filling out the necessary paperwork. With his task complete, Jake decided to see how the other teams were doing before starting another unit.

Curt and Rob were mapping a jumble of rib bones and vertebrae in their unit. A few yards away, Heather and Al were clearing away some loose soil and brushing the bones clean in preparation for a photo. Sam, his trowel little more than a blur, was scraping soil away from a skull fragment while Susan knelt nearby, attempting to corral the dirt in a plastic scoop.

Michelle and Pam were topping off the soil in a bucket, with another full pail sitting nearby. Their screen was already half full, so Jake decided to give them a hand. Slipping on his gloves, he cautiously pressed the soil down against the mesh screen, while watching for the telltale signs of pale bone and shiny lithics. He deposited the bone fragments and stone flakes in different bags, noticing an increasing number of the former as he worked. Once the screen was empty, he set the artifacts bags to one side, cleaned out any remaining twigs and pebbles, and dumped the next pail of soil into the screen. As he worked, he took a close look at the exposed bone in Michelle and Pam's unit. Jake spied some articulated lower leg bones, fragments of at least two mandibles, and a few other elements.

"Looks like the remnants of a discard pile," Jake said, pausing to pull another small flake from the screen.

Michelle looked up, simultaneously brushing away a mosquito with the back of her hand. She left a smear of dark brown soil across her forehead. "I think so too. There are three separate jaws here, including one I pulled out earlier." Michelle pointed to a thick bone with a complete row of gleaming teeth, nestled in a tray formed out of aluminum foil. "Pam has uncovered some toe bones over there."

Pam sat back on her calves, grinning. Her Rosie the Riveter T-shirt was caked with mud, and her arms were peppered with mosquito bites.

"Having fun on your vacation?" Jake asked wryly.

"You bet. Joke if you will, but this is a blast. Beats the monotony of day-to-day police work anytime."

"If you say so. Personally, I wouldn't mind a few quiet days behind a desk right about now. After you've dug frozen soil in a snowstorm for an emergency salvage project, the thrill of the job starts to wear off."

"Gee, Michelle, is he this much fun in class?" Pam said with a wink. "There must be a mountain of drop slips outside his office after the first day."

Michelle suppressed her laugh, but it took some effort. "Professor Caine is honest but fair," she said. "And that's the only comment I have until my grades are posted."

Jake gave her a frown, but she could tell his heart wasn't in it. He turned back to Pam. "Seriously, I do appreciate your help. It's really nice to have you here. Uh, as a volunteer, I mean."

Pam gave him a big smile, dimples showing. "So, Professor, Michelle said this is all part of the butchering process. Care to explain?"

"Well, it's not practical to try and move an animal weighing upwards of 2,000 pounds, so they did some initial butchering at the kill site. The choicest portions, those with the most meat like the limbs and rib cage, would be cut loose and moved to a nearby camp to be processed further and filleted."

"Why didn't they do all the butchery right at the kill site? Wouldn't that save time?"

"Yes, but the kill location isn't always the best spot. If you drive the bison into a wet bog, that might work to trap and kill them, but it would be a mess to try and butcher and fillet the meat in the same spot."

"There could be another site, like a small camp or processing station, right near here," Michelle added.

"Any chance you could find it?"

"Not likely, but maybe," Jake said. "It could be in any direction, and we can't be sure how far away it might be. Probably on a rise or high spot, somewhere. But even if we found it, unless there are bones preserved there it might be hard to tie it to this kill site."

Pam nodded. "So, these bones got left behind because they didn't have enough meat on them?"

"Essentially. Depending on the weather, the meat can spoil pretty fast, so the Native Americans would have had to work fast to remove what they wanted. Once at the camp, they could dry or smoke the meat in order to preserve it."

"Why are they piled up like this?"

Jake shrugged. "Probably moved the unwanted portions to the side, just for room to work. They'd take the hides, too, for blankets and clothing."

"Wait a sec," Pam said, reaching for the jawbone Michelle had placed on the foil. "Michelle said this one has cut marks on the inside. Doesn't that mean they were butchering the heads, too?"

"Brains were used for tanning hides, and bison tongues were considered a delicacy. Those cuts are from where the tongue was removed."

"Ew. Hard pass."

Michelle chuckled, then used her trowel to draw Jake's attention to some partially buried bones along the edge of the unit. "What do you make of this, Jake? There are a bunch of limb elements here, like they didn't even bother with this one."

Jake studied the bones. "Are they from a juvenile? Sometimes they wouldn't bother processing a calf, because of the limited amount of meat compared to an adult."

"No, it's definitely an adult," Michelle said. "The end of the humerus is fused, same with the other bones that I can see. Maybe it was diseased?"

"Hmm. Maybe. After you finish these two units, open a 2-by-2 unit over that area. Let's see what else turns up."

Before Jake could add anything further, their attention was drawn to the sounds of tires rolling across gravel, and the slow approach of a large white SUV.

It was the first time Jake could recall Michelle swearing. He was a bit surprised at how good she was at it.

CHAPTER 10

Recognizing Matt Walker's vehicle, Jake sprinted across the excavation area. A certain amount of caution was necessary to avoid the maze of open units, exposed bones, dig kits, and other paraphernalia scattered over the site. Sam's yelling, coupled with other voices raised in concern, did not help the situation. Instructing everyone to stay put, he crossed under the flagging tape barrier and walked up to the SUV.

Matt Walker stood calmly outside his vehicle. Jake saw Ryan and Laura sitting within, watching, but it did not appear that they were about to join their boss.

"I'm sorry, but today isn't a good day for a visit."

"Professor Caine, please, before you say another word, allow me to apologize for my rather churlish behavior yesterday."

Jake eyed him with suspicion but didn't reply.

"It was an arduous trip up here from Snelling College," Walker said, shaking his head. "And we were quite exhausted. Didn't mean to start a row, or cause any offense. Of course, Sam's violent over-reaction to my arrival, I have to say, did not . . . um . . . improve the situation."

Jake felt a little embarrassed. Despite whatever past relationship these two had, Sam's behavior was extreme, and hardly professional.

"I understand," Jake said, keeping his guard up. "All this travel can definitely wear on a person."

"The significance of this site, I have to admit," Walker said, smiling, "may have clouded my judgment. The reported bone preservation and the age; simply extraordinary! Perhaps that also factored in to my less than appropriate behavior."

"It is an amazing site," Jake acknowledged, and then described in brief some of their more recent finds, noting the condition of the remains and some of the interesting patterns that were coming to light. Walker nodded and listened attentively while Jake spoke.

"It truly does sound like a fascinating discovery," Walker said. He took a sly glance over Jake's shoulder, in the direction of the excavation. "Now, how about that tour? Perhaps Doctor Noggle could be entreated to depart, for a brief while?"

It took Jake only a moment to realize he was being played. "No, that's not going to happen. Not today." He folded his arms across his chest. "Perhaps another time."

The pleasant look on Walker's face disappeared in an instant. "Come now, Professor Caine. We're both men of science. Be reasonable."

"I think I am. It's my responsibility to run this excavation properly, and that means caring for the cultural material as well as those working here. At this time, your presence is going to do more harm than good. I'm sorry."

"I didn't want it to have to be this way, but you leave me no alternative," Walker said. "It isn't going to be long before I'm overseeing this project. All of it."

Jake was doubtful, but nonetheless concerned. "How, exactly? The Wisconsin State University survey team has already investigated the Emerson property thoroughly, and we have the only permit for archaeological work at Ghost Bog. Our Memorandum of Agreement with the landowners and the state covers all this in detail."

"Perhaps. And perhaps not," he said, with a cunning smile. "You *may* have a lock on this particular site, Mr. Caine, but that hardly prevents our project from investigating more significant locales nearby."

"Such as? To my knowledge, this site is unique."

Walker snorted, causing his wire-rimmed glasses to waggle on his long, thin nose. "With due respect, Professor, my knowledge of the Pleistocene and Holocene vertebrate paleontology of this region far outstrips your own. It would take very little effort to uncover a bone deposit that would put this jumble to shame."

"Best of luck to you with that project. I look forward to reading about it at some point. If you'll excuse me, I need to get back to work."

Walker stamped his foot, but quickly regained his composure. "Thank you. Of course, I'll be much too busy right here, cleaning up this mess of an excavation."

"That is *not* going to happen."

"We'll see. Let's just say I have an 'in' with regards for this particular property," Walker said, opening the SUV door. "An 'in' I will take advantage of in the very near future."

"That's all he said? An 'in'?"

"Yes, Sam," Jake said, sighing. "No matter how many times you ask, that's all he said. Claims he has info on similar or better sites in the area, and that he thinks he's going to take over here."

"Sound like a load of sour grapes to me," Heather said, and Curt and Rob both nodded their heads in agreement. As soon as Walker's vehicle was out of sight, the entire crew surrounded Jake, demanding answers.

"He can't take over, can he?"

"No, Al. The University holds the permit, and everything is signed and sealed with the Emersons. Besides, they would have told me if they had been talking to another researcher."

Sam muttered something about landowners and dollar signs to Susan, but Jake didn't hear it clearly enough to comment. A cascade of other comments and questions flew back and forth among the crowd.

"Okay, that's enough. There's no sense getting all worked up over nothing. Let's just get back to work; if anything does happen, I will make sure each and every one of you is informed."

The archaeologists had started to disperse, with some reluctance, when another car drove into the parking area. An audible groan went up from the group, as they all stopped to stare at the new visitors.

Peter Holcombe got out of the driver's side, smiling and waving at the archaeologists assembled nearby. An unrecognized man got out on the passenger side. Peter's smile faded when he saw the grim looks on their faces.

"Is something wrong? I'm sorry if we came at a bad time."

"Oh, no, Peter," Jake said, with a half-hearted smile. "Just busy today, and we had a little problem with an earlier visitor."

Sam and Heather both voiced their agreement, in no uncertain terms, before joining the rest of the crew as they marched back to their units. Jake was about to explain further when Peter's companion reached him, hand outstretched.

"Hi. I'm Keith Emerson. You must be Professor Caine! I'm so thrilled to finally meet you."

Keith Emerson was in his late twenties or early thirties, with wavy sandy brown hair and a round, boyish face. He grinned like a kid at an amusement park while he shook Jake's hand.

"Keith is the on-call legal counsel for the Town of Scenic," Peter said. "He was in St. Paul when we visited a few days ago, so I promised him we'd stop by when he was in town. Are you sure this is a good time?"

"Of course, no trouble at all. C'mon, I'll give you the grand tour."

Jake took Keith and Peter on an extended tour of the dig. Keith had a solid grasp of the basics of archaeological fieldwork, so Jake was able to provide more details on the excavation and the unusual nature of their finds. Michelle pulled some butchered bison bones and spearpoints for Keith to examine, which he photographed with his phone. After loaning him a pair of gloves, Jake let Keith screen for a while. His dress shirt and slacks were spattered with mud, but he couldn't have cared less. Keith's enthusiasm was infectious.

"I can't wait for Frank to see all this."

"Frank?"

"Frank Russell, my best bud from college. We took some archaeology classes together, in between all the boring pre-law courses."

"He's an attorney, too?"

"No, he's an agent with the Wisconsin Bureau of Investigation. His office is in Madison, but he does a lot of work up north. Sometimes we go fossil hunting together, but not often enough."

Keith dropped another flake in the artifact bag, then removed his gloves so he could mop his brow with a handkerchief.

"Whew! This is tough work, especially in this heat."

"It is warm today," Jake said. "Your aunt was right about the cold snap we had the other day, though."

"Speaking of which, I'd better stop now and get cleaned up before we head over there." Keith stepped away from the screen with some reluctance and took a few minutes to brush away the worst of the dirt from his clothes.

"I'll have to come back when I'm better dressed, if I can work it into my schedule."

"Scenic's criminal element keeps you pretty busy?" Jake said, laughing.

"No, I don't do criminal cases, and the city has a separate guy on retainer as a prosecuting attorney. My private practice is spread all over, so I spend a lot of time chasing back and forth between here and the Twin Cities. Of course, I like to check in with my aunt and uncle as much as I can."

"We should head over there soon," Peter said, checking his gold wristwatch. The face had a large crimson S on it, similar to the one Jake once saw on the town flag. Jake noticed Keith wearing a similar watch, but with a slightly different face.

"Yeah. Just one second." Keith stopped by Sam and Susan's unit and took a few more photos. Sam kept his head down, but Jake was happy that he wasn't complaining.

"Well, you're welcome back here any time."

"Thanks. Boy, hate to admit how much I miss archaeology," Keith said, looking around the dig. "At least I can jaw about it with Peter sometimes. He's the real expert on local history and geography."

Keith shook Jake's hand, took a few steps away, then stopped and turned back. "Speaking of experts, I almost forgot. Did Doctor Walker from Snelling College ever get in touch with you? When he called me a few weeks back I . . ."

"You told him about this?" Sam roared, throwing his trowel down with a heavy clunk.

Keith's eyes went wide, and even Peter took a step back. Jake interrupted before Sam could say anything further.

"Walker was the source of the trouble I mentioned earlier. Not a big issue. He's somehow under the impression that he should over-see this dig, and that he was maneuvering to take over."

"I'm sorry. Really. I didn't mean to cause any trouble. He just seemed so interested in this project . . ."

"I'll bet," Sam said, spitting. He was still glaring at Keith, and behind him Susan was likewise shooting daggers at the young lawyer.

"My aunt and uncle are committed to having you guys excavate this site," Keith said. "I even went over the contracts with them. There's no way anybody else is going to work on Ghost Bog, I assure you."

"That's what I said, too," Jake said, including both Keith and Sam. "I'm sure there was no harm done. More than likely Walker heard about the discovery through the professional grapevine, and then contacted you in the hopes of gaining access."

Keith nodded in agreement. Sam continued to glower.

"Well, I am sorry if I caused any trouble," Keith said, handing Jake one of his business cards. "If you do have any problems with Doctor Walker, just give me a call. I'll set him straight."

CHAPTER 11

THE STRESS OF THE DAY'S EVENTS, coupled with the hard work put in by the crew over the six-day work week, warranted an extended evening on the town. Although tired, everyone felt the need to blow off steam. Even Susan, normally content to retire to her shared room with Al, agreed to come along. Curt and Rob nominated their favorite local sports bar, located only a few blocks from the crew's hotel. After cleaning up, the archaeologists reconvened at the Scenic Bar and Grill and fortified themselves on delicious bar food and a somewhat heroic intake of alcoholic beverages.

The crew made short work of the appetizers purchased by Jake, and then entertained themselves at the pool tables and dartboards, talking and laughing. For Jake and Sam, sitting at one end of a long table, the conversation invariably returned to work.

"I just don't think it's anything we have to worry about further," Jake said, as he sipped his beer. So much for a relaxing evening out, he thought. "Walker is just blowing smoke, and his whole scheme to 'take over' is solely based on talking once or twice with Keith Emerson. It's over."

"Maybe," Sam said, scraping the label off his beer with his fingernail. "We still don't know what else he may be up to. And I don't particularly trust that Emerson kid, either."

"He's fine. He's pro-archaeology, and I can't see him doing anything to cause problems."

"He could try and convince his aunt and uncle to push us aside, or even to just let Walker start poking around on the property. That'd be bad enough. People are awful fickle when dollar signs start dancing around in front of them."

"The Emersons aren't like that. I've talked to them a dozen times since this project started, and money is the last thing on their minds."

"Yeah, but what about the kid? You don't know him at all." Sam took a final swallow of beer and slammed the bottle down a bit harder than expected. The sound carried across the bar, despite the ambient music, conversation, and blare of the wall-mounted televisions.

Sam flushed, then gave Jake a weak smile. "Sorry. Guess this is all getting to me some. Must be too old for this crap."

"Enough of that talk. You're too grouchy to let old age take over your life. Heck, you're still in your prime. Maybe not as prime as me, but still."

Sam laughed, starting to relax. "Fair enough. I think it's having Walker around. That guy just pushes my buttons; always has."

"What's the deal with you two?"

"Not really sure," Sam said, scratching his head. "We first met years ago at a conference. Don't remember the specifics, but right after that I heard a rumor he was bad-mouthing the paper I gave."

"Not a surprise in this field. Happens all the time."

"I know, but this was different. More personal. A few months later, he published a paper criticizing some early rockshelter fauna that I analyzed. The editor was a friend of mine, so he let me publish a rejoinder that shredded Walker's arguments. Things just escalated after that."

"Peer review can be messy. Too many big egos and personal attacks."

"You got that right. After that, we butted heads just about every time we crossed paths. Most of the time I went out of my way to avoid him."

"He's not an archaeologist, though," Jake said, refilling his beer from the nearby pitcher. "Your two fields shouldn't intersect all that much."

"True. He really only seems to get in my face when I'm dealing with an older assemblage, something with late Pleistocene or early Holocene bones."

"That would explain his interest in Ghost Bog."

"Yeah, but this site is too important to let him or anyone else interfere," Sam said, slapping his palm against the table. "I'm not going to let anything mess this up. Anything."

"Everything okay over here, guys?" Pam sat down next to Jake, sliding an empty plate to one side. "You're not talking shop, are you? We're supposed to be here to relax and have some fun."

"Archaeology isn't just a job, you know," Sam said. "It's a way of life. Can't separate the two."

"Maybe not, but even as a cop you have to be off duty sometimes, or the stress of the job starts to beat you down. Take some time for the people around you, maybe make their day a little brighter. You'd be surprised at how much it helps."

"I suppose you've got a point," Sam said. He glanced down to the far end of the table, where Susan sat munching on a plate of wings. "Guess I'll go over and thank Susan for working so hard. Plus, she's had the hardship of suffering alongside yours truly," Sam said, grinning.

He made his way to the bar, bought a longneck for himself and a cocktail for Susan, and plopped down in an empty chair next to her.

Pam turned her attention back to Jake. "You sure everything is okay? That sounded pretty intense."

"Eavesdropping isn't a very nice habit, you know."

Pam smiled. "Oh, you know all too well I have my devilish side. Besides, it's part of my training to keep my eyes and ears open for trouble."

"Doesn't that contradict your earlier idea of taking time off of work? Ouch!"

Pam punched Jake playfully in the shoulder and laughed. "Don't crack wise with me, mister, or I'll run you in. Besides, if you don't treat me right, I'll just pack up my dig kit and head back home."

"Well, I definitely don't want that," Jake said, hands raised in surrender. "You're too good a digger to let you escape that easily."

"Thanks. Glad I can match up with a professional crew."

"Besides, it's nice having you around."

"About time you noticed." Pam smiled broadly. She moved her chair a little closer and leaned in. "It's nice being around you, too."

Jake smiled in return. "So . . . no problems getting time off, then?"

Pam leaned back in her chair. "No, I had some leave time banked up, and it's been pretty quiet back home. Too quiet, in a lot of ways. I've actually been thinking about whether I should move on."

"Sheriff Rostlund wouldn't want to lose his star deputy, would he?"

She shrugged. "I think the novelty of us solving that cold case has kind of played out. Other than the trouble during the Waconah field school, not much crime around Donovan, Wisconsin. Traffic hassles, petty burglaries, some drug issues, but mostly just dealing with the tourists. It gets tedious, to be honest. No challenge."

Located on Taylor Lake, the Waconah site was a prehistoric Oneota village and the site of Jake's archaeological field school. Years earlier, archaeologist Jacklyn Wardell died while leading her own investigations at the site. During Jake's field school, the Wardell case heated up, and Deputy Pam Hauser played a big role in bringing the case to a close.

"It was unfortunate that we had to cancel the second field school at Waconah due to the pandemic," Jake said. He paused to refill her glass, and then topped off his own. "You would have had fun volunteering."

"It is interesting work. Not sure I'd want to do it full time, though."

"It can be tough. Lots of travel, especially when you're first starting out. And you'd need an advanced degree to land a permanent job."

"Hmm. Maybe you could give me some 'private' tutoring? I think I'd enjoy that." She gave him a wink, and Jake choked on his beer.

"It might be a good time for me to strike out on my own," Pam continued, seeming to ignore Jake's discomfort. "I mean, I never had a chance to move away, after my dad's death and having to help out with my siblings." When Jake first told Pam about the Wardell cold case, he was a bit surprised by her immediate interest and offer to help. She later revealed that her father had been killed during an apparent hunting accident, a crime that was never solved to her satisfaction.

"It wouldn't hurt to explore your options," Jake said. "Do you have anything specific in mind?"

"I was thinking of maybe applying with the FBI," Pam replied. "Lots more chances for advancement, maybe do some real investigative work. Could be exciting."

"You'd be great as an FBI agent," Jake agreed.

"But now I'm intrigued by your suggestion, Professor Caine." Pam leaned in close again. "Late night study sessions at your place. Excavating side by side during the day, then analyzing ancient treasures with you in the lab until the wee hours of the night. Very tempting."

Pam laughed, bell-like tones that sent an electric shiver down Jake's back.

"Seriously, Jake. Any job would be great if it meant I could spend more time with you." She slid her hand over his arm and grasped it warmly.

Jake's free arm trembled slightly.

"Okay, now you're in trouble!"

Jake and Pam both jumped, startled by Curt's announcement. He stood on the opposite side of the table, weaving a bit, flanked by Rob on one side and Michelle on the other.

"Look, boss. Heather and Al are kicking our butts at the pool table." Curt raised the pool cue in his hand, as if that gesture made clear his intent. "Doesn't matter how we team up, but they keep winning!"

Jake looked past Curt and saw Heather and Al at a nearby pool table, holding cues and looking quite smug. In unison, they each drew a finger across their throats, and laughed.

"We need you, Jake. C'mon, just one game with Rob. If we can beat them once, the tide will turn!"

Curt's hangdog expression was almost too much to bear. Rob, a bit more sober than Curt, chimed in. "Please, Jake. You know what Heather gets like when she's on a winning streak. She's going to be unbearable to be around."

Jake considered that aspect of Heather's rather competitive personality, and agreed to give it a shot.

Curt turned back to Heather and Al, who were now waving their arms like drunken chickens. "Ha! Got him, ladies. I'm bringing in a ringer!"

Jake turned to Pam. "You in?"

Pam gave him a little smile, but it wasn't matched in her bright blue eyes. "No, you go ahead without me. It's cool. Just going to relax here for a while."

Beer in hand, Jake left Pam and joined the others at the pool table. Michelle hung back. "Sorry, Pam. I tried to tell them you two were talking."

Pam shrugged her shoulders. "It's okay. Maybe another time, I guess."

"Want to go shoot some darts? You can't just sit here."

Pam took a glance over at the pool table, where a loud clack and yells of approval signaled Jake's successful break.

"Sure, why not?" Pam said, pushing her disappointment aside. "Let's do it. Besides, you know the old saying: Unlucky at love, lucky at darts!"

CHAPTER 12

Sunday dawned a bit late for the archaeologists, all of whom were spent from the revelry of the previous evening. Other than a communal jaunt to the local laundry, they split off into small groups or kept to themselves. Sam barricaded himself at his desk, pouring over notes and paperwork from the dig, while Susan opted to undertake a solid day of rest in her room. Curt, Rob, and Heather, all rivalry from the billiard contest now forgotten, planned to check out a nearby state park famous for its waterfalls. Pam, Michelle, and Al decided on a shopping trip in the Twin Cities, topped off with a fancy dinner at an elegant restaurant. They invited Jake to join them, but a withering look from Sam convinced him that his wisest course of action would be to stay put.

On Monday, the refreshed archaeologists were back to work at Ghost Bog. The warm autumn weather continued, and they made good progress on the excavation. Several large, contiguous units were now open, and for the most part cleared of bones and artifacts down to the damp, sterile subsoil. The number of spearpoints found had doubled since the first week, and the crew identified at least five spots where Native Americans had sharpened or reworked stone knives and scraping tools. Just that morning another hearth had been uncovered, bringing the total number of cooking fires up to a dozen. Large bones were exposed in all the open, unfinished units, revealing an amazing picture of the past, where slain bison had fallen, carcasses were processed, and portions were redistributed and discarded.

About mid-morning, Sam carried a full box of artifact bags, filled with bison bones and stone artifacts, into the shed. After he emerged, he waved Jake over.

"What's going on?"

"Getting mighty full in the shed, Jake," Sam said, wiping his brow with kerchief. "Still some room on the one shelf, but the other one is full. And we aren't going to get many more boxes on that pallet in the back, either."

Jake stuck his head in the door and looked around. In addition to the pallets and shelves laden with artifact boxes, there was a large folding table covered with equipment, several tool boxes and containers, and scattered piles of miscellaneous gear covering most of the floor.

"Yeah, does look like she's about ready to burst," Jake said, turning back to Sam. "If we could spare someone, I'd be tempted to send them down to the University with a load of boxes."

Sam shook his head. "I'd rather avoid that. Can't afford to lose anybody, not for a whole day like that. Maybe we could move some boxes back to the hotel."

"The rooms are pretty packed with stuff already, not to mention everyone's personal gear. Plus I don't think the hotel would appreciate us using the rooms as storage lockers for bones and soil samples."

"Well, we could just move a few things, like the lithic artifacts. But it wouldn't make much of a dent in there."

Jake rubbed his chin, considering their options. "If we get a rain day, you know, a good soaking where we can't excavate, then we could transfer a bunch of stuff to the University."

"I suppose," Sam said, looking doubtful. "Still hate to lose any digging time." He took a sip from his water bottle and surveyed the dig.

"Much as I hate to admit it, you were right about Pam. She did a pretty good job last week."

"I tried to arrange for more volunteers, but Pam was the only one who could make it work. She really started getting in to archaeology after Waconah."

"Heather's not a fan of her, though."

"No, not so much," Jake said. "They'll be fine, as long as we keep them apart."

"Speaking of woman troubles, I was sorry to hear about you and Amanda breaking up."

Jake was unsure how to reply. "Thanks," he said, after a moment. "It was hard being apart all the time. She was busy at the History Center, and I typically have a full class load and students to advise at the University. Guess I should have seen it coming. It was a complicated situation."

"Archaeology is complicated, Heck, life's complicated," Sam said. "Well, none of my business. Better get back at it."

Jake watched Sam walk back to his unit, considering what he said, as well as what he hadn't said. He didn't need any more complications in his life.

Heading back to his small unit on the edge of the dig, Jake first stopped off to chat with each pair of diggers, starting with Heather and Al at the opposite end, before moving on to Curt and Rob. He asked everyone about his or her recent finds, and discussed which units to open up next. When he reached Sam and Susan's units, he made an effort to chat with her in particular, realizing he hadn't had much chance to speak with her since she arrived. Susan was pleasant if somewhat reserved. She still seemed a bit out of place but in better spirits than the previous week.

"Jake? Got a couple of things over here for you to check out."

"Okay, Michelle. Be right over." Jake said goodbye to Susan and made his way over to Michelle and Pam's 2-by-2 meter unit along the eastern edge of site. They were each working on a mass of bones, at opposite ends of the unit. "So, what do you have?"

"Me first," Michelle said, excitement in her voice. "Take a look at this!"

Michelle held up a large, corner-noted spearpoint almost four inches long, made of a dark golden brown, translucent stone. Amazingly, unlike most of the other points recovered so far, this one was completely intact.

"Wow! That is a beauty. Looks like a Kirk point, so a perfect fit for the Early Archaic. Where did you find it?"

Michelle pointed to a spot near some ribs, marked with a golf tee. "Don't worry, I got some photos of it before I moved it."

Jake took the point and held it up, letting the sunlight dance across its surface. "Hmm. Looks like Knife River flint, believe it or not."

"Really? Here in Wisconsin?" Michelle asked, rising to her feet.

"Sure looks like it. Makes a pretty strong case for a western connection."

"Um, how about a little explanation for a newcomer?" Pam asked. She stopped brushing the small bones in front of her, waiting for a reply.

"Knife River flint, or chalcedony, is a kind of stone found in the Dakotas. The only way it gets this far east is if someone went out there to collect it, or traded for it, or brought it with them when they traveled east across Minnesota."

"I didn't realize people were moving around so much 7,000 years ago."

"The Paleoindian and Archaic peoples were highly mobile, and moved around quite a bit before they started settling down in the big river valleys. But it is unusual to find Knife River in Wisconsin, this early."

"It strengthens the theory that the people hunting bison here in Wisconsin may have started out in the Dakotas," Michelle said.

"Certainly possible," Jake said. "Although I think Sam is of the opinion that this was a local group, hunting a small bison herd that was eking out a living in the northern forest. Better go show this to him, and make sure everyone else gets a look. Nice job."

Michelle grinned proudly, and walked over to show off her discovery.

"Gee, That's a tough act to follow," Pam said, leaning over to clean more bones. "My bones are going to pale by comparison."

Jake knelt beside her. "Let's see what you've got."

"I took out that section of backbone over here, and then underneath I found these smaller ribs, all lined up. It doesn't look like they were butchered at all. They're small, so I guess they're from a juvenile bison, right?"

Jake nodded, then reached over to examine a small piece of bone that Pam had exposed with her brush.

"What do you make of this bone, Jake?" She jabbed at it with a wooden pick, simultaneously shooing away a pesky mosquito with her other hand. "It has a funny curve, and it's not flat like the rest of these ribs."

Jake stared at the element, and brushed a bit more dirt away with his hand. "No, it's definitely not a rib," he said quietly. "That's a clavicle."

"A bison clavicle? Neat."

Jake sighed, and his shoulders dropped. "Bison don't have clavicles. But humans do."

CHAPTER 13

"SO, EVEN THOUGH WE KNOW THE remains are contemporaneous with the bison kill, state law requires that we alert the local authorities. That's why we called you."

Sheriff Grace O'Neil stared at Jake, then looked at the partially exposed skeletal remains next to him. She glanced at Sam, and then turned her attention back to Jake.

"If these bones are old, what do you need me for? Do I have to call someone, maybe the coroner?" Sheriff O'Neil was in her late forties or early fifties, with red hair streaked with silver and a pale complexion. She stood a little less than six feet tall, with narrow shoulders and wide hips, although it was hard to judge as she kept shifting her weight from one foot to another. The dour expression on her face suggested she would have rather been almost anywhere else at that moment.

"It's just a formality, sheriff. We want you to be aware of the presence of human remains at the site. Because of the age, it isn't necessary to notify the coroner." Out of the corner of his eye, Jake saw Sam running his fingers through his hair, a sure sign that he was growing (even more) frustrated. Probably why his hair is so thin, he thought. "If it helps, I called and left a message with the State Archaeologist. That's also required under state law. And she'll give us the official word on how to proceed."

The sheriff gaped at him for a moment, then peered around him to look at the bones. She glanced around the excavation, searching for anything familiar. Finally, she shook her head in annoyance.

"I'm going to need to get Legal in on this. Stay here."

"Redheads always give me grief," Sam said, scuffing the ground with his boot as the sheriff walked back to her vehicle. She got inside and started talking animatedly into the radio.

"She's probably just never had to deal with anything like this before, Sam. Doesn't know what's expected, so she's unsure of how to proceed." Jake stepped back into the open unit and knelt down next to the remains. "Wasn't your second wife a redhead?"

"Don't remind me. Been trying to forget about that one for a long time now." Sam sat down on a nearby overturned pail, wincing as he did. "So, how are we going to handle our new friend here?"

Jake shrugged. "Depends on what Liz has to say. Considering this area will be destroyed when they extend the access road, I think she'll agree that it would be best to remove him. Or her."

"It's going to slow us way down, Jake. We're already falling behind schedule."

Jake gave the older man a puzzled look. "No, I think we're doing okay. Pam's arrival means an extra pair of hands, and we already opened more units than I planned. Everything beyond this point is a bonus."

Sam mumbled something under his breath, and kicked away a small pebble. The unoffending stone bounced off the toe of Pam's boot as she approached.

"Jake? I'm really sorry about this. I, I didn't mean to cause any problems."

Sam stood and shuffled back to his unit. Jake eyed him for a moment, watching as Susan patted Sam on the shoulder. Susan was glaring at Pam, but she turned away when she realized Jake had noticed.

"It's okay. Those bones were going to turn up at some point, and they're going to have to be dealt with. It's actually good they were found now, rather than on the last day of the dig." He smiled, but she didn't see the humor. "The old joke in archaeology is that the most important finds only show up on the last day of work, usually about ten minutes before quitting time."

"Are you going to have to shut down? I mean, isn't that what happens at construction sites, when human remains are found?"

"Sometimes, but that's not the case here. Usually work is stopped in the immediate vicinity of a find, but only to preserve the remains until they can be examined in detail. State agencies and Native American tribes have to be consulted, but it normally goes pretty quickly. And Liz Pond, the Wisconsin State Archaeologist, is an old pro dealing with these issues. It can be an inconvenience for the builders, but good archaeologists try to make it as painless as possible."

"But don't you have to leave the body in place? I mean, isn't there some rule about not disturbing graves?"

"The law is flexible because not ever situation is the same," Jake replied. "If a graveyard is going to be destroyed and it can't be avoided by redesigning the project, then a decision might be made to remove the remains. Other times . . ."

Jake's cell phone rang, and he checked the caller ID. "State Archaeologist's office. This'll be Liz."

Pam nodded, and Jake took a few steps closer to the human remains. He spoke for a few minutes, answering questions and adding more details, before ending the call. As he finished, Sheriff O'Neil returned.

"I just spoke to Keith," the sheriff announced. "He's confirmed that all . . . this . . . is above board."

"Keith Emerson?"

"Yes, Keith Emerson," Sheriff O'Neil snapped. "He's legal counsel for Kohl County. Anyway, he says what you're doing with the bones . . . the human ones . . . is exactly what the law says you should do."

The tone of her voice made Jake feel as if he were being lectured, which he didn't particularly appreciate, since he had been the one to call and enlighten her after the remains were found, but he decided to let it pass.

"Well, thank you, sheriff. The State Archaeologist has also given her approval, so we'll carry on with the excavation."

"Fine. Keith said something about stopping by again one of these days, so if you have any more questions you can take them up with him." With a brusque salute, the sheriff strode back to her vehicle and drove away.

Jake waved his hand and called out for everyone's attention. "Okay, we're set. The local authorities are aware of the situation, and I don't anticipate any problems."

"Liz has signed off, too?" Sam asked.

Jake nodded. "It'll mean generating a separate burial report for her files, but Liz agrees that since the remains can't be avoided, we'll have to excavate. She offered to send a notification letter to the tribal offices and will let me know if any of them have concerns. We may end up reburying them nearby at a later date, but we'll cross that bridge when we come to it."

"What about the Emersons?" Heather inquired. "Aren't they upset about what *she* found?"

"When I spoke to them after phoning the sheriff, they were fine with it," Jake said sternly. He didn't appreciate the accusatory tone aimed at Pam, who stood off to the side, alone. "In fact, they both seem pretty excited about the discovery. And it really is an amazing find. Early Archaic human remains, in direct association with a bison kill site. The bones are well preserved, so there's the potential to uncover a lot of important information."

"Maybe this is how Ghost Bog got its name," Al offered. Heather scoffed at the idea, pointing out the thousands of years that had passed. Curt and Rob each chimed in with their thoughts, and soon a small but heated debate had erupted over oral tradition and social memory.

"Alright, alright," Sam yelled, clanging his trowel against an empty bucket. "Can we shelve this squabble until after work? These bison bones aren't excavating themselves!"

"Sam's right," Jake agreed. "Everyone back to their units, please. Michelle, you and Pam keep working on the bison remains in the other half of this unit. I'll start working on our friend here."

Michelle nodded, and glanced over her shoulder as everyone resumed working. "Uh, Jake? I'm sorry I didn't recognize the bones as human," she said, eyes downcast. "So much for thinking I should specialize in zooarchaeology."

"Hey, knock off that negative attitude. Ribs are always hard to identify, especially when they're half-buried in black, mucky soil."

This brought a smile to her face. "Besides, Pam said you commented on how small they were, and that they might be from a young bison calf. You knew right off something wasn't kosher."

"I suppose that's true," Michelle said, confidence returning.

"Besides, you were distracted by having to work with the rookie on the crew," Pam said, gently poking Michelle in the arm.

"In any event, you can make it up me by helping me excavate the skeleton. It'll go faster with two of us, but you'll still have to supervise Pam's work. Okay?"

"Sure, great. I've never excavated human remains before."

"Fine. There are some skeleton recording forms in the brown file box in the shed. Could you go grab a couple, and some more graph paper? I want to document everything as is before we expose more of the skeleton."

Michelle scurried across the site toward the equipment shed.

"You're a big softie, you know that?" Pam remarked, favoring him with a dimpled smile.

Jake grinned. "I don't know what you're talking about. I just doubled her workload. I mean, it's for her own good. Good experience, that is."

"Mm-hmm, anything you say. Guess I'd better get back to work before you take out your wrath on me next."

CHAPTER 14

THE ARCHAEOLOGISTS WORKED STEADILY THROUGH THE rest of the afternoon, savoring the unseasonably warm autumn weather. As the day drew to a close, Jake cautioned the crew to keep mum about their discovery of human remains, in order to prevent unwelcome interest in the site. He also visited the Emersons and asked them to keep an extra close watch on the site during the evenings. They happily agreed, and thanked Jake several times for giving Keith a tour of the dig and letting him help out. It was all he could talk about during his last visit with them.

By late morning the following day, most of the human skeleton had been revealed. Working in tandem, Jake and Michelle documented the exposed bones and then carefully uncovered more of the remains. The crew, excited by the impact of their discovery, used any excuse they could to wander over and check on their progress. Even Heather was drawn to the find, but she downplayed her enthusiasm if Pam was within earshot. Sam, however, was largely immune to the significance of the 7,000-year-old skeleton.

"Still at it, huh," Sam said, glancing down at the remains, frowning as Jake and Michelle brushed away loose soil from each side. "You know, you could pop out some of those ribs right now, get the arm bones loose after that. Easy enough to clean them good back at the lab."

Jake rolled his eyes, and Michelle pretended not to notice. "We could, Sam, but it's not the best way to do it. There are less than a dozen human skeletons this old, and none in this condition anywhere in the Midwest. I want to document everything we can about this find before any of it comes out of the ground." He leaned back, and tried to work a stubborn knot out of his shoulder. "In any case, it won't take more than another day to finish."

Sam didn't respond, but knelt next to Michelle and peered at the skeleton. "Lots of busted bones, though. Preservation really isn't that great."

"It's better than I would have expected. Look here, and at this set of breaks over here—all green fractures. I think our friend here had a pretty violent end."

"You sure? Could just be taphonomic, crushed under the weight of the soil."

"No, I don't think so. The fracture edges on these ribs are clean and sharp. Definitely perimortem."

"Find something good?"

"Hey, Pam. Michelle and I think this person had a rather traumatic death. About half of the ribs show multiple fractures, and there are visible fractures on some of the forearm bones, too."

Michelle held up the skeletal analysis form she had on her clipboard and pointed to a series of jagged lines drawn on various bones. "See? We've recorded them on the form, and if you use these as a guide it's much more clear."

"Wow, yeah, I see what you mean," Pam said, looking from the clipboard to the skeleton. "They're all over the place."

"Haven't seen many on the legs yet, but we still have more bones to expose," Michelle said. "But the pelvis is broken up quite a bit, which is consistent with a massive impact."

Sam abruptly stood and returned to his unit without another word. Pam watched him leave, and then looked questioningly at

Jake. He shrugged his shoulders, and shook his head.

"What were you saying, as I walked up? Perry-something?"

"Perimortem," Jake said. "Means that the injuries occurred right before or at the time of death. We don't see any evidence of healing."

"I'm impressed. On top of all your other qualities," Pam remarked, "You're a prehistoric forensic scientist, too."

"No, not really . . . nothing that specialized. Archaeology is all about reconstructing the past, but most often we look at 'big picture' patterns, not something as specific as a crime scene."

"That's pretty much what you've got here, right?"

"I suppose so. It's not often that archaeologists get to look at specific moments in time. You know, like Pompeii and Herculaneum, for example."

Pam nodded, and knelt next to the edge of the unit to get a closer look at the remains. "So, you have the probable cause of death. What about the basics? Male or female? And an adult, right?"

"Definitely an adult. The long bone ends are fully fused. Not a ton of wear on the teeth, at least from what I can see, so probably not very old. And male, I think. The cranium and mandible are pretty rugged, but that can be subjective. Measurements of the pelvis, once we get it out of the ground and reassemble it, will be more definitive."

"And you're sure the body is as old as the bison kill?"

Jake thought for a moment, considering the evidence. Michelle, who had been engrossed in cleaning some dirt from opposite side of the skull, was now listening carefully. "It looks like it. The human and bison bones are in the same strata, with no indication that the body was deposited later on. And the discoloration of all the bones is consistent, which suggests they've all been in the ground from the same amount of time."

"And we have some small bone fragments that we can submit for radiocarbon dating," Michelle said, indicating a small plastic vial. "The results should prove the bison and the body are contemporaneous."

The now-familiar sounds of tires rolling over gravel ended their discussion, and Jake stood with reluctance, wincing a bit as his back muscles protested this position change. Sam glared at him, shaking his head, but Jake ignored the look and followed the well-trod path to the parking area.

Jake was a bit surprised to see Keith Emerson climb out from behind the wheel. His passenger, a man Jake didn't recognize, walked around the back of the car, scanning the clearing through aviator sunglasses. Both men were dressed in dark, well-tailored suits.

"Hi, Keith. Nice to see you again." Jake made a show of looking at Keith's attire. "I'm going to take a guess that you're not planning on screening this time."

Keith laughed, shaking his head. "No, afraid not this time. Meeting this morning, and I have to be in court this afternoon. But I had to bring Frank over to meet you while I had the chance."

"Frank Russell. Nice to meet you," Frank said, extending his hand. He stood about six foot-five, a few inches taller than Jake, with a slim but athletic build. His hair was dark brown, cropped short, and he had a grim, squared-jaw face that contrasted with Keith's youthful appearance, despite their close ages. "Keith's been going on and on about your dig. I had to get over here soon, or he was going to explode."

"Don't listen to him, Jake," Keith said. "He had a million questions as soon as I told him about the bison kill, and it got worse after he found out I got to work at the site. He's worse than a big kid."

Jake took a second look at the tall, quiet man. Big kid was not the term he would use to describe him. "Come on, I'll give you a tour and show you some of our finds."

Jake led Frank around the Ghost Bog site, describing the excavation and some of their more interesting finds. Keith chattered away behind them, embellishing on Jake's standard presentation and terminology. He also introduced Frank to the crew, all of whom were polite but not overly friendly. Some of the recent visitors had left the archaeologists leery of newcomers, and the stoic guest with the tight smile did not seem inclined toward jovial conversation.

"All very interesting, Professor Caine," Frank said, as they stood near Heather and Al's open units. "But Keith informed me that some human remains were also discovered. Might I have a look at those?"

Jake was a bit surprised, and took a quick glance at Keith, who was chatting with Al about a series of foot bones she had uncovered. Obviously Keith was aware of the find, as Sheriff O'Neil had contacted him during her visit. "Of course. Follow me over here."

Jake led Frank on a sinuous path through the boggy soil until they reached Michelle and Pam's units at the far end of the excavation. He made introductions and then pointed out the partially excavated skeleton, describing some of the traits they had noted thus far. Frank seemed quite interested in their discovery, and asked a series of follow-up questions about the extent of the injuries, the cause of death, and other specific details. It was akin to a forensic examination, which Jake attributed to his presumed background in crime scene investigation.

"Jake?" Pam gestured him over, tapping her clipboard. "Got a sec for a quick question?"

Jake excused himself, leaving Frank in Michelle's capable company. Pam had her back turned and seemed engrossed in a problem with her paperwork.

"What's up?"

"Everything okay, Jake? That guy is carrying a sidearm."

Jake turned his head quickly, while Pam put a cautionary hand on his arm. "It's on his left side, at his belt."

It was hard to spot, but Jake caught a glimpse of the black leather holster when Frank's jacket fluttered in the breeze.

"Jake?"

"It's okay. Frank is a Wisconsin Bureau of Investigation agent. I think he and Keith are just making a quick visit here in-between some official business in Scenic."

Pam exhaled, relieved. "Good. I really didn't want to see any more trouble here."

Jake smiled. "Me, neither. And thanks for keeping your eyes open."

KEITH AND FRANK LEFT SOON AFTERWARDS and work resumed at the Ghost Bog site. No other visitors came, and Jake and Michelle exposed most of the skeleton by the end of the day. As they closed up the site, they covered the bones with white muslin and several thick tarps, and over that they put a large, heavy board provided by Harold Emerson. The crew covered the board with another larger tarp, weighed down with sandbags and logs. It would take several people a fair amount of time to uncover the burial, if they were even able to locate it in the darkness.

Jake felt quite pleased with the day's progress, and decided they should celebrate at The Hop, a 50s-themed diner in Scenic. His suggestion was met with a muted response from the crew, but Pam thought it sounded like fun and agreed to go.

About an hour later, Jake and Pam sat across from each other in a padded vinyl booth, serenaded with rock and roll music. The Hop was richly decorated with advertisements and knick-knacks from the 1950s and 1960s. Neon lights glistened off chrome trim on the tables and countertop, and servers on roller skates brought burgers and malts to hungry patrons parked in the car-service area. Inside, the diner was over half full, with an equal distribution of youngsters and seniors.

"So, how did you find this place?" Pam asked with a grin, picking up a menu. "If I had known it was here, I would have packed my poodle skirt and saddle shoes."

"That sounds like a cute look. I'd like to see that sometime," Jake said. "I ran across it when I was up here last fall, dealing with some permit issues and meeting with the Emersons. Just fell in love with the style; it's like something out of *American Graffiti*."

"How's the food though? I noticed there wasn't much enthusiasm when you suggested it at the site."

Jake frowned. "Oh, these young people today, no appreciation for classic 50s' décor. Just look at that jukebox over in the corner. I think it's an original and—hey, are you laughing at me?"

Pam shielded her face behind the menu, but she was turning red from stifling her laughter. "No, no. Course not. Just appreciating your . . . enthusiasm for this place."

Jake tried to maintain a stern look, but when Pam rolled her eyes, they both burst out laughing. They managed to regain their composure when the waitress arrived to take their orders.

"Fine, I guess I'm a big nerd," Jake said, after the waitress had left. "Now you know my terrible secret. Happy?"

"Very. But don't worry, I'll keep your secret from all the 'young people' at the site. What's that all about, anyway? You're not much older than most of your students."

"Sorry. Guess being cooped up with Sam all week has started to rub off on me." Jake explained Sam's earlier soul-bearing, and his concerns about nearing the end of his career. He also summarized Sam's antagonistic history with Matt Walker.

"He's not exactly elderly, but I suppose he's closer to that age than we are," Pam said, pausing to take her cherry fizz from the waitress. "I guess that explains why he's in such a rush."

Jake nodded. "I think he'd be a little more relaxed if Walker and his two shadows would stay away. I hope I made it clear that they aren't welcome at Ghost Bog."

Before Pam could answer, a figure appeared at the edge of their booth.

"Ah, Professor Caine, so nice to see you here."

"Hello, Peter. Good to see you. And please, call me Jake."

Peter tilted his head in Pam's direction. "And this is?"

"Oh, sorry. Peter Holcombe, this is Pam Hauser, a new volunteer at the site. She helped out during a recent field school near Donovan."

As Pam and Peter exchanged greetings, Jake noticed a tall, lanky youth in a black leather jacket standing oddly close to Peter. He wasn't paying attention to their conversation. Rather, the youngster was ogling some pretty girls sitting at a nearby table.

Peter caught Jake staring past him, and turned slightly. "Where are my manners? Professor, Pam, this is my son, Eric." He stepped back, and Eric shuffled forward and mumbled a greeting, not bothering to hide the perpetual sneer on his thin, sallow face.

Jake and Pam both said hello, but it was Peter who continued the conversation.

"I've been telling Eric he simply has to make time to visit your site."

Eric barked out a short laugh and rolled his eyes. Peter ignored his response. "He's quite busy with his own little projects, of course. And he doesn't have the passion for natural history that I do. It's not all that popular with the younger generation."

Jake smiled, nodding in nonchalant agreement. Eric appeared to be in his early twenties, with a greasy appearance and tough-guy manner. His attention had already returned to the girls at the nearby table, who were stealing glances back at him, frowning. Jake didn't envision an academic career in Eric's future; a courtroom setting seemed more likely, and not as a judge.

"I hear you have another exciting discovery at Ghost Bog," Peter said, drawing Jake's attention. "Just think, a 7,000 year old human skeleton right here in Kohl County. Amazing!"

Jake was a bit startled, but tried to hide it. "Yes. Yes, it is quite the find. We're trying to keep it quiet, of course," he said, lowering his voice. "How did you, um, happen to hear about it?"

"News travels fast around Scenic, Professor. Sheriff McNeil brought it to our attention at the town planning meeting yesterday. I hope that's not a problem?"

"No, of course not," Jake said. Obviously, he had no control over whom the sheriff might have told, but he hoped he could minimize the damage. "We just don't want the information to spread too much. It's a security issue."

"I understand completely," Peter said. "Rest assured it will go no farther."

"Don't be too worried," Pam said. "Jake and Michelle removed the last of the remains late today, so there's nothing else out there."

Jake started to speak, but Pam nudged his leg with her foot.

"Oh, good. I was hoping to get a look at the remains, but I understand the need for secrecy."

The waitress arrived bearing Jake and Pam's food, ending any further conversation. Peter said his goodbyes and left the diner with Eric in tow.

"That was a little weird," Jake said, before taking a bite of his cheeseburger.

"I'll say," Pam said, pouring a large dollop of ketchup over her fries. "I got a really bad vibe off Eric. Hard to believe he's prim-and-proper Peter's son."

"Yeah. But I was thinking more about Peter's comments about the skeleton. By the way, nice save there, telling him that all the bones have been removed."

"Classic misdirection technique," Pam said with a satisfied smile. "A simple lie takes away their motivation for snooping around, and don't give out any information about where the remains have gone. If they ask more questions, it makes them look suspicious."

"I don't think we have much to worry about with Peter."

"Maybe not him, but what about Eric? I thought his ears perked up when Peter mentioned the human remains. Other than that, he couldn't have cared less about what was being said."

Jake chewed thoughtfully on an onion ring. "It'll all be over soon. Michelle and I will remove the bones tomorrow, so even if word does spread it won't make much difference. That should be the end of human remains at Ghost Bog."

CHAPTER 15

As Jake turned the Wisconsin State University van on to the gravel entryway, he wasn't surprised to see Pam's old Camaro already in the parking area, as she had dutifully arrived on site early each day since her arrival. Spotting Matt Walker and his assistants standing outside their van, shovels in hand, was decidedly not a welcome sight. His passengers let out a chorus of groans and swearing as they also saw the intruders.

"Okay, let's not get excited," Jake ordered, as he pulled to a stop and turned off the engine. "Business as usual while I take care of this. Heather, go unlock the shed, and on your way over take a look and make sure nothing has been disturbed. Michelle, check on the burial but don't uncover it just yet. Rob, Curt, pull the tarps off your units and set up the screens."

Heather shook her head. "But what about . . ."

"If I need you guys, I'll give out a yell. C'mon, let's go."

Jake walked across the lot toward Matt Walker. Pam, arms folded and leaning against the back of her car, nodded her head but made no move to join him or the newly arrived crew. It was apparent that she planned to remain on guard until instructed otherwise.

Jake sighed as he reached Walker, who stood smiling. His assistants, dressed for fieldwork, seemed calm but not necessarily at ease.

"And what do we have here?" Jake asked, as politely as he could manage.

Walker looked surprised, or at least made a good mimicry of it. "Why, we're here to help of course. You're not going to turn down three more volunteers, are you?"

"I appreciate the offer, but we're doing quite fine as it is. Well ahead of schedule, to be honest."

"But you are using volunteers, aren't you?" Walker inclined his head toward Pam, who continued to monitor the situation. "Your blonde friend there, for example, seems to be both digger and guard dog. She was quite adamant that no one entered the excavation area until you had arrived."

"Just following the rules," Jake said. "In any event, we don't have the space for three more volunteers. And we both know it would only lead to trouble."

"Come now, Professor Caine. Many hands make light the work, as they say. And you must be somewhat shorthanded, what with the human skeleton you discovered."

Jake's jaw dropped slightly, but he soon regained his composure. "And how did you hear about that?"

"Oh, you know how news like that tends to travel. And I am particularly well connected, after all." He gave Jake a theatrical wink.

Jake frowned and folded his arms across his chest. At that moment, he could only think that he needed to drink more coffee in the morning if this is how his days were going to start.

"Under the circumstances, I don't see how you can refuse my assistance," Walker said, returning to the haughty tone of his prior visits. "And to be blunt, if I pursued the matter I would imagine the administrators in Madison would be inclined to turn this entire project over to me, especially with the human remains to consider."

So, that was it. Intimidate me into thinking he can take over if he really wants to, thought Jake.

"Nice try, but I don't think so," Jake said. "Wisconsin is strict about the excavation and analysis of human remains. There is a list, updated annually, of those qualified for inclusion. I'm on that list. So is Sam, and Heather, my assistant. I do know for a fact, however, that you are not on that list."

Walker's smug demeanor vanished as he realized his little trick wasn't going to succeed.

"And in any event, the human remains were completed excavated yesterday, and are no longer of concern."

Walker's eyes darted to the left and right of where Jake stood. "And I suppose if I push matters, you'll have your thugs rough me up, is that it?"

Puzzled by this remark, Jake turned to see Heather, Curt, Rob, and Michelle lined up at the edge of the excavation area. They stood ramrod straight, each grasping a shovel, glaring at Walker and his team.

Walker's shoulders dropped and he let out a long, exaggerated sigh. "Well, it's quite obvious that my expertise is not appreciated here." He brushed invisible dirt from his hands in a showy fashion. "Time to move on to Plan B: An extensive paleontological survey of Kohl County. The results of which I am quite certain will put this little grave-robbing expedition to shame. And you need not worry about the proper permits, as I have all that taken care of already."

Walker patted the breast pocket of his khaki vest, before turning away. He ordered Ryan and Laura to load up their equipment and get back in the van.

"We won't be bothering you again, Mr. Caine," Walker called over his shoulder as he climbed behind the driver's seat. "Luck to you. You will need it."

As they drove off, Jake turned to the crew and made it clear that he didn't appreciate their behavior, even if they meant well. The last thing he needed was a violent confrontation. He didn't yell, but it was clear to all that he was not pleased. They scattered when he sent them back to work, all except Pam, who stood a few yards away.

"Sorry about all that, Jake. They showed up a few minutes after I arrived. I wouldn't let them on to the site, and I was about to call when I saw your vehicle."

"It's okay, it's over now. Just glad they weren't poking around here without us around."

"No, everything was quiet when I arrived. Where are Sam and the others?"

"They were running late. Their van needed gas, and it was their turn to pick up coffee and doughnuts. They should be about ten or fifteen minutes behind us. Boy, it couldn't have happened on a better day."

"Speak of the devil," Pam said, gesturing to the Lewis and Clark Museum van as it rolled to a stop. She picked up her backpack and walked over to help Michelle uncover their units.

Jake saw the look on Sam's face and knew he hadn't escaped unscathed.

"Jake, I just saw Walker driving out of here! What's going on?"

As succinctly as he could, Jake explained what had happened. In between Sam's cussing, Jake stressed how it appeared that Walker had finally given up getting access to Ghost Bog. Sam continued to fret and fume, until Jake was sick of the entire situation. After a few minutes, he walked off to his unit, leaving Sam to complain to empty air.

Jake resumed work on the skeleton, and with Michelle's assistance they made good progress documenting and removing the elements. By early afternoon, their task was completed and the human bones were stored in the Wisconsin State University cargo van, ready to transport back to the hotel.

Their primary task finished, Jake put Michelle back to work with Pam, and started on a small unit a few yards away. He was polite when called upon, but for the most part avoided interaction with the rest of the crew. Some dark clouds rolled in as dusk fell, so he ordered everyone to pack up a little early, just as the first raindrops began to fall. The team covered the open units, locked up the equipment in the shed, and left the site in record time. After locking the boxes of human remains in the footlocker in his room, Jake washed and snuck out of the hotel to a small bar and grill about a mile down the road. He found a secluded corner table, ate and drank in relative solitude, and let the stress of the last few days melt away.

CHAPTER 16

J AKE'S MOOD HAD IMPROVED BY THE next morning. The sun
was shining again and while cool in the early hours, the weather
forecast predicted unseasonably warm temperatures for at least
another week. He greeted everyone happily, raising a few curious
stares, but most assumed his bad mood had passed and he was
back to normal.

At the mid-morning break, Pam refilled her coffee mug and sat
down next to Jake as he munched on a leftover bagel.

"You're in a chipper mood this morning," Pam said, nudging
him with her elbow. "Makes me wonder what you were up to last
night, after you ditched the rest of us."

"Sorry about that. Nothing personal; just needed some alone
time."

"I get it. Pretty stressful job, running an excavation like this,
tons of paperwork, and then guys like Walker causing even more
problems."

"True, but it isn't all that bad," Jake said, brushing the last
crumbs from his hands. "With luck, we've seen that last of Walker
and his toadies."

"Oh, I don't think they'll be back, not after your crew showed
that they've got your back," Pam said, smiling. "What you need is

a nice, relaxing evening on the town. How about if I pick you up and we . . ."

"Hey, Jake, we got a spearpoint lodged in some ribs!" Heather's shout was probably heard in the outskirts of Scenic. "Come on, check this out!"

"Duty calls," Jake said, as he rose and walked over to join the crowd around Heather and Al's unit.

Pam watched him leave, then poured out her lukewarm coffee and went back to work.

ABOUT AN HOUR LATER, JAKE CHECKED in on Pam and Michelle as they were finishing work on their current unit. Michelle was scraping the last of the soil into a dustpan, while Pam was recording the artifact counts in their paperwork.

"Looks like you're just about done here," Jake said.

Michelle nodded. "Maybe one more pail of soil to finish this level, and that's it. We only had a few scraps of bone in here, and a couple of flakes. Nothing spectacular."

"Sounds good. I think I'll have Pam start . . . over there, in Unit 68. Michelle, you can finish up on your own."

Pam looked up from her clipboard. "Trying to get rid of me?"

"No, not at all. We need to get this whole section cleared out, and that unit has already been started. We stopped digging there when the body was found. Most of the topsoil has been removed, so you should be right on top of the bone bed."

"Okay. I'll get started in a second," Pam said, scribbling a few more notes on the dirt-smeared page in front of her.

"Everything okay?"

"Fine. Just tired, I guess," Pam said, setting the clipboard on a nearby tool kit. "Don't worry, I'll have that unit excavated in no time."

Pam took the paperwork for Unit 68, grabbed her dig kit, and went over to work on her new unit. Jake gave Michelle a puzzled look, but she just shrugged and went back to her troweling.

Jake returned to his own unit a few meters away, and worked

contentedly for the next hour or so. He was picking some soil away from a bison mandible when a shadow fell across his unit.

"Uh, Jake?"

"Yeah, Pam. What's up?" He continued scraping, ever so gently, along the smooth underside of the large jawbone.

"Promise you won't be mad."

"Uh, oh." Jake stopped working and sat back on the edge of his unit. "What happened?"

"I think I've got more human remains. Can you come and take a look?"

Jake nodded, and grabbed a stiff brush from his dig kit. "Did Michelle check them?"

"No, she's still finishing up our old unit," Pam said, leading the way. "She found some more flakes by the wall, so she wanted to dig down a bit into the subsoil."

Jake nodded, glancing over to see Michelle laying on her stomach, peering at the yellow soil in front of her. Reaching Pam's unit, Jake knelt and immediately recognized an unmistakable series of human rib bones, joined at the sternum.

"Ho-boy. Yeah, you've got another one, I'm afraid."

"I am so sorry, Jake."

"Hey, not your fault. One of us was going to find him—or her—eventually." Jake looked up at Pam, and gave her a smile. "Actually, this is really amazing, finding two human skeletons at a 7,000 year old bison kill."

Pam let out a sigh. "Good. I was afraid you'd be upset, you know, 'cause it will slow things down."

Jake glanced over at Sam and Susan in their expanding central unit. "Well, Sam will grouse a bit, but that's second nature to him." He scraped and brushed some more dirt away from the upper part of the skeleton, exposing the clavicle and proximal end of the humerus. His brows furrowed ever so slightly.

"Hmm. Bones aren't quite the same color as the bison bones, or even the other skeleton. And the preservation seems better."

"Is that a problem?"

"Don't know," Jake said, continuing to expose the bones of the left arm. He worked his way past the elbow joint, and followed the radius and ulna downward.

"It sure looks like these bones are a bit more shallow than the rest of the bone bed. How many bison elements did you remove so far?"

"None," Pam said, glancing over his shoulder. "These were the first bones I hit, so I started exposing the ribs, like Michelle showed me. Is this skeleton not part of the bison bone bed?"

Jake stopped and straightened up. "No, definitely not," he said, pointing the tip of his trowel at the metal watchband encircling the wrist bones.

CHAPTER 17

Jake watched, mesmerized, as the station wagon crept into the parking area, now packed with vehicles. The new arrival tried to squeeze in between Sheriff O'Neil's patrol car and the Lewis and Clark Museum van, but soon abandoned that and attempted to maneuver into a spot next to Keith Emerson's car. Keith, standing a few feet from Jake, winced as the station wagon inched closer to the front of his own car. Agent Frank Russell, who had arrived with Keith, calmly remarked that the driver had at least a few inches of clearance but that did little to placate his companion. Jake had been surprised to see them, but they explained that they were in a meeting with Sheriff O'Neil when he called. Under the circumstances, it had been agreed that it would be best if they tagged along. After the trio had arrived and inspected the discovery, the sheriff contacted one of her deputies to "help secure the scene" and ordered everyone away from the skeleton until the coroner came. She did, with some reluctance, allow work to continue elsewhere at the dig, at Jake's request. Sam was already irate about this latest find and halting work entirely would have pushed him over the edge.

As they waited, Keith and Agent Russell each made several calls, while the sheriff wandered around the perimeter of the dig glaring at the archaeologists, when not busy checking her watch and staring at the roadway leading into the site. O'Neil's deputy, a gangly youngster barely old enough to purchase alcohol, followed her around, awaiting instruction. He had arrived within ten minutes of her call, but now present she seemed to have no immediate use for him.

Finally, the wagon had settled to a stop and a gray-haired man with extremely bushy eyebrows exited the vehicle and walked over to the group. He did not look pleased.

"This better be good, Grace, dragging me all the way out here. Hello Keith, Frank. Gangs all here, huh. Where's the deceased?"

"Over this way, Doc. These here archaeologists found . . ."

"Hold it, let me grab my notebook. Left it in the car."

"Doctor Wheeler is the local sawbones," Keith explained to Jake while they waited. "He's the acting county coroner."

"Okay, let's go."

Sheriff O'Neil led the group around the well-worn path at the edge of the excavation and then crossed over to the unit in which the remains were found. Doctor Wheeler did a double take when Jake removed the protective tarp.

"What the hell is this, a joke? I don't do prehistoric stuff!"

"Look closer, Doc," Agent Russell said. "This one's wearing a watch."

The coroner leaned down and inspected the remains over the top of his glasses. "Hmph. Well, this still isn't my area. Body's dead, I'll agree to that. Otherwise, you're on your own dealing with this one."

Doctor Wheeler flipped his notebook open, pulled a pen from his pocket, and turned to Jake. "You found the body?"

"Yes. Well, one of the crew, Pam, was the first to uncover the bones. I confirmed the remains as human, and cleaned off more of the soil."

"Fine, fine. Get her over here, will you?"

Pam came over and gave her personal info to the coroner, who scribbled it in his notebook. He then jotted down Jake's name, title, and other relevant data. He wrote for a few more minutes without speaking, and then closed the book.

"Well, I have all I need. Grace, I'll send you the paperwork in a couple of days."

"What am I supposed to do with this now?"

The doctor shrugged. "Not my call. If it were recent, I'd say call Charlie at the funeral home, but I'm not sure he could handle this. This guy has been out here for years, minimum."

"Should I just dig it up, and take it back to the station until we figure this out?"

"Even though these bones are recent, there is important archaeological material right underneath" Jake said quickly. "I don't want to see that damaged."

"He's right, Grace," Keith said. "Technically it could be construed as destruction of archaeological resources. We need to proceed with caution."

A minor squabble erupted as each person voiced his or her concerns and thoughts on how to proceed. Jake's primary concern was maintaining the integrity of the site, and he insisted that the archaeologists would have to be involved in some fashion during the removal of the remains.

"Lot of hassle over a bunch of bones," Doctor Wheeler said, as he looked around the clearing. "Probably some out-of-state hunter, keeled over from a heart attack. Is this here state or federal land?"

"Not sure," Sheriff O'Neil replied.

"Technically, the Emerson still own the property on which the site is located, but they're in the process of selling it to the state," Jake said. "This excavation is part of the legal requirements for the transfer process."

The coroner's eyes glazed over at the extended explanation. "Pretty much all of the bog and forest around here is state-owned, right? Why not let the Department of Natural Resources handle it?"

"We talked to them and they don't want it," Agent Russell said.

"They're spread pretty thin since the last round of layoffs. Officially, they aren't under any obligation until the land purchase is final."

"Damn jurisdictional crap," the doctor said, swatting away a few mosquitoes that had intruded on the discussion. He gestured at the badge on Agent Russell's belt with his other hand. "You're the state bureau agent up here. Why don't you take charge, and then pass it along to the DNR later on?"

"Hmm. That could work," he said, with an exaggerated expression of reluctant acceptance.

Sheriff O'Neil shot him a suspicious look. "Wait a minute. I think it's up to me to decide who's in charge here. I'm, I'm not sure . . ."

"Look, Grace," the doctor said, his frustration evident. "You said a minute ago you don't have the manpower to deal with an old cold case. Why pick up another headache that you don't need?"

"It's entirely up to you, Sheriff," Agent Russell said. "Last thing I want to do is encroach on your turf."

"Going to all be state land before long anyway, Grace," the doctor added. "What does Mike want to do about it?"

Sheriff O'Neil chewed at the corner of her lip. "The mayor is out of town again. I couldn't get hold of him." She looked at each man in turn, and gave Jake a particularly hard look. "Fine, whatever. Frank, this is your problem now. Do you need to get this cleared first?"

"No, that won't be a problem. I called Madison when we arrived. Before I knew for sure if the property was still in private hands," he added.

"Oh. Okay. Well, be sure you keep my office informed. Copies of all records, photos, notes, all that sort of thing."

"Of course."

"Grand. Now that everyone's happy, I'm getting the hell out of here," Doctor Wheeler said, digging for his car keys. "And I don't want to hear from any of you about any more damn skeletons!"

Sheriff O'Neil mumbled something under her breath and then yelled to her deputy, who met her at the edge of the parking lot.

They watched the coroner extract his car from its spot, spoke briefly, and then left. As the deputy's patrol car reached the highway, Agent Russell turned to Jake.

"So, Professor Caine. How long will it take you to excavate the John Doe?"

"Me?"

"You are qualified to excavate human remains, I believe."

"Yes, I am, but as a crime scene doesn't this require extra precautions?"

Agent Russell tilted his head and shrugged his shoulders. "It's not an active crime scene, in the traditional sense. Archaeologists are trained in detailed recovery techniques, so I'm sure you'll be able to locate and collect anything that might be relevant to identifying this individual. And you're the only one here who can distinguish what might be associated with the body and what is from your bison kill."

Jake nodded, relieved that the integrity of the bison bones would remain intact. "That does make sense. I suppose one or two days ought to do it. Anything special instructions, specific for a crime scene?"

"Technically, we don't have any proof that this is a crime scene. Could have been an accidental death, like the doc said. Just record everything you do, and collect everything that doesn't fit in naturally with the area or the archaeological site."

Agent Russell turned his attention to Pam, who had been standing a few feet away. "You are a deputy county sheriff, correct?"

"Yes, over in Donovan. I'm taking some vacation time."

He nodded, and Jake thought he noticed the barest hint of a smile. "You worked some crime scene investigations, I presume?"

Pam described her background and police training. Most of it involved traffic accidents and burglaries, but Agent Russell seemed satisfied.

"Between the two of you, you have more than enough practical experience to handle this. Deputy Hauser knows the protocol necessary to maintain a clear evidence chain. I'll be in and out of the area for the next few weeks, so you can contact me if you run into any problems." He handed one of his cards to each of them. "You can always relay a message to me through Keith, too."

Agent Russell reminded them to keep everything collected in a secure location, and to avoid any comments to the media, should there be any inquiries. He and Keith began to leave, when he stopped and turned around.

"One word of caution, Professor Caine," Agent Russell said. "Concentrate on removing the remains and any associated items, but limit it to that, if you would."

Jake gave him a puzzled look. "I'm not sure what you mean."

This time Agent Russell was definitely smiling. "Let's just say your reputation in this area precedes you."

"My reputation?"

"Cold case investigations, Professor. Let's not have any . . . surprises, please. I think we understand each other."

With that cryptic remark, Agent Russell and Keith walked back to the parking area and were soon gone. After watching them depart, Jake turned to Pam.

"What did he mean by that? Was that in reference to Waconah?"

"Had to be, I think," Pam said, frowning. "I'm surprised he knew about it. I mean, it was big local news, but how would the Wisconsin Bureau of Investigation have gotten wind of it?"

"Maybe he just ran across a news posting online."

"Probably. I'm sure he just meant it as a joke. So, should we get started?"

Jake nodded, and the pair started organizing the paperwork necessary for the excavation of human remains. But in the back of his mind, Jake was more than a bit concerned by Agent Russell's remark, and the possibility that he was missing something important.

CHAPTER 18

WORKING TOGETHER, PAM AND JAKE DEVISED a system for removing and screening the surrounding soil, and made quick progress excavating John Doe's remains. After exposing a larger area around the skeleton, Jake was able to discern a slight shift in color that allowed him to locate the edges of the much younger burial pit. It was easy to follow and it was soon apparent that there was no real impact on the bison kill site.

Dealing with the living people at the site, however, proved to be much more challenging. After the departure of Sheriff O'Neil, Agent Russell, and Keith Emerson, Jake gathered the crew together and explained the plan for removing the human remains. When Sam began to protest, Jake stressed the need to excavate the skeleton without damaging the bison bones, and that having the work done by the archaeologists was preferable to watching the sheriff or her deputy hack away with a pick and shovel. They all agreed on that point, but some unease was still evident, beyond Sam's continued grumbling. For good or ill, Ghost Bog was starting to live up to its name.

At the end of the day, Jake, Pam, and Michelle covered and concealed the human remains as best they could, in the same manner as that of the ancient, Early Archaic bog body. Jake, accompanied by Pam, checked in with the Emersons to see if they had any questions following their talk with Keith, but they seemed to have taken the recent discovery in stride. Pam suggested that she and Jake meet up for a working dinner, to compare notes and review their paperwork in order to complete the excavation the next day. She, too, had sensed the tension among the crew and assumed things would return to normal once their work was finished.

THE NEXT DAY, WORK BEGAN WITH an undercurrent of anxiety in the air. Even the birds seemed subdued, and the usual chatter and laughter by the crew was replaced by whispering and muted conversation. Unlike the Early Archaic skeleton, the crew showed little interest in the modern John Doe. Even their regular finds of ancient bison bones and stone tools seemed to generate only minimal excitement.

During the mid-morning break, Jake decided to loosen his stiff joints with a short walk out to the highway. On his return, he paused to refill his water bottle when he overheard Heather speaking to Susan in the sheltered doorway of the equipment shed.

"It was just like this at Waconah, you know."

"Really? Sam mentioned there was . . . trouble there but didn't go into much detail. Alyssa did say it was quite the scandal in the archaeology community for a while."

"It probably was," Heather said, "but none of it was Jake's fault. Deputy Hauser caused most of the trouble, right from the start. She got him all worked up over Professor Wardell's death, and that led to more problems."

Jake listened with increasing disbelief as Heather unfolded a heavily biased tale of the Wardell investigation, with more than a few outright lies about Pam thrown in. According to Heather, Pam practically ordered Jake around at gunpoint, disrupted the Waconah field school every chance she could, and drove Amanda away so she could make her play for Jake.

"That's terrible! What an awful thing for her to do," Susan said, clucking her tongue. "She should be ashamed."

"She's a jinx, that's for sure. Things were going along fine here until she showed up, right? I mean, who found both bodies? She did."

"That's true," Susan said. "And I know for a fact that this is causing poor Sam no end of worry. This dig is so important to him."

"I believe it. A bison kill this old, right here in Wisconsin. Site of a lifetime."

"No, it's more than that. Budgets have been tight the last few years, and they keep talking about layoffs and early retirements. There are some people at the museum who think it's time Sam thought about retiring."

This was news to Jake. In all their recent discussions about the Ghost Bog site and work in general, Sam never mentioned pressure to step down. He was pondering whether or not to step in and say something when he spotted Sam heading in their direction. Jake took a few steps away from the shed, made a 180-degree turn, and then acted as if he had just arrived.

"Hey, Sam," Jake yelled, with the intent of alerting Heather and Susan to his presence.

Sam gave him a curious look, obviously wondering why Jake was wandering around aimlessly. "Have you seen Susan? I've got a screen full of dirt piling up."

"No, haven't seen her. Did you look . . ."

"I'm coming, Sam," Susan said, stepping out from the doorway. "Just helping Heather move some boxes in the shed."

On cue, Heather appeared behind Susan, and waved to Sam. Her eyes widened when she spotted Jake, but he just nodded at her and they both continued on their way.

Ducking under the flagging tape at the edge of the excavation, Jake decided it best if he talked to Heather about her comments later, out of earshot of the rest of the crew. No need for a possible confrontation that would make everyone else uncomfortable, and he wasn't exactly sure how to approach the situation. While Heather was entitled to her opinion, spreading nasty gossip wasn't going to make the current excavation go any smoother. It was a delicate, no-win situation.

"Everything okay, Jake?" Pam looked at him with genuine concern as he reached their unit.

"Sure," he said, smiling. "Back is just a bit sore, that's all. Occupational hazard. Plus I'm a bit concerned about getting our friend out of the ground soon, you know, before Sunday when no one is around."

"I don't think that will be a problem. All the bones are exposed except for the right forearm, which is positioned under the body. But we can get to that soon enough."

Jake knelt next to her. "Hmm. It looks like John Doe landed on his side when he fell. That would explain why his arm is underneath."

Pam nodded. "It could be that he was thrown into a depression or hole, too. I mean, if it is a crime scene."

"We might not know that for sure until the bones are examined in detail. Now that I think about it, Agent Russell didn't say if he expected us to analyze the remains."

"He might want you to. I imagine a case like this would be low priority at the state crime lab. If you were willing, it would speed up the investigation."

Jake shrugged. "I'll ask him the next time we see him. For now, let's dig under the right side some more. If we cut back the soil here, we should be able to expose part of the right arm before we start removing the ribs."

Working in tandem, they scraped the soil back from the skeleton and screened it, checking carefully for bits of bone and scraps of clothing. Little was found until Jake brushed some dirt away from the now-exposed right hand. He followed the edges of each brown-colored bone until a shiny bit of gold appeared, partly hidden behind two finger bones.

"Got something here," Jake said, probing a bit deeper with a sharpened wood dowel. "Might be a ring. Let's get some photos before I dig any further."

Pam handed him the camera and a photo scale, and he took several close-up shots of the bones and the object. After each shot, Jake removed a bit more dirt until most of the hand bones were exposed.

"The finger bones are tucked underneath," he said. "I don't think it's a ring, it's too large."

"So, it's something clutched in his fist?" Pam asked, peering over his shoulder. "Maybe a set of keys?"

"Maybe. Here, wait a second." Jake dug gingerly underneath the thumb bones and made a small opening at the top of the fist. His efforts were rewarded with a large portion of a shiny, flexed band. "I think it's a watch."

Pam frowned. "A watch? But he's already wearing a watch on his other arm."

Jake brushed away some loose soil and took a few more photos. He then removed some of the overlying bones and freed the item. "Yeah, it's a watch. Looks just like the one he's wearing, in fact."

"So, we found a dead watch salesman? Sure, I can see it clearly now. John Doe was selling a watch to a bog-dwelling hermit, they argued over the price, and the result was *murder*."

Jake laughed out loud but felt a bit embarrassed given the context and stopped. "I'll let you take credit for that theory with Agent Russell. Look how twisted the band is, over here. Maybe it got pulled off in a struggle."

"That's a possibility. Not as intriguing as my idea, but not bad for an amateur."

"Thanks, deputy," Jake said, rolling his eyes. He turned the watch over, examining both sides. It was a man's watch, but the size of the band suggested someone smaller than himself. He scraped the mud off the front and saw a stylized S on the watch face.

"Hey, this watch looks a lot like the ones Keith and Peter were wearing. See this big red S? It's on the Scenic town flag, and it was on both of their watches."

Pam took the watch from him and looked at it closely. "If you're right, that could mean that this John Doe was a local. So much for the 'official' ruling that this was some out-of-state hunter."

"We should find out where these watches come from. Maybe it's something they sell in town or give away to town officials."

"If it's something common, it might be hard to track," Pam said, handing it back to him. "And it's not in very good shape."

Jake stared at the back of the watch, then scraped at it gently with his thumbnail. "There might be some lettering visible on the back, under all this grime."

"Can you clean it?"

"Maybe. Have to be careful or I could make it worse."

"What about electrolysis? I saw someone clean some old tools that way on one of those antique shows."

Jake shook his head. "That only works on metals that are ferric or iron-based. This is stainless steel. Using electrolysis on stainless steel releases poisonous chromate. Very nasty stuff."

"Okay, scratch that idea. What do you want to try?"

"There are commercial cleaners out there that might do the trick, if we're careful. I'll do some research online before I try anything, on either watch," Wrapping the watch in tissue paper, Jake slipped it into a bag and then placed it inside a small cardboard box. On the outside, he recorded the site name, date, and location of the find, and wrote *'found clutched in John Doe's right hand'* at the bottom. He looked at the exposed skeleton again and frowned. Then it dawned on him.

"Wait a second. We're looking at this all wrong," Jake said, almost in a shout. "This isn't the watch from the victim; that watch is on his left hand, around his wrist bones!"

Pam's bright blue eyes widened as the full implication dawned on her. "This watch could be from his killer."

CHAPTER 19

B Y THE END OF THE DAY, Jake and Pam had removed all of John Doe's bones from the ground. Jake brought them, along with the two watches, to his hotel room where he secured them in a large storage trunk. On Saturday, Jake and Pam carefully screened all the dirt from the surrounding area but found only some scattered bits of decayed cloth and some rusted pieces of metal. They bagged and boxed these items and set them aside to join the bones back at the hotel. An hour was spent adding more details to their already copious notes, until it was decided that they had accomplished all that could be expected. Jake called Agent Russell to tell him the news, but only left a short message after getting shunted to his voice mail.

As some dark clouds began to roll in, Jake and Pam started excavating the bison bones positioned below the human remains. They had been working for a short time before a rumble of thunder echoed across the clearing and large raindrops began falling. The crew swiftly covered their open units and stashed the equipment in the shed before retreating to the vehicles, as the storm opened up with a vengeance. Irritated over the loss of a half-day of work, Sam launched into a lengthy argument for returning to work on Sunday, despite it being their only scheduled day off. No one, even Susan, showed much enthusiasm for the idea. Jake smoothed things over by suggesting that he and Sam spend Sunday reviewing the notes, updating their maps, and planning out their strategy for the final few weeks of the excavations.

Sopping wet and exhausted from a long week of work, the archaeologists disappeared into their rooms after returning to the hotel. The storm continued throughout the afternoon, and most everyone chose to stay in rather than brave the storm. Jake spent some time Saturday evening online, researching ways to remove corrosion from stainless steel. He found some good tips, including a few that recommended the use of cleaning materials available at most grocery stores. He made a short list of items to pick up Sunday morning before his meeting with Sam.

Jake tried to take Heather aside to discuss her conversation with Susan but never found an appropriate moment. Someone was always nearby, or the timing didn't seem correct. He finally decided he would take care of it during the week, as soon as he could. If he let it pass, it might get worse.

Sam was in good humor on Sunday. He was genuinely pleased with the progress made once Jake pointed out just how much of the site had been excavated. Only minor changes were needed on a few maps, and the bag and photo logs were error-free. Jake and Sam added margin comments to many of the excavation forms, pulling together information from the perspective of the site as a whole. Most of these were focused toward the analysis and final report. Sam was insistent that they push for a quick turnaround, while Jake advocated a slow and steady process, to better fit his already crowded schedule.

Sam even—somewhat grudgingly—admitted that Pam was doing a more than adequate job. Her contributions had increased their output, despite the inconvenience of dealing with the two sets of human remains. Jake was about to reassure him that the odds of another body turning up were astronomical when there was a sharp knock on the door.

"I got it," Sam said, tossing a small stack of papers onto the bed. He shoved aside a half-empty box of office supplies with his foot and pulled open the door. Pam and Michelle stood outside, smiling.

"Hi, Sam," Pam said cheerfully. "Thought we'd find you two in here."

Jake sat up from his editing and waved. Michelle waved back. "What can we do for you?"

"It's past noon, and you two have been cooped up in there most of the morning. Thought we'd see if you'd like to join us for lunch."

Suddenly feeling ravenous, Jake was about to accept when Sam spoke up.

"Sorry, we've got way too much to do today. These nice days aren't going to last much longer, so we have to make them count. Maybe next time."

The disappointment was evident on Pam's face. "Sure, I get it. Maybe another time." She had barely finished speaking before Sam had closed the door.

"What was that all about? We're almost done with the notes, and I'm not planning to starve myself over paperwork and site maps."

"There are crackers and chips on the table," Sam snarled, pointing to some smashed bags of salty snacks. "You'll be fine."

Jake just stared at him for a moment. "That's not the point. Everything is under control, in the field and with the paperwork. In fact, we're way ahead of schedule. You need to let up a little."

"I don't see it that way," Sam said, as he settled back down in his chair. His face was twisted and drawn, and Jake was concerned that he might be hiding a back or hip injury.

"Yeah, we're ahead of the game right now, more or less. But what happens when the weather turns?" Sam stopped to stretch out his right leg, grimacing as his knee cracked. "I can feel it in my bones, Jake. A few more days, maybe a week, but something big is coming our way. Real big."

Jake shrugged his shoulders. "Maybe. We've had a nice long spell of warm weather, and it can't last forever. But even if we have to wrap up early, we already recovered a ton of material, more than enough to interpret the site. If you push people too much, it's going to backfire and they'll start messing up."

"All the more reason to push harder now, while we can."

"We'll keep at it until the weather turns bad," Jake said, then fixed him with a steely gaze. "Look, Sam, we've been friends for years, and this isn't like you. Something else is bothering you, I can tell. C'mon, out with it."

Sam looked like he was about to protest, but the look on Jake's face changed his mind. "I . . . I don't know, exactly. It's just, well, things are changing around me, and I'm getting left behind. My career is almost done and I'm freaking out about what little I have to show for it."

"That's nuts. You have plenty of good years in you, Sam. Hell, you're too stubborn to ever retire. And you've accomplished more in your career so far than most scientists ever do."

"Maybe. It's more than that. After a while, you start to notice you aren't as sharp as you used to be. New articles and books come out that trash ideas you've held as sacred for decades. I don't know, I feel like I've lost my edge, if I ever had one."

Jake stared at Sam in genuine concern. It was disturbing to see him like this, uncertain, doubtful of his own abilities. It explained why he was pushing so hard and why this excavation seemed so paramount. "I understand how you feel, but . . ."

"That's just it, Jake, you really can't! I'm not blaming you, but you've got most of your career ahead of you, and I'm looking at most of mine in the rearview mirror."

Sam leaned back in his chair, pulled open the door of the mini fridge and took out a can of beer. He offered one to Jake, but he shook his head. "About two years ago, the Lewis and Clark Museum got a huge interdisciplinary grant to do some climate and eco-logical modeling research. With the money from that, they hired some hotshot young scientist to develop a paleoecology-commu-nity modeling project, apparently one of the key parts of this new research. Anyway, the kid gave a presentation to the staff about some computer model he developed, and it was all statistics, algorithms, and patterning theory. I was lost after about ten minutes."

Sam took a long drink of his beer, then chuckled. "Marla Colbert, the vertebrate paleontologist, zinged him pretty good, though. She asked him point-blank if he had done any actual field studies, you know, put a shovel in the ground somewhere to 'truth' his model. Kid looked stunned, like the idea of doing real fieldwork was totally foreign to him. He hemmed and hawed a while, mumbled something about using existing data sets to test his results, but the answer came back pretty flat."

"It's just one incident," Jake said. "You're making too much out of it."

Sam was silent for a moment, staring past Jake but not focusing on anything in particular. "Maybe. But mark my words, I'm not going to let anything mess up this excavation. I'll back off—some—if it'll keep you off my back, but it had better be smooth sailing for the rest of the dig. If not, I just don't know what I might do."

Jake smiled, nodding. "Fair enough. No more surprises, I promise."

CHAPTER 20

T HE SUN ROSE A BIT LATER than usual on Monday, and the chill temperature carried more than a hint of autumn shifting toward winter. Jake began to wonder if Sam's predictions the day before had been correct, but by mid-morning it had warmed up some and everyone was humming along with their work. The excavated areas of the site were now in the majority, leaving a patchwork of unexposed ground ready to be dug.

Sam appeared to have taken Jake's suggestions to heart. He was cordial and complimentary to everyone, and never once groused about time lost during breaks. He even regaled the crew with anecdotes about his youthful field adventures and had them roaring with laughter on more than one occasion.

Sam's mood was infectious. Heather, too, was in fine feather and seemed to have gotten over her negative attitude toward Pam, or, at the very least, she was making more effort to conceal her true feelings. Unfortunately, that only lasted until lunch, when Heather went on a lengthy discourse about Amanda, her work at the History Center, and how perfect it would be for her to design an exhibit around the Ghost Bog site. Her status as Jake's former girlfriend was noted more than once. On the surface, it appeared quite innocent, but Jake had the feeling much of the discussion was designed specifically to irritate Pam. It proved ineffective, however, as Pam merely nodded on occasion and gave no outward indication of unease.

After the lunch break, the rest of the day passed without incident. As the sun dipped below the trees, the crew started closing down the site and packing up. Jake was collecting the last of the day's paperwork when Pam walked over.

"Here you go, chief. I should have that last level out tomorrow morning."

"Great, thanks." Jake took the forms and added them to his clipboard. Pam stood there, motionless. "Is there something else?"

"Care to take me to dinner tonight?" Pam said, smiling to show off her dimples. "Maybe steak and seafood?"

Jake hesitated, caught off guard by her invitation. "Sure, I suppose. But . . ."

"You know, I heard that on fancy archaeological tours, the site director *always* treats volunteers to dinner, to show their appreciation," Pam said, folding her arms across her chest. "I think it's in your best interests to follow their lead."

She looked stern, but Jake caught the hint of a smile on her face. Her blue eyes sparkled, and Jake mused once again about how striking Pam was, even with smears of mud decorating her rosy cheeks. "Well, if it's mandatory I guess I have no choice."

"Nope, none at all."

"I suppose one fancy dinner won't kill me or our budget. And if it keeps the volunteers happy, it'll be worth it." Jake turned to Sam, sitting a few feet away, checking his phone. "What do you say, Sam, up for an evening out tonight?"

Unnoticed by Jake, Pam's face fell. Sam looked at her carefully before smiling and shaking his head.

"No, I don't think so. I'm going to recheck the maps for the orientation of the skeletons in the central units. If we have them right, the herd was moving due east when they hit the bog. And I need to deal with a couple of these phone messages; could end up important. You kids go ahead."

PAM DROVE JAKE BACK TO HIS hotel and agreed to pick him up a half hour later. He showered, shaved, and put on the cleanest (and only) dress clothes he found stuffed into his duffle bag. The khaki pants were a bit wrinkled and his dark green shirt had a mismatched button, but it was the best he could manage under the circumstances. Jake was adjusting his frayed black tie for the third time when he heard the knock at the door.

Jake swung open the door and stopped short. "Wow, you look great!"

Pam smiled and tilted her head. "What, this old thing?" She did a little pirouette, showing off a short black skirt and V-neck burgundy blouse. Her sleek high heels contrasted sharply with the hiking boots she wore at the site.

"Did you have some place fancy in mind? I don't have a sports jacket or anything . . ."

"Not necessary, you look fine. Very handsome, in fact," Pam said, hooking her arm through his. "I thought we could go to the supper club by my hotel. Nothing fancy, but the food is great, according to the front desk."

"Sounds good." Up close, Jake caught the enticing aroma of her perfume and smiled.

Jake and Pam enjoyed a delicious meal of steak and seafood, and several glasses of wine. The conversation flowed easily, and Jake even managed to avoid droning on about their progress at the site. The lights were low, and other couples occupied most of the other tables. Jake surmised that the candlelight kept the tourist families at bay, much like a citronella candle and mosquitoes.

Pam laughed at every little joke he made, and Jake felt happier than he had been in a long, long time.

"Well, it took a while, but I finally got you alone for a date," Pam said, raising her glass in a mock toast before taking a sip.

"What about our dinner at The Hop? That was just the two of us."

"While I appreciate your fondness for all things . . . antiquarian, it wasn't exactly a romantic encounter."

"Okay, I'll give you that," Jake replied, glancing around the intimate setting. "I'm glad we managed to stay in touch after Waconah."

"Me, too. Nothing like a cold case mystery to bring two people together."

They both laughed, and Jake raised his glass. "To you, then, Officer Hauser."

"To us, Professor Caine. We make a pretty formidable couple."

Jake's smile faded at the word couple.

"Are you okay?"

"Sorry," Jake said. "Thinking about Waconah . . . and 'couple' . . . reminded me of . . . Amanda."

Pam's face fell. "Oh. Sorry, I didn't mean to bring up a bad memory." Jake had told Pam, via email, that he and Amanda had broken up. Not wanting to pry, Pam sent her condolences, but didn't ask about specifics. Instead, she wished him well and let him know she was there if he wanted to talk.

"It's alright," Jake said. "We were having so much fun, I kind of . . . well, I mean . . ."

"I get it," Pam replied. An uncomfortable silence hung in the air, but only for a moment. "Jake, I didn't want to push things at the time, but it is over between you two, isn't it? I mean, you're not getting back together, are you?"

After a pause, Jake exhaled, and the candle flickered in protest. "I guess not. Erin—you know, the lab curator from Waconah—went up to La Crosse right before the fall semester started, to supervise transfer of some Waconah artifacts to the History Center for their exhibit. She and Amanda spent a lot of time together, during work and afterwards, and Amanda admitted that she had started dating Sean, one of the historians."

"Ouch. I'm sorry, Jake. You didn't know, did you?"

"I kind of suspected, based on how Amanda acted the few times we spoke, before she broke things off," Jake said, and then he smiled. "Erin blurted it out a few days after she got back. She felt sick to her stomach about the whole situation. Guess she's not one to share government secrets with, huh?"

"I like Erin. She's a character." Pam took a sip of her wine. "I'm sure she was just trying to help. Maybe she sensed how you were feeling, and decided she had to speak up."

"I suppose. Anyway, that's when I realized it was really over."

Jake was silent for a moment and slumped back against his chair. "That's the first time I said it out loud."

Pam reached across the table and squeezed his hand. Jake stared back at her, watching the flame of the candle dance in her bright, blue eyes.

CHAPTER 21

"NICE OF YOU TWO TO GRACE us with a visit. Finally."
Sam's greeting echoed across the clearing, and Jake had little doubt that it was audible as far as the Emerson's home at the edge of the marsh. The assembled archaeologists all looked up in unison, breath steaming in the cold morning air. So much for a quiet arrival and slipping in unnoticed.

"Sorry. Got a late start this morning," Jake said, as Pam opened the trunk of her Camaro. She reached in and pulled out several large bags and a square coffee carafe.

"We did bring some bagels and doughnuts," Pam announced, handing the carafe to Jake. "Think of it as a peace offering for us being tardy today."

Based on how quickly the crew helped themselves to the snacks, it was evident that no hard feelings were felt. Only Sam and Heather showed any reluctance, but they soon joined the others at the edge of the excavation area.

Jake and Pam spent the night together in Pam's hotel room and overslept the next morning. Jake needed to return to his own hotel room for his field clothes, which only compounded their delay. Before leaving Scenic, Jake decided to purchase some baked goods and coffee as an excuse for their late arrival, and to thwart questions about why they were together at such an early hour. Pam was thoroughly amused by Jake's unease and needled him mercilessly on the drive to Ghost Bog.

"Everyone's been doing such a great job," Jake said, pouring coffee for the group. "We just thought you'd all enjoy a little treat this morning."

"You deserve a reward, too, Jake," Pam commented. "I mean, I think you're doing great yourself." She gave Michelle a sly smile. "Plus you've really been going at it in the evenings."

Jake turned beet red, spilling some of the coffee he was pouring for Susan.

"Uh, on maps, and, um, paperwork. I've been checking the field forms every night. That's all. But having a great crew makes all the difference."

"Don't be modest, Jake," Pam interjected, a winsome smile playing at the corners of her mouth. "I think you're fantastic."

Jake stammered to reply as Heather pushed forward with her battered travel mug. "Yeah, yeah, you're Super-Archaeologist," Heather snarled. "Can I get a refill here, or are you going to spill the rest all over the dig?"

Jake handed her the carafe, then headed for the shed to get his dig kit and clipboard. He almost collided with Sam as he exited the building a few minutes later.

"Pretty late this morning."

"Yeah, sorry about that. Got going late and had to stop at the bakery," Jake said, brushing past Sam, who fell in step behind him, chewing on a bear claw.

"Only have a few weeks left, Jake. If we start losing days to rain, or . . ."

"It was just twenty minutes," Jake said, pausing to pull the sandbags and tarp from the top of his unit. "I'll stay out an extra hour tonight if you'll just drop it."

"I just want to get as much excavated as we can. Who knows if we'll ever be able to come back out here again."

"Obviously our talk on Sunday has been brushed away, I see," Jake snapped. He was tired, more than a bit embarrassed, and in no mood for a repeat of Sam's favorite lecture topic.

Sam looked a little hurt. "No, I meant what I said about easing up. My phone call and trip last night amounted to a whole lot of nothing, so I guess I'm still a bit perturbed by that. While you were dining out and oversleeping, I spent last night driving all over northwest Wisconsin trying to locate a collector."

Jake looked up, puzzled. "Collector? What collector?"

"Said he had some boxes of bones and a few notched points from a site close to here. Thought it might be related. But the directions were nuts. I think I crossed into Minnesota once. Hell, maybe twice! Anyway, maybe I'll give it another try tonight."

"Don't be too mad at Jake, Sam," Pam said as she joined them. "I had a rough night and just couldn't get moving this morning, so I was late picking Jake up. We could have skipped the bakery, but I knew you'd want the crew to know how much you appreciate their hard work."

Sam looked at her, then back at Jake who was scraping soil into a dustpan. His features softened. "No real harm, I guess," Sam replied. "Besides," he whispered, giving Pam a wink, "They'll work even harder now."

Pam squeezed his arm before returning to her screen, which Michelle was filling with soil. "Nice gal you've got there, Jake. Might be good to keep her around, if you know what I mean."

Jake stopped working, then nodded. "You may be right. Definitely something to think about."

"We can hash it over tonight, during that extra hour you mentioned."

"Sure," Jake said, shaking his head as Sam walked toward his own unit.

JAKE WORKED SOLO THAT MORNING, HAPPY with the solitude as he mapped a small pile of jumbled bones, likely from an area where larger meat portions were cut down into smaller units for dispersal and transport. His mind, however, was racing as he considered the events of the previous evening, making it difficult to concentrate. Right before the morning break, he caught a whiff of Pam's perfume and looked in her direction, only to see her staring back at him while screening for Michelle.

A rustling in the tall grass behind him caught his attention, as Gypsy and Shadow trotted out of the marsh to join them at the dig. Gypsy led the way as usual, with Shadow trailing in her wake. Tails wagging, they began their usual routine, visiting each archaeologist in turn and begging for treats.

"Well, looks who back. C'mere, sweetie."

"Boy, it's like clockwork with these two, whenever there's food around."

"Do you suppose they smelled the doughnuts from the Emerson house?"

"It's awful far."

"Beagles have great senses of smell, about the best of any dogs," Pam said as she removed her gloves to scratch Gypsy's ears. "We thought they might show up, so we also bought some of these doggie bagels." She fished into her pocket and handed one to each dog. They wolfed them down and returned to their begging.

"Guess you should have brought more."

"Next time I'll know better."

Laughing, the archaeologists resumed their work. With their food source shut down, the beagles soon found other distractions. Gypsy picked up an interesting scent near the edge of the clearing and wandering into the woods, nose to the ground. Shadow watched her depart, then fashioned a bed out of Al's sweatshirt and lay down for a nap.

Jake settled back into his routine. He mapped a few errant bones, removed the upper layer, and began to brush away some sticky soil from the second layer of bison remains. Sam walked over, took a glance back toward the center of the dig, and then squatted down next to Jake.

"You didn't make it home last night," Sam said.

Jake considered bluffing his way through with a lie, but then shrugged his shoulders in response. Sam knew him too well, and would see through any story he might concoct on the spur of the moment.

"Sorry, I didn't call . . . Dad."

Sam gave him an evil grin, and snuck a peak back at Pam, working a few yards away. "Don't worry, I can keep a secret—for a price. I do enjoy fine scotch."

"Fine, fine. Just don't make a big deal out of this."

"And don't let your amorous escapades get in the way of this excavation, either. We need to pull a lot more bone out of this bog to get the sample I want."

"We'll have plenty. The shed is ready to burst and we still have a few weeks to go. Should be more than enough data for the grant report, and any articles you want to publish after that."

Sam ambled back to his unit and work resumed. After an hour, Jake sat back to check his map one last time before he removed the lower level of bones. He was updating his notes when Gypsy returned from the woods and sat down beside him.

Jake mumbled a greeting, not looking up from his paperwork. "Hi, Gypsy. Had enough exploring for a while?"

Gypsy cocked her head and put her paw on his leg. When he didn't respond, she nudged his arm with her nose.

"What's up? I think you had enough of my breakfast for one day."

She thumped her wet, muddy paw down hard on his leg. Jake turned his attention to the dog, and noticed some dark red spots on the white fur of her paw. Similar splotches decorated her muzzle, with smears of color across both front legs.

"Did you get something in the bog, Gypsy? Maybe a rabbit?"

At the word rabbit, Gypsy let out a low, deep howl and began to paw Jake with renewed enthusiasm. She let out a few short, chirped barks, so much so that Shadow began to take notice.

"Okay. I guess you're not going to let up until I see what you got. Right, girl?" Jake rose and Gypsy started dancing around, barking. He followed her toward the trail she had explored earlier that morning.

The barking and movement caught Sam's attention. "Now where the hell are you off to?"

"Just going to stretch my legs. I think Gypsy treed something and wants me to see. Only be a sec."

Sam continued to speak, but Jake tuned him out and followed Gypsy onto the brush-choked trail. His forward progress was soon halted; while there was ample room for a dog, it was not easy going for a tall adult male. As he pushed aside the whip-like branches, Jake resolved to speak to Sam once again about his attitude. Jake was the official excavation director, as the state contract and grant were through him and Wisconsin State University. Sam's tendency to get bossy when aggravated or anxious was starting to wear thin.

After about thirty yards, the brushy foliage gave way to open forest and Jake was able to stand straight and increase his pace. As he spotted Gypsy a few yards ahead, the smell reached him.

"Whew, that's bad enough that even I can smell it now. What did you find, Gypsy? A dead deer, maybe?"

In a small clearing, Gypsy stood next to the dead body of Matt Walker, flies buzzing around the large bloody stain in the middle of his chest.

CHAPTER 22

"Professor Caine? Follow me this way, please."
It was phrased as an invitation but felt like an order. Agent Russell led Jake back to the location of Walker's body, following a circuitous route through the clinging vegetation. The path was much easier than the one used by Gypsy, as this one had been trampled by Agent Russell and Sheriff O'Neil, then Doctor Wheeler, and a small army of police officers and crime-scene technicians. Given the obviousness of the path, the miles of police tape strewn everywhere seemed like overkill. Jake wondered if it was biodegradable, or if future archaeologists would find it one day and puzzle over its significance.

The two men paused as they reached the clearing. The body was now covered with a light tarp, but the outline of the deceased was still visible. In his mind's eye, Jake could still see the gruesome sight that greeted him only a few hours prior.

Agent Russell took a step off to one side, and nodded at an older woman dressed in a bright yellow Tyvek suit, scribbling on a clipboard. Three other techs, also attired in protective crime-scene clothing, were moving about the body, taking photographs and collecting evidence in small plastic bags. Sheriff O'Neil and a green-gilled young deputy stood on the opposite side of the clearing. Jake could make out other forms moving beyond the clearing, hunched over as they studied the ground for clues.

Agent Russell's stern voice broke through his reverie. "If you would, Professor Caine, run us through exactly what occurred. Again."

Jake nodded, all eyes fixed on him, and repeated his account of the discovery. He reached the point where he left the clearing in order to call the sheriff's office when the lead technician interrupted.

"And you didn't disturb the body in any way? Maybe move an arm, even slightly?"

"No. I knelt down . . . right there, and put two fingers on his neck, to confirm that he was dead."

"You couldn't see that from looking at him?" Sheriff O'Neil's accusatory tone was high-pitched, even for her. Jake thought her deputy was about to be sick.

"Was the body warm or cold?" the lead technician said, before Jake could answer the sheriff.

"Cold."

She nodded, and made another note on her form. "And the time?"

"A few minutes after ten. I checked the time as I walked back to the dig."

"There's the source of our trouble," Sheriff O'Neil said under her breath but loud enough that all could hear.

Agent Russell turned to the lead technician, and they spoke for a few minutes. He then gestured for Jake to leave, falling in step behind him. Sheriff O'Neil followed, after first barking an order for her deputy to stay put.

As he reached the edge of the Ghost Bog site, Jake released an exhausted breath. He scanned the excavation, finding everyone looking back expectantly. Well, Sam was still on his knees, troweling in his unit, while Heather stood at a nearby screen, half-heartedly pushing dark soil back and forth. Al was squatting near the

LC van, comforting Susan, who was slouched over in the back seat. Pam, Michelle, Rob, and Curt stood near their own units, barely attempting to feign activity.

"How fast are you going to be able get all this closed down?"

Stunned by Sheriff O'Neil's question, it took a moment before Jake realized she was addressing him. "Wait. What . . ."

"It won't be necessary to shut down the excavation," Agent Russell announced. He took a few steps past them, reaching the folding table set up by the crime-scene crew when they arrived.

"What do you mean? This is a crime scene!"

"No, Sheriff, it is not." He paused to take a sip from a bottle of water. "The victim's body was found over fifty yards from here. And Doctor Walker was not killed in that location."

"Huh? How do you know that?"

"One, the position of the body. Two, no trace evidence consistent with a shooting in that location. Three, the pooling of the blood – according to the forensic team – indicates the body was moved post-mortem. Four, . . ."

Jake nodded in agreement as he followed Agent Russell's reasoning. Sheriff O'Neil was less impressed.

"Well, how do we do know *they* didn't drag the body from here to there?" She jerked her head in Jake's direction, for emphasis.

"Again, no evidence. Moving a body from here would have left a considerable mess in the brush. My team found no blood, no broken branches, nothing consistent with what you are implying. The only footprints visible before our arrival were Professor Caine's, one set going in and one set coming out."

Sheriff O'Neil frowned, at a loss as how to continue but unwilling to concede.

"And before you ask, the victim was not killed out here, either. The crime-scene personnel walked the excavation area, and inspected the vehicles and the storage building. All clean."

Jake was surprised to hear about that aspect of their investigation, and looked around to see if anything had been disturbed.

Agent Russell picked up on his discomfort. "Don't worry, they were careful around the bones. They know their job." He turned his attention back to the sheriff, and picked up a large evidence bag from the table. "And four, we found this about 75 yards beyond the body, along a deer trail."

The bag contained a folding metal frame with two large wire wheels, one on each side. Squinting, Jake could see that it was battered and bent, with rust visible in places.

"That could have been out there for months," Sheriff O'Neil said. "Maybe years."

"Perhaps. There are bloodstains on it, and we did find some fresh wheel marks a bit farther on. Definitely worth checking out in the lab."

The sheriff shrugged and seemed to put the matter aside. "So. You're going to take jurisdiction?"

"Yes. According to the GPS, the body is located on state land, so no choice. But of course you can cover the local aspects," he added, smiling. "Track the victim's movements, see who he was talking to in Scenic, and work with us when we talk to his colleagues. Usual stuff. A little teamwork will go a long way."

"Uh-huh. Well, I think you ought to order these people out of here for the time being. How do we know they won't go up there and mess up the crime scene?"

Jake was about to respond when Agent Russell raised his hand. "I trust Professor Caine will give us his word that neither he nor his crew will go anywhere near the crime scene, Sheriff."

"Of course. I . . ."

"How do I know he'll keep his word?"

"If you're that concerned, Sheriff, I advise you to post a deputy up there. That's standard procedure."

"I can't do that. I only have two deputies. This is ridiculous!"

"It's my call, Sheriff, so that's the way it's going to be."

Sheriff O'Neil's mouth snapped open and then clamped shut, eyes bulging. Before she could erupt, two crime-scene technicians emerged from the brush, struggling with the stretcher carrying the recently deceased Matt Walker. She opted to turn her frustration on them.

"Where's Deputy Martin?"

"Back there, off the trail, losing his breakfast," one tech remarked, gritting as he maneuvered around the table toward the parking lot.

As the sheriff entered the brush, shouting for her wayward officer, Agent Russell turned to Jake and shook his head.

"It's fortunate Walker's body was found on state land. A little closer, and she would have shut you down—hard."

"I think you're right. I suppose multiple bodies, no matter how old, can have a disturbing effect on some people," Jake said. "By the way, thanks for getting here so quickly. How did you get here before her?"

"Just luck. Keith and I were on the road outside Scenic when I got your call, so we had a good head start. It was smart of you to call me, after the sheriff."

"Thanks, but Pam deserves the credit for that. She thought we'd be in better hands with someone more, um, experienced with this sort of thing."

Jake glanced in Pam's direction and gave her a wave. She nodded in return, but made no move to join them.

"She's right about that. You're fortunate to have her around."

Mentioning Pam reminded Jake of another concern, forgotten in the chaos of the morning. "I called and left you a message on Saturday, after we finished removing the second skeleton."

"Hmm? Oh, the John Doe." He paused to check an incoming text on his phone. "The Walker investigation will have to take priority. Just hang on to the remains and documentation for now. If you'll excuse me, I have a bit more to do here."

"Sure," Jake said, watching him depart. "And now to deal with the fallout over here."

Jake walked across the excavation area, calling to the crew as he did. Within moments, most of them had joined him by the water jug outside the storage shed. Al showed up a minute later.

"How is Susan?"

"Still pretty upset," Al said. "She stopped throwing up, but she can't stop crying and shaking."

"Is she in shock? Should we call the paramedics?"

Al shook her head. "I don't think so. She was responsive when the cops asked her about medical treatment. I think she's all shook up, and just exhausted. This was probably the last straw."

"Okay," Jake said. "After this, I'll have you run her back to the hotel and stay with her. If she isn't better soon, we'll take her into the emergency care center."

"So what's our status, Jake?" Sam asked, drumming his fingers together. "They going to shut us down?"

"No. We have to stay clear of the . . . scene . . . but Agent Russell doesn't think it is necessary. They'll probably be in and out of here for a while, but it shouldn't interfere with us finishing our work."

"Any chance they might change their minds?" Pam asked. "Sheriff O'Neil didn't look too thrilled when you three came out of the woods."

"That is a bit of an understatement." Jake gave the team an abbreviated account of her comments but stressed that Agent Russell was running the show.

"About the best I can say is just focus on your work, and be cooperative if they need to ask us any questions." Jake stopped to check his watch, a bit surprised to see that it was now late afternoon. "Al, go ahead and take Susan back to the hotel now. The rest of us will put in another hour or so, and then call it a day."

Everyone nodded in agreement and walked back to their respective units. Pam stayed behind, then reached out to squeeze Jake's hand. "You doing okay?"

"Yeah, sure. Well, good as can be expected." Jake spotted Keith Emerson wandering back from his aunt and uncle's home on the far side of the wetland. Jake waived as he reached the clearing, but Keith only gave a curt nod and hurried into the woods to join Agent Russell.

"To be honest, I'm feeling exhausted all of a sudden," he said, stifling a yawn.

"I'm not surprised, given all that's happened," Pam said. "And you missed lunch, too, now that I think about it. How about if I treat you to dinner? Nothing fancy."

"Sounds good. Thanks."

THE ARCHAEOLOGISTS, MINUS AL AND SUSAN, finished off their day with little enthusiasm. After returning to the hotel, they scattered to their rooms, feeling no desire for socializing. Jake found Susan resting and more embarrassed than anything. Al had picked up some dinner for them both at the local sandwich shop, and that alone seemed to have calmed her nerves. Susan apologized for her reaction at the site, but Jake brushed it aside and told her to take as much time off as she wished.

Pam drove over from her hotel a short time later to collect Jake. He barely had time to shower and change, and seriously considered just giving up on the day and climbing into bed. Sam sat on his own bed, sipping a beer as he stared blankly at the television. Jake's attempts at communication received only terse responses, and he didn't respond when Jake left.

Jake and Pam ended up at a nearby café, made small talk about everything except Walker's murder, and picked at their food. Jake opted for coffee over alcohol, and despite several refills was still struggling to stay awake when the bill arrived. Pam drove him back to his hotel, gave him a big hug and a good night kiss, and offered to drive him to Ghost Bog in the morning. Jake entered his room only to find Sam passed out in the same spot as when he left. He doused the lights and turned off the television, and soon collapsed into his own bed. Despite the exhausting day, Jake slept fitfully, tossing and turning as he wrestled with nightmares until the early hours of the dawn.

CHAPTER 23

"**Y**OU LOOK TERRIBLE."

"I'd argue with you," Jake said, blowing on the lid of his travel mug, "but I feel pretty terrible. Like I didn't sleep at all."

"Bad dreams?" Pam said, slowing down for a blind curve a few miles from the site. Jake nodded. "I had a few myself."

"Guess it's to be expected. By the way, thanks again for picking up this coffee. Good and strong, unlike the hotel packet stuff."

"Thought you might need it this morning." She gunned the engine as they reached a straight stretch of road. "How are the others doing?"

"Not sure. Sam was just getting going when you arrived. I think he had quite a bit to drink last night. Heather and the others were just loading up their van, so they shouldn't be far behind us."

"Heather is probably starting a petition to have me exiled from Ghost Bog. I'm a jinx, you know."

"You heard about that, huh?"

"Mm-hmm. She's not exactly subtle."

"True. I've been meaning to talk to her but haven't had a chance," Jake said, then smiled. "If it matters, I think you're being here is one of the best things that has happened to me in a long time."

Pam rewarded Jake with a dimpled smile, and then focused her attention on slowing down and turning into the gravel driveway leading to the site. "I feel the same way," she said as they rolled to a stop. She squeezed his hand and leaned over for a kiss.

They got out of the car and surveyed the scene. The yellow police tape was still visible on the far side of the dig, but otherwise there was little to remind them of the events of the previous day.

"Guess they finished up last evening, after we left," Jake said, blowing on his hands to warm them. "Cold this morning. Probably only going to have a few more nice days before winter gets here."

"They were talking about snow flurries west of here," Pam said. She rounded the back of the car to where Jake was standing. She gave him a cheeky smile. "Just the two of us. Want to climb into the back seat and make out?"

"Very tempting offer," Jake said, putting his arms around her waist. He smiled back and snuggled close to her. "But not a good idea. We'd never hear the end of it if we got caught."

"Spoilsport. Maybe later?"

"Definitely." He let her go, just as the crunch of tires on gravel announced the arrival of the Wisconsin State University van.

Pam popped the trunk and pulled out their backpacks while Jake walked to the shed and removed the padlock. On impulse, he peered into the darkness, just to confirm that nothing had been disturbed. He grabbed some dig kits and buckets, and started moving equipment to a spot outside the shed.

"Morning, boss."

"Hi, Michelle. Cold this morning, huh?"

"I'll say. I took one step outside, ran back into my room, and changed into my heavy leggings." She found her dig kit, set it off to one side, and helped Jake with the other gear.

"I suppose we won't be out here much longer if the weather gets worse, huh?"

"Probably not, but it depends on just how bad it gets," Jake said. "A little cold and flurries are one thing, a ton of snow and frozen ground are something else. Are you in a hurry to get back home?"

"Not really. I could use a break from hotel living, though."

"Yeah, I know what you mean. There's hardly any place to walk in my room, and Sam snores like a defective chainsaw."

Michelle laughed out loud, pausing slightly when Curt walked up to grab his equipment. He only shrugged, though, before joining Rob at the edge of the site.

Jake saw Heather and Pam at opposite ends of the dig, each struggling to uncover their respective units. He shook his head, wishing the two could get along but realized it wasn't likely to happen. "Guess we'd better get over there and give them a hand."

Michelle nodded and they joined the others. The archaeologists had been at work for about fifteen minutes when it dawned on Jake that they were still short a few bodies.

"Hey, any of you know where the others are?"

A few heads turned his way, but it was Heather who responded. "Al told me Susan overslept, and Sam was just starting to load up his stuff when we were leaving. And I think they needed to stop for gas on the way."

Jake thanked Heather, checked his watch, and got back to work. Probably delayed by a line at the gas station, he thought, or maybe they stopped to pick up some snacks for the morning break. If they didn't show in another fifteen minutes, he'd call and make sure everything was okay.

Concentrating on his work, over thirty minutes passed before Jake realized that the Lewis and Clark Museum crew was still absent. He reached for his phone when the sounds of tires on gravel caught his attention. The van sped into the parking area and jerked to a stop in the middle of the clearing. Al and Susan jumped out and ran up to Jake. Both women were shouting, and Jake could only make out scattered words and panicked pleas for help.

"Calm down!" Jake yelled, hoping to shock them into some manner of coherent behavior. "What's wrong? What's happening?"

"Sam's been arrested!"

CHAPTER 24

"WE HAD THE VAN LOADED AND were ready to go, when the police car pulled in behind us, blocking us," Al said, sipping coffee with both hands wrapped tightly around the mug. Upon hearing the news, the entire crew converged on the trio, pelting them with questions and exacerbating the already tense situation.

It took a few minutes before Jake gained control. He told everyone to quiet down, and then asked Heather and Michelle to pour them some coffee. Pam found two buckets that they could use as chairs, and Rob shut off the van, which they had left running in their rush to tell Jake the news.

"Sam got out to see what the trouble was, and then the sheriff pulled up in another car, right next to us," Al continued. "She got out, spun Sam around by the shoulder, and handcuffed him!"

"She said he killed Doctor Walker," Susan said, almost in a whisper. Her eyes were focused on the brushy woods at the far edge of the site, where the police tape swayed gently in the breeze.

Al nodded. "She said she was arresting him on suspicion of murder in the death of Matthew Walker."

Voices were raised in alarm, and Jake shot his hand up to silence them.

"Then what happened?"

"Um, well, they put Sam in the back of the police car. He didn't say anything."

"He didn't know what was happening," Susan added. "He was pretty upset."

Al nodded, then continued. "One of the officers asked about us. Sheriff O'Neil glared at us for a few minutes, then told him not to bother with us. I took a few steps toward them and asked where they were taking Sam."

Al reached into the pocket of her bulky hooded sweatshirt and pulled out a laminated card. "Sheriff said he was going to jail, and shoved this card in my face."

Jake took the card and read it. The address of the Scenic Jail was listed, adjacent to the municipal building. Phone numbers for the sheriff's office, two judges, and some local lawyers were listed on the opposite side.

"Well, this is useless," Jake snapped. He handed the card to Pam. "Assuming Sam has been arrested, what going's to happen to him now?"

Pam shrugged. "Depends on the department, but if he was arrested rather than brought in for questioning, he'd be booked, fingerprinted, phone call, the usual. And then arraignment, when the judge will determine bail. Could take a while."

Pam turned to Al and Susan. "Did they have an arrest warrant? Show you any paperwork?"

They both replied in the negative. Tears were starting to well up in Susan's eyes.

"We've gotta do something!" Heather yelled, a statement echoed by the rest of the crew. No one, however, seemed to know what the best next step would be.

Jake took the card from Pam and moved a few steps back from the group, and called the non-emergency number for the Scenic sheriff's office. After a dozen rings, someone answered and he was immediately put on hold. Minutes passed until he was reconnected. He had barely explained who he was and the purpose of his call when the operator cut him off, explaining that active police investigations could not be discussed through that number. As he started to ask whom he should call, the operator ended the call.

After expelling a few choice curse words, Jake hit redial and after a lengthy interval was connected to the message service. On a whim, he tried Sam's cell phone but it went to voice mail, suggesting his phone was turned off. He was about to try the emergency number when Pam approached.

"Any luck? It's getting pretty tense over there."

Jake looked past her and sighed as he saw Heather and Curt arguing, and Rob and Al chiming in their opinions. Michelle stood a few feet back, arms wrapped tightly together. Susan was immobile, still perched on her bucket.

"Not good. They wouldn't tell me anything, and now I'm getting sent to voice mail. No luck with Sam's phone, either. I was about to dial 9-1-1."

"Hang on a second." She took the card from Jake, scanned it, and then called on her own phone. "Hi, this is Mary over at the *Scenic Sentinel*. Sheriff Grace told me she caught the man who killed that poor geology professor. Thought I'd get some details for the paper."

Jake waited patiently during her call, catching only the limited responses from Pam's side of the conversation. Finally, she said thanks and ended the call.

"Well?"

"They have made an arrest but they won't release any details to the public right now, to 'protect the on-going investigation.' He did say that they're positive they got the right guy, an out-of-towner who has a 'violent history' with the victim."

"Oh boy. I can see how that might look bad." Jake rolled his eyes and scuffed at the ground with his boot. "Mary?"

"It's a common name, so there might be a Mary on staff. I couldn't say I was John Smith, you know."

"Very devious, but I definitely approve. So, I suppose now . . ."

"Jake, what are we going to do?"

Heather's inquiry, harsh and with a tinge of panic, was a demand for action. The rest of the crew crowded around her, giving the appearance of an outnumbered band resolved to storm the castle regardless of the consequences. Even Susan, lagging behind the others, had a determined look on her face.

"We got through to the sheriff, but they won't give us any information. Let me try Agent Russell."

Jake entered the number, but the call went to his messaging system. He explained the situation as best he could and requested that Russell contact him as soon as possible. Jake repeated the process when he contacted Keith Emerson, but found he had to speak quite a bit louder to overcome the heated discussion going on behind him.

"We just can't stay here, doing nothing!"

"None of these people are going to give us any help."

"This whole town has a creepy vibe, ever since we got here. They're probably going to try and arrest us next!"

Jake slipped his phone into his pocket, before addressing them in a clear, deep voice.

"The last thing we want to do is panic or jump to any conclusions. Someone's obviously made a mistake . . ."

"Yeah, a big mistake."

"Fine," Jake said, in a tone that brooked no further discussion. "I'm going to drive into Scenic and see what I can do."

"We're going too," Heather snapped, and her chorus nodded in agreement.

Jake shook his head. "No, we can't all go. It would just cause a scene and make things worse."

"How can things get any worse?"

It was Heather who spoke, but the others chimed in almost immediately. Mild panic was starting to set in when Jake first spotted the flashing red lights of the two police cars pulling into the parking area.

CHAPTER 25

JAKE LED THE PROCESSION OF ARCHAEOLOGISTS as they walked over to meet the unwelcome arrivals. Pam was on his right side and Heather on his left, while Curt, Rob, and Michelle trailed behind like ducklings. Al and Susan brought up the rear, with Al comforting the again-distraught older woman.

Sheriff O'Neil stood waiting, hands on her hips, flanked by two deputies. Jake recognized one as young Deputy Martin, who had gotten sick the day before. The other deputy was older, shorter, and much heavier across the midsection. He was sweating heavily, despite the cool morning temperatures. As they neared, Jake noticed that he placed one beefy pink hand on the butt of his pistol.

"Sheriff, can you tell me . . ."

"We have a warrant to search these premises," Sheriff O'Neil announced, eyeing the group. She brandished a small sheaf of papers in one hand, waving it like a small flag. "You will stay clear of our search or you will be arrested."

It sounded well-rehearsed, Jake thought, but oddly inappropriate as you could hardly call an archaeological dig in a wooded bog any sort of premises.

With a sneer, O'Neil handed the warrant to Jake. He glanced at it but soon found himself lost in legal jargon. It did appear to be properly signed and sealed, as best he could tell. He handed it off to Pam, who started reviewing it line by line with her finger.

"What are you looking for?"

"The weapon used in the homicide of Matthew Walker," she said tersely, as she surveyed the area.

Jake glanced at Pam, who nodded to confirm the target of the warrant. He turned to the crew, waiting a few feet away. "Everyone go back to your units and wait there. Don't interfere and everything will be fine."

They moved away grudgingly, but Jake was sure they would avoid any trouble. In the meantime, Sheriff O'Neil was ready to proceed.

"Tuttle, you check out the van. Make sure you look under the seats."

"Shouldn't you have done that during the arrest?" Pam inquired with feigned innocence.

O'Neil glared at Pam but didn't reply. "Martin, you come with me and we'll look in that building."

Jake followed the sheriff and her deputy as they marched to the storage building. Pam and Heather fell into step behind him.

Sheriff O'Neil paused at the doorway. "There any lights in here?"

"No. We never hooked up any power lines since we only use it to store equipment," Jake said, standing a few feet back. "There are a couple of flashlights on the table by the door."

O'Neil and Martin each took a flashlight. Jake watched uncomfortably as they staggered around the crowded room, but for the most part they avoided moving any of the larger artifact boxes. Minutes passed, and Jake considered asking if they needed help, if only to get them out of the building before they caused any real damage.

"Aha! Got it, Martin."

Jake leaned in, to see Sheriff O'Neil grab Sam's leather shotgun case. She carried it closer to the doorway, where the light was better, and unzipped the end. A cloud of dust filled the air as she handled the case, but the butt of the shotgun was visible. She closed it, a triumphant smile on her face.

"Looks like we've found what we came for," O'Neil said smugly, as she walked out of the shed, tossing her flashlight to Jake. She reached into her jacket pocket and pulled out a large red tag with "EVIDENCE" stamped on it in big, black letters.

Jake felt sick to his stomach. He had forgotten about the Lewis and Clark Museum's field shotgun, stashed away in the shed at the beginning of the dig.

"Sam only uses that for specimen collecting," Heather blurted out from behind him.

The sheriff gave her a withering glance, and then pointed out a small luggage tag on the handle. "Yes, thank you, but I can see that for myself. Definitely belongs to Sam Noggle."

The tag listed Sam's name, museum ID number, address, and date he borrowed it. It did seem to implicate Sam, but Jake couldn't believe his old friend was responsible. He was about to protest when a voice called out from inside the shed.

"Sheriff, do you want me to grab this box of shells?"

Deputy Martin's shout put a damper on Sheriff O'Neil's jubilant mood. She realized she had focused too much on the shotgun and missed some important potential evidence . . . and it was clear to her that the archaeologists knew she had erred.

O'Neil ducked back into the shed and after a few minutes of yelling, she and Deputy Martin exited, the latter holding an evidence bag with the box of shells. Pam leaned forward and studied the contents. The deputy helpfully held it up so that she could get a better look, until Sheriff O'Neil noticed what he was doing and ordered him to stop.

Pam smiled at the deputy and thanked him sweetly, before stepping back behind Jake. She pulled a notebook from her pocket and wrote something down, apparently quite pleased about something.

Sheriff O'Neil looked peeved but didn't seem to want to make an issue of her actions.

"Well, I think we have all we need, Martin. This will tie everything up just right."

"Does Agent Russell know about this?" Jake demanded, his ire rising. Things were moving too quickly, and he wanted answers.

Sheriff O'Neil's eyes bulged, and Jake braced himself for the explosion. "I don't answer to him, or you, for that matter! Now move aside or I'll arrest you too!"

Jake was about to let loose his own tirade when Pam grasped his arm, pulling him back a half step. She locked her blue eyes onto his and shook her head.

"Let it go. It won't help."

The sheriff gave them each a nasty look, and then stomped off toward the parking area, her deputy hurrying to catch up.

"I, I'm gonna make sure they didn't mess up the shed," Heather said, voice breaking, as she dashed through the door.

Jake exhaled, running his hand through his hair. "Thanks. I guess I was about to really step it in, huh?"

Pam smiled, then took a quick glance over her shoulder to confirm that the sheriff and her deputies were leaving. "Well, you did seem to be building up a pretty good head of steam. No sense letting you take a swing at her."

Jake was mad, admittedly, but striking a county sheriff hadn't been on his mind. He was more embarrassed about how upset he was. His hands were shaking.

"Sorry. I'm just so damn frustrated," Jake said. "Not even sure what to do next. It all looks hopeless."

"Actually, things might not be as bad as it seems," Pam said, tapping her open notebook with her pen.

"What do you mean?"

"Lots of little things, which any good attorney can turn into major issues, if it even comes to a trial. First, the gun case was covered with dust, so it obviously hasn't been touched anytime recently. And that shotgun is a .410, which is as small as they come. Sure, you could do some damage with a gun like that, especially at close range, but it would still require a heavy slug. The ammo box—which was unopened, I noticed—only had small birdshot loads. Getting hit with that would sting, but depending on the range the pellets wouldn't even penetrate heavy clothing."

Jake brightened, but was still concerned. "But couldn't they argue that it was the murder weapon, and he used shotgun slugs from another box, to cover his tracks?"

"Possibly. I'm not a forensic weapons expert. But the hole in Walker's chest was pretty large, more like what I'd expect from a 12 gauge, loaded with a slug or #00 buckshot."

"You're brilliant, you know that? I could kiss you."

"Now you're thinking. Better save it for later, okay?"

At that moment, Heather returned from her inspection of the shed. Her eyes were bloodshot and teary. "It doesn't look like they disturbed anything," she said, wiping her nose with her sleeve. "Just a few boxes out of place. So, what, what are we going to do now?"

"Pam noticed a bunch of problems the sheriff's recovery techniques," Jake said, and summarized what Pam had told him.

"In addition," Pam added, pointing to her notepad, "O'Neil didn't recover the weapon *with* Sam when he was arrested, which means anyone out here at the site could have had access to it. And all of this took place in front of the three of us."

"When you put it all together, it sounds like reasonable doubt to me," Jake said, grinning.

Heather seemed pleased with Pam's observations, even if the source was not her favorite person. "Good, that's really good. Just let me know what you need me to say or sign. I'm going to tell the others."

"For now, just tell them that the sheriff made some mistakes and things look good for Sam," Jake said. "No sense going into details, and we should probably keep those to ourselves."

Heather nodded and headed over to the dig.

"I think the Scenic Sheriff's Office is in way over their heads," Pam remarked, tucking her notepad back into her jacket. " I was watching the other deputy, Tuttle, while the other two were in the shed. He took a quick look in the front seat and the floor, but barely glanced through the rest of the van. He was leaning against it most of the time, until O'Neil came back out. The murder weapon could have been in the back seat and he would never even have seen it."

"So, plenty of holes in their case against Sam."

"That's what I'm thinking. At least, as far as their search goes. We don't know what other evidence they have, if anything."

Jake ran his fingers over his goatee, considering the situation anew. "You know, all this makes me think that Agent Russell isn't involved in this at all. There's no way he'd allow something so slip-shod, right?"

"I'd have to agree. I think Sheriff O'Neil is running all this behind his back."

"He's not going to be too thrilled when he finds out."

"So, what do you want to do now?" Pam asked, gesturing in the direction of the excavation. "I think the crew is still pretty anxious."

Jake looked over, only to see Heather and the others clumped together, obviously discussing the latest developments. It did not appear that anyone was all that interested in work.

"Well, I'm still thinking I should drive it to town and see what I can find out. Heather can keep things under control here, I think."

"Why don't I go over there instead? I know my way around a sheriff's office, and I might be able to find out things that you can't. The crew isn't going to care if I'm gone, and without you here I don't expect they are likely to stay put."

Jake had to agree with that. They'd probably catch up to him before he was even a mile down the highway.

"Okay, makes sense. See what you can find out; call me if you need anything."

Pam squeezed his arm, gathered up her belongings, and headed toward her car. Jake trudged over to the dig area, hoping that the whole situation would be resolved by morning. Deep down, he knew it wasn't to be.

CHAPTER 26

FOR THE REST OF THE DAY, time slowed to a crawl. The archaeologists went about their work robotically, in near-complete silence. Jake jumped every time his phone rang, which heightened the tension that permeated the site. The first call was from the department secretary, inquiring about a delivery delay for a textbook Jake had ordered for a spring class. Pam called about an hour after that, to relate a complete lack of progress. She had spent most of her time cooling her heels in the waiting area, with no sign of Sheriff O'Neil. Jake convinced her to hang around until four, and then return to the site and bring him back to the sheriff's office. Pam agreed, but cautioned that she didn't think it would do much good.

Shortly before they began to close up for the day, Keith Emerson responded to Jake's earlier message.

"Hi Jake. Finally got your message. I was in court most of the day, and meeting with clients after that."

"I understand. Were you able to straighten this out? I don't want Sam to be locked up overnight."

"I called O'Neil and the mayor, but neither one could take my call. No straight answers from anyone, to be honest." He let out a loud sigh, clearly audible above the background city noise. "I'm still in St. Paul, and I have an evening deposition that I can't miss. I'm sorry, but there's no chance I can get back to Scenic tonight to sort this mess out."

Jake tried to keep the frustration out of his voice, but was successful. "So he's stuck there? What if I . . ."

"Jake, look, for now the best thing to do is sit tight and stay calm. I'll drive back first thing in the morning and get you some answers. I promise."

"What about Agent Russell? We're pretty sure that O'Neil is doing all of this on her own. Doesn't he have jurisdiction and all that?"

"Frank is tied up in Madison this week, but I left him a message about the situation," Keith replied. "I guarantee he is not behind this. No way he'd condone something like this, not Frank."

"Alright." Jake said after a slight pause. "I'm not happy about it, but I understand. My crew is none too happy, either."

"Just a little time, that's all we need. Day or two at the most, maybe three, and we'll get it all worked out, I promise."

Keith rang off, and Jake walked over to relay what he had learned to the anxious archaeologists. He tried to put a good face on the news, but it was apparent that no one was hopeful of a quick resolution. As they were discussing the situation, Pam arrived. Jake told her what Keith had said while the rest of the crew started closing down the site.

"Doesn't sound too promising, does it?"

"That's an understatement," Jake said, kicking at a small clod of dirt. "Keith sounded upset, but I think he's too tied up with his cases to make this a priority. And Agent Russell is stuck in Madison for a while, so no help there, either."

"I suppose we could try to hire a lawyer on our own. To be honest, it might not be a good idea to put too much faith in Keith Emerson."

"Why not?"

"He does work as an attorney for Scenic, after all. There could be a conflict of interest."

Jake shook his head. "He only does that part time, I think. It's more of an on-call situation. Besides, I don't think he's behind any of this."

"Maybe," Pam said with a shrug. "So, what do you want to do instead?"

"I told the crew to steer clear of the sheriff's office," Jake whispered, "but that doesn't mean you and I can't head back over there. Maybe we can get in to see Sam."

Pam nodded, but wasn't enthusiastic. "We can give it a shot, I suppose, but don't get your hopes up."

"IF WE COULD JUST SPEAK WITH Sheriff O'Neil," Jake said, struggling to keep his voice level, "I'm sure we could get this all worked out."

"Told ya before, Sheriff's out on a call and won't be back until tomorrow," the deputy behind the desk replied, not looking up from his sports magazine.

Jake glanced at Pam, who shrugged her shoulders and mouthed, "told you so" in response. As she had predicted, Jake's arrival failed to make any impact on the situation.

"We've been trying to get through to her all day," Jake said. "What do you do in an emergency?"

"This isn't an emergency, is it? Best to call and leave a message."

"Our friend has been arrested."

"Visitin' hours are 10 to 4 on weekdays. You'll have to come back." The deputy's attention returned to his magazine.

Jake inhaled deeply, about to unleash a tirade of pent-up frustration. Pam put her hand on his shoulder. "What about bail, for our friend?"

"Have to talk to the judge about that," the deputy muttered.

"Well, where can we find the judge?" Pam asked.

"Ain't here. Judge only comes in when there's court business."

"Like someone being falsely arrested and held illegally?" Jake asked, slamming his hands down on the desk.

That caught the deputy's attention. Eyes wide, he tossed the magazine away and stood up. He tried in vain to assert his authority, but as Jake stood nearly a half-foot taller, the deputy wasn't about to cower him with his physical presence.

"Look, mister," the deputy said, voice cracking, "until Sheriff O'Neil or the judge tells me otherwise, the old guy stays in his cell, and nobody goes back there 'cept on official police business. Okay?"

"C'mon Jake, we can show ourselves out," Pam said, tugging at his arm. "We'll be back," she said pleasantly over her shoulder.

Outside, Jake let out a stream of curse words as the door slammed shut behind them. Pam took his hand in hers. He hadn't realized he was shaking until that moment.

"Take a deep breath, hon, and let it out slow."

"Do you believe that guy? What the hell is wrong with this town?"

"Beats me," Pam said, starting to walk toward her car. "I've never run into a sheriff's office like this before. It's like something out of a bad movie."

"I suppose I should thank you for getting me out of there," Jake said, a bit sheepishly. His temper cooled, and he began to realize how close he had come to lashing out physically.

"You might have felt better if you had knocked him around, but that wouldn't have gotten Sam out of jail, you know."

"I know, I know." Jake folded his arms and leaned back against the car. "So, what do we next? Find an all-night bakery that makes cakes with files inside?"

Pam laughed out loud, despite the gravity of the situation. The long day had been emotionally and physically draining for both of them.

"I'm partial to cheesecake, myself, but I think the file might spoil the taste." She moved close and put her arm over his broad shoulders. "We could try and hire an attorney, but we might not have much luck tonight, especially in this town."

Jake sighed and glanced at his watch. "I suppose we ought to let Keith have a try. He knows all the people in Scenic government, so that should help. Right?"

"I guess. So, we're back where we started," Pam said. "Come on, I'll buy you some dinner. Maybe things will look better in the morning."

CHAPTER 27

Unfortunately, Pam's wish fell upon deaf ears. After a subdued evening meal at a local bar and grill, she and Jake decided to call it an early night and each returned to their respective hotels. With Sam gone, Jake felt out of sorts. Each member of the crew stopped by at some point for news on Sam, and Jake felt worse after each negative reply. He spent an hour catching up on paperwork, but his heart wasn't in it.

There was a palpable tension in the air the next morning as Jake and the crew loaded up their vehicles. He was surprised to see Susan, eyes red and bloodshot, out with the others, until Al whispered that Susan wanted to "stay busy" to keep her mind off their troubles. The journey to Ghost Bog was draped in silence, a moody quiet that continued throughout the cool autumn morning. Jake's incoming phone calls were few and none had any connection to Sam's arrest. Without telling the others, Jake tried to call both Keith and Agent Russell around noon but was redirected to voice mail each time. A call to the Scenic Sheriff's Office was likewise non-productive. The crew monitored his actions throughout the day, hoping to hear some positive news but none was forthcoming.

As the sun started to dip low in the western sky, Pam broke the unspoken taboo.

"I take it you haven't heard anything," Pam said, handing Jake a small packet of field forms.

He shook his head. "No, nothing. I even called the sheriff's office, as if that would do any good. I was hoping that we would have heard from Keith by now."

Heather and Michelle, arms filled with artifact bags, approached as Jake was speaking.

"I don't think we should rely on Keith Emerson," Heather announced. "I mean, he's one of *them*, right?"

"Them?"

"You know, a local. This whole town has a creepy feel. You notice it more and more the longer we're here."

"I don't think it's that bad," Jake said. "The sheriff's office is messed up, sure, but everyone else is friendly enough."

"Maybe not," Michelle said, looking from side to side as if someone might overhear. "Curt and Rob went to that sports bar down the road last night, and they said it went dead silent when they walked in, and people kept watching them the whole time they were there."

Jake sighed and his shoulders slumped. Trouble between the crew and the locals was not something he wanted to see, with the end of the excavation so close. Of course, having one of his team arrested was not exactly anticipated, either.

"It could be just a coincidence. Maybe they felt anxious because of what's happened."

"Whatever. I just don't think we can trust anybody who isn't one-hundred percent on our side."

"Heather has a point, Jake," Pam said, pushing a loose strand of blonde hair back behind her ear. "It seems like Keith is working on our behalf, but how can we be sure? We don't even know where he is."

"Fine. Look, why don't I call the county building? They should be able to tell me where Keith is, and that should give us an idea of what he's done."

The group agreed, with some reluctance, and moved away to secure the site while Jake punched in the number.

"Hello, Scenic Town Hall," a cheery voice answered. "How may I direct your call today?"

Jake recognized the voice immediately, having spoken to the receptionist on many occasions when they were organizing the permits for the project. "Hello, Nora, this is Professor Caine, from the archaeology dig."

"Oh, hello Professor! So nice to hear from you. Are you finding lots of dinosaur bones at your dig?"

Jake rolled his eyes, having explained to her several times prior that they weren't looking at bones quite that old. "The excavation is going quite well, all in all." Obviously she wasn't privy to the recent difficulties at Ghost Bog. "I was wondering if you could connect me with Keith Emerson. It's important that I speak to him right away."

"Hmm, well let's see now." He could hear the squeak of chair wheels, as she rolled back to inspect the official status board located opposite the city/county mail cubbies. "It looks like Keith is still out. There's a note that says he'll be in the Twin Cities until sometime next week."

Jake nearly dropped his phone. Keith had all but assured him that he would be back in Scenic immediately and would make sure Sam was released. Did something else come up? Did Keith deliberately mislead him?

After a moment of silence, Nora spoke up. "Would you like me to transfer you to his voice mail? I think he checks his messages pretty often."

"No, that's okay," Jake said, mulling his options. Leaving yet another message seemed futile, but how else could he get any answers? Then an idea occurred.

"Nora, is Mayor Greene in his office? Maybe he can help me out."

"He's here. Let me see if he's available."

There was a loud click, followed by rather tinny elevator music, interspersed with a recorded message extolling the wonders of Scenic's tourism industry.

"Hello? Mayor Greene is swamped at the moment, but he'd be more than happy to see you tomorrow. If you can, he said you should stop by his office around nine. Is that okay?"

Jake thanked Nora for her help and agreed to drop in the next day. Heather approached as he put his phone away, smiling.

"Good news? What did Keith say?"

"Ah, Keith wasn't available, but I have a meeting scheduled with the mayor tomorrow morning. With luck, I can convince him this is all a big misunderstanding, and he can order the sheriff to let Sam go."

Heather frowned, less than impressed by the results of Jake's phone call. "That's good, I guess. But wasn't Keith supposed to be there today to clear all this up?"

"Something probably came up, or he got delayed," Jake said, hoping to forestall an argument. "I assume you can get the crew rolling tomorrow and take care of things here? I want to head over there first thing."

"Sure, no problem. Do you need us to drop you off?"

"No, I'll have Pam drive me over. We'll meet up with you at the site after the meeting."

The frown turned into a deep scowl at the mention of Pam. "I suppose that's cool, She should help out more, especially after all the trouble she's caused."

"Trouble? Come on, Heather, that's not fair."

"Isn't it? She found the first skeleton, which only slowed us down. Sam really freaked out about that. You know how worried he is about finishing this dig."

"Yes, but we're way ahead of schedule anyway and have already opened up more ground than we planned," Jake said, trying to keep calm. "Besides, finding an Early Archaic skeleton is a major discovery. We'll be doing research on those remains for years to come."

"What about the second skeleton, that hunter or whatever? That really made a mess of things. It turned the whole town against us!"

"You can't blame that on Pam either. Any one of us might have been the one to dig in those spots. We would have had to deal with the remains regardless of who found them."

"Well, things always seem to get screwed up when she's around. She's a jinx!"

"Heather, I know you don't like Pam. That's been obvious since the Waconah field school. But you can't let your feelings cloud your judgment."

"But I—"

"Let me finish," Jake ordered, folding his arms across his chest. "Once you start your professional career, you're going to have to interact with a lot of different people. Some you'll like, others you won't be able to stand. But it will hurt you professionally if you can't work with other people, so you need to learn to keep a lid on your personal feelings."

Heather jutted her chin out but didn't reply. Jake thought he saw her eyes watering, and he regretted the bluntness of his remarks.

"You're a fantastic archaeologist, Heather, and I know you're going to be great one day," Jake said with a smile, clapping her on the arm. "I've always been proud of your accomplishments. We just need to polish off a few of your rough edges. Look, we're all tired and stressed out about Sam, so take what I said with a grain of salt. Just remember what I said, okay?"

"Okay," she said, chewing on her lower lip. "Everything will be better once Sam's back out here."

And hopefully that will be sooner rather than later, thought Jake. The shiver he felt down his back at that moment, he tried to convince himself later, was merely from the chill of the evening air as the sun disappeared over the trees.

CHAPTER 28

"I DO NOT LIKE THIS SITUATION, PROFESSOR. I do not."
Jake bristled at Mayor Greene's condescending tone and his emphasis on the last three words, but he held his temper in check. Pam, sitting on his right, placed her hand on his arm.

"I understand your feelings, but we aren't responsible for what has happened."

"Hah!"

The mayor raised his eyebrows at Sheriff O'Neil's response, but said nothing in rebuke. She took a step forward from behind his chair and placed her palms against the oversized desk.

"All of the trouble in Scenic started when you . . . people arrived, and started muckin' around in that swamp. I had my concerns right off, just ask anyone."

Mayor Greene nodded his head. "Three dead bodies since you got here. Hardly good for Scenic's image."

"One of those bodies is over 7,000 years old, and another at least twenty," Jake said. "I don't see how . . ."

"Potential tourists aren't going to care about specifics, Professor. They do an Internet search for 'Scenic, Wisconsin' and up pops 'three dead' and they'll move right on to the next listing. I guarantee no one will vacation here with that kind of reputation."

The three other people in the office, all dressed in suits, nodded in agreement. The mayor had introduced them as members
of the chamber of commerce or tourism or something similar,
but Jake was so shocked to see them that he had blanked on their
names. He had assumed the meeting would be between himself
and Mayor Greene; instead, it was an ambush. Pam had insisted
on accompanying him inside the building and elected to remain
when it was clear that the Scenic officials had no intention of a
nice, friendly visit.

"You didn't seem too upset with us when we first arrived," Jake
said, a bit of heat in his voice. All of it—the strain of the dig, the
murder, Sam's arrest, even the recent confrontation with Heather—
was finally getting to him.

"Well, that was before, before all this."

Pam removed her hand from Jake's arm and tapped her fingers together. "I think we're all unsettled about recent events." She
smiled at the mayor and nodded her head. "But you have to realize
how concerned we are for our friend Sam. If we could just speak to
him for a moment, or perhaps arrange for an attorney . . ."

"He's not getting away on bail, you can bet on that," Sheriff
O'Neil snapped. "We've got solid evidence that he's the killer."

Pam turned her full attention to the sheriff. "And your evidence
is?"

Sheriff O'Neil gave Pam a nasty look, but still chose to answer.
"The victim, Walker, was killed right near your dig site. The suspect, Noggle, had multiple run-ins with the victim while you were
there, and has a history of antagonism with the victim. He has no
alibi for the night of the murder, and he had motive."

"What motive?" Jake didn't really want an answer, but he was
tired of letting the sheriff ramble on unchallenged.

"Noggle was worried that Doctor Walker was going to take
over the Ghost Bog dig site." The sheriff had a triumphant look on
her face, as if this were the clincher that tied it all together. "With
control of your old bones and some other better sites that he had

found, Walker was going to discredit Noggle. That would have destroyed his standing and ruined his livelihood."

"That was never going to happen," Jake said, shaking his head. "Archaeological studies don't work like that. There's no fame or fortune involved for scientists. And we're the only ones with permits to excavate at Ghost Bog."

"But when you're done, the property goes to the state, correct? And at that point you wouldn't be only ones who might be able to dig out there, right?"

"Technically, yes," Jake said. "Any reputable scientist could apply for a permit to conduct excavations at the site."

"So there you are."

"It's not that simple. The application process isn't first come, first served. Officials at various levels have input, and primary consideration is afforded to archaeologists with prior experience at the site. And Walker is a paleontologist; archaeology and paleontology are two different fields of study. The recovery of an Archaic skeleton also marks it as a burial site, which adds another layer of red tape."

The sheriff rolled her eyes. "I'm not particularly interested in either of the old skeletons you dug up. What's past is past, I say. But the murder of Doctor Walker is happening now, and could be a danger to the Scenic community."

"But following your argument, Walker was killed because he had a beef with Sam. If Sam is responsible, no one else is in any danger."

"We can't take that chance. Who knows what a deranged killer might do if let loose?"

"The same thing is true if Sam isn't responsible," Pam added. "If someone else, maybe a local, is involved, they are still at large."

"No one around here even knew Walker before all this happened, so it doesn't make sense that a local would have killed him."

"You can't know that for sure," Jake said. "And you aren't even considering the possibility that there could be other suspects."

Sheriff O'Neil stopped short, struggling to find an appropriate answer to their argument. After a moment, she sidestepped the issue.

"Finally, Noggle had the murder weapon in his possession when we arrested him," she said, reveling in what she perceived as the nail in the coffin.

Jake and Pam glanced at each other, each thinking along similar lines. "You took *a* shotgun, but not necessarily *the* murder weapon," Jake said.

"And the shotgun in question was recovered from the supply shed at the site, after Sam was arrested at his hotel. It was *not* in his possession," Pam added. "Technically speaking, that is."

The sheriff was now clenching her fists, growing more annoyed by Jake and Pam's counter arguments. Mayor Greene looked uncomfortable, not happy with the direction the meeting had taken.

"Look, as far as I'm concerned, Sam Noggle is the most logical suspect for the Walker homicide," Sheriff O'Neil said. "And until I feel otherwise, he's going to stay locked up. Period."

"However you want to spin it, folks," the mayor said, "There's more than enough evidence to hold your friend until we can sort all this out. And the judge who signed the warrant agrees, so that's that."

Jake didn't appreciate ultimatums. "Maybe I ought to run all this by Agent Russell and see what he thinks."

Sheriff O'Neal blurted out something about placing them both under arrest, but was shut down. Mayor Greene raised his hand, and she took a silent step back. He turned his attention to Jake and Pam. "You go ahead and do that, if you feel that way. But our job is to keep the folks of Scenic safe, and that's what we're going to do."

USHERED OUT OF THE MAYOR'S OFFICE, Jake and Pam were walking down the hall toward the main entrance when a side door swung open, almost striking them.

"Eric, we're not done here!"

"Later, man! Got things to do." Eric Holcombe burst through the doorway, nearly bowling over Jake in his haste. He scowled at the two archaeologists, barely slowing down as he hurried away. A slight man in a gray suit emerged from the office.

"But this is important. We have to . . . oh, hello, Professor Caine," Peter said, putting on a smile. "Didn't expect to see you out here."

"Bit of a surprise for us, too. Hope we're not intruding."

"No, of course not." Peter glanced past them, brows furrowing as Eric disappeared through a side exit. "I must apologize for Eric. Impetuousness of youth, I'm afraid."

"Don't worry about it. It's, um, been a rough couple of days for us, too."

"Oh, yes. So I've heard. Terrible business about Doctor Noggle, just terrible! Please let me if there's anything I can do."

Jake thanked him for his offer, and Peter retreated into his office, closing the door softly behind him.

As they stepped out of the building into the cool morning air, Pam looked back over her shoulder. "I wonder what that was all about."

Jake shrugged. "Peter probably wants Eric to find a job. I suspect being a punk in a small town doesn't rake in the cash. Maybe he can land a position as deputy mayor or something."

"Ouch. Someone's a little bitter this morning."

"Sorry. Didn't appreciate the ambush set up by the sheriff and the mayor."

"I think we handled it pretty well, all things considered," Pam said, pulling her keys out as they walked over to her car. "And we have a pretty good idea of the sheriff's theory of the crime, as flawed as it is."

"But we weren't able to see Sam, let alone get him released. The crew is not going to be pleased."

Pam leaned over and kissed him on the cheek. "Can't win them all, hon. Do you want to try something else, or do we just head out to the site?"

Jake mused on the situation as they got into Pam's car, and she started the engine. Pam checked her phone for messages, allowing him to gather his thoughts.

"I can't believe I'm saying this, but I think it's up to us. Again."

A hint of a smile played at the corners of Pam's mouth. "I was hoping you'd come around to that conclusion. I don't see any other option, myself. And we do make a great team."

Jake rolled his eyes, but he had to admit that she was right.

"So, where do we start?"

"I think a two-pronged approach will work best. Three, if you include keeping up with work at Ghost Bog. We do have to finish the excavation, and it will keep the crew occupied and out of trouble. First, I want to keep calling Agent Russell and Keith. We'll flood them with messages until we get some action."

"Sounds good so far. And if we don't have any luck with them, we should hire an attorney for Sam. A non-local attorney, maybe someone from Eau Claire or Minneapolis."

"Agreed. Let's give them until the end of the day on Monday. On Tuesday, we can start making some calls."

"Another thing I thought of before but didn't want to mention in the mayor's office. Anything that Sam may have told the sheriff will get tossed, since he wasn't allowed to have an attorney present."

Jake nodded, starting to feel that things might not be as hopeless as they once thought. "Second, you and I are going to track down who really killed Matt Walker."

"That's a tall order, partner," Pam said, drumming her fingernails on the steering wheel. "I mean, not that I don't think we could do it, but I should point out that I'm way outside my official jurisdiction here, and we're not dealing with a cold case this time. We're strictly amateur investigators on this one."

"All I'm saying is let's pull together any evidence that might be useful, and we'll see where it leads. We can start by documenting the whereabouts of the crew on the night of the murder, what they saw and when. We should also talk to Walker's two assistants."

"The crew might not appreciate you checking on their alibis. Are you comfortable with that?"

Jake considered the question, then nodded. "Yes. It's important enough that I don't think anyone will mind. We'll just say that Agent Russell has requested it, as a way to help Sam. I don't think anyone will object."

"Unless, of course, they happen to be involved in the crime." With that, Pam put the car in gear and began the drive through town toward the Ghost Bog site.

Jake hadn't considered the possibility that someone on the crew might be involved, even peripherally. He knew Heather and Michelle well enough to know they couldn't be involved. Curt and Rob had been on the Wisconsin State University archaeology crew for several seasons, and although he had only worked with them on occasion, Jake doubted they were mixed up with murder. Al and Susan, on the other hand, were strangers.

The squeak of the wipers against the windshield jarred Jake from his musings. Some intermittent spatters of sleet and rain were falling, and the sky was filling with dark gray clouds.

"Looks like that storm they promised is on its way," Pam said. "Glad I packed my heavy sweater this morning."

"The forecast said snow showers tonight, and maybe more wet weather tomorrow. If it gets real bad, we'll plan on working from the hotel instead of going out to the site."

"Fine with me. I don't really want to catch pneumonia on my vacation," Pam said. "By the way, I suppose you'll need me to account for my whereabouts on the night in question, just as a formality. Well, I have an iron-clad alibi, as I was deeply entranced in a romantic interlude with the man of my dreams."

Jake blushed furiously as Pam offered to provide a detailed description of their evening together.

CHAPTER 29

A T THE SITE, JAKE TOLD AN abridged version of his meeting with Mayor Greene and Sheriff O'Neil. He tried to keep it positive, but the overall poor tenor of the encounter was evident. In order to forestall further bad feelings, Jake added that he was in contact with Agent Russell and Keith Emerson, both of whom were striving to get Sam out of jail. It was a small lie, he told himself, but necessary and it did seem to placate the archaeologists as they returned to work.

After lunch, Jake spoke with Heather and Michelle about their activities during the evening Walker was murdered, while Pam did the same with Curt and Rob. Michelle accepted that it was for Agent Russell and answered candidly, but Heather was suspicious. She accused Jake of playing "amateur detective" again and blamed Pam. Jake sidestepped the inevitable argument and managed to get the information he wanted, but it wasn't easy.

The scattered showers turned to a persistent, cold rain by mid afternoon, so Jake decided to close up early. As the last of the equipment was locked in the shed, he told the archaeologists to meet at his room tomorrow morning. The weather forecast almost assured that they wouldn't be able to do any fieldwork on Saturday. Jake climbed into Pam's car as the others drove off.

"How did you make out with Curt and Rob?"

"Not bad," Pam said, pulling the notebook from her pocket. "They both accepted that it was just a formality, on orders from Agent Russell. Let's see. They rode back from the site in the big van with Heather and Michelle, and Sam, Al, and Susan were about five minutes behind them in the LC van. They unloaded their gear and asked if anyone was interested in grabbing dinner, but everyone declined. This was about 5:30 or 5:45. They got cleaned up and had a beer each before driving over to the pizza place in Curt's car. After dinner, they drove back to the hotel to see if anyone wanted to head out to the bar and watch football. This was about 7:00, although Rob thought it was closer to 7:30. Heather and Michelle were gone, and so was the WSU van. They talked to Al, but she and Susan said they were going to stay put. There was no answer at Sam's room, and since the Lewis and Clark Museum van was gone, they figured he had gone out to eat. After that, they walked over to the bar and stayed there until almost 11:00, after which they came back and crashed until morning."

"That fits with what Michelle and Heather told me. After getting back to the hotel and showering, they drove off about 6:30 and ate at the Chinese restaurant on Main Street. After that, they picked up some groceries at the sprawl mart on the edge of town and were back to the hotel by 8:00. Michelle said the Lewis and Clark Museum van was gone but thought she saw Curt's car down by their room. Heather didn't recall one way or the other."

"She didn't see the cars, or didn't *not* see them?"

Jake shrugged his shoulders. "I think she was being intentionally obtuse. By not saying one way or the other, she probably thinks she's helping Sam. Besides, she wasn't very forthcoming."

"I suppose it doesn't matter. I think it's unlikely that either of them are involved, or Rob and Curt, either." Pam started the car and looked at Jake. "Do you want to head to your hotel and talk to Al and Susan next?"

"Let's stop by the Emersons first. I want to tell them we won't be around tomorrow, and we should ask if they saw or heard anything the night of the murder."

Pam agreed and a few minutes later they found themselves in the Emerson kitchen, petting the excited beagles and enjoying the aroma of fresh-baked treats.

"So, with the bake sale next week, I've been busier than ever," Vera said, wiping her hands on a well-worn apron. "Otherwise we would have brought something over for you kids."

"That's alright," Jake said with a smile. "It's been a hectic week for us, too."

"Told you, Vera," Harold said, sipping a beer at the opposite end of the table. "They don't need us buttin' in, fattening them up."

"You hush, now. Professor, you and your lady friend will take some banana bread with you, won't you?"

"Of course, thank you. Um, like I said, we probably won't be around tomorrow because of the weather, so if you can keep an eye on the site until Monday, we'd appreciate it."

"No problem at all," Harold said. "Gypsy and Shadow head in that direction every time I take them out anyway."

Jake thanked him, and made sure the Emersons had his cell number in the event of any problems. With some misgivings, Jake decided he had better follow through with his earlier idea.

"By the way, did either of you hear or see anything over at the site the night, the night . . . it happened?"

Harold and Vera looked at each other for a moment but didn't seem upset.

"Nope, not a thing," Harold replied. "Even the dogs were quiet that night."

Vera nodded her head in agreement. "We didn't see anything out of the ordinary. That's just what we told Keith's friend Frank, when he asked us."

Obviously, thought Jake, Agent Russell would have checked in with the Emersons, given their proximity to the site. Before he could respond, Pam followed up.

"Neither of you heard any shots, nothing like that on Monday night?"

"In these woods, you hear shots echoing all over the place, especially before hunting season," Harold said. "Boys are busy sighting in their rifles and such. But nope, nothing close by that night."

LOADED DOWN WITH TWO LOAVES OF banana bread and several bag of cookies and muffins, Jake and Pam dashed back to her car as the cold rain pelted down even harder than before.

"Nice of them to give us all these treats," Pam said as she started the car. She filched a cookie from a nearby bag as Jake fastened his seat belt. "Too bad they didn't notice anything the night of the murder. That could have been helpful."

"It does confirm that the actual shooting probably took place away from the site, which is good. Shows that Sam didn't lure Walker out here."

"True, but it doesn't mean that Sam wasn't involved, somewhere else. Hotel?"

Jake nodded, a bit despondent over Pam's remark. It wasn't going to be easy to demonstrate Sam's innocence without some direct evidence that someone else was responsible. He felt a bit guilty, deep down. If he hadn't gone to dinner with Pam that night, Jake would have been with Sam, providing him with a solid alibi. As it stood, Jake and Pam had no clear idea of where Sam was the night of the murder. That alone was their biggest obstacle. Until they could speak with him, they weren't going to overcome it.

CHAPTER 30

B ACK AT THE HOTEL, THE ARCHAEOLOGISTS were in the final
stages of unloading when Jake and Pam arrived.

"About time you showed up," Heather said, tucking a sheaf of
damp paperwork into a binder. "This rain isn't making things any
easier, you know."

"Sorry. Had to stop by the Emersons to let them know we
wouldn't be at the site tomorrow," Jake said. He grabbed one of the
few remaining artifact boxes in the van and carried it to his room.

"We do have some baked goods from Vera, though," Pam
said, arms laden with the still-warm treats. "C'mon over, help
yourselves."

The crew approached and soon relieved Pam of most of the
items. Jake returned and collected the day's paperwork.

"So we're not going out tomorrow?" Michelle said, in between
cookies.

Jake nodded. "They're predicting rain all night, maybe snow
showers or worse tomorrow. No sense pushing it when we're
far ahead of schedule anyway. We'll put in a half day on notes
and maps, and then you can have the rest of the weekend to
yourselves."

They all seemed pleased with that arrangement, and after

acquiring a few extra snacks started to disperse toward their rooms. Jake gestured to Pam, and they fell in step behind Al and Susan.

"Al, got a second?"

"Sure. What's up?"

Jake looked over her shoulder as Pam reached Susan, and the two of them took a few steps into Susan's room. He turned his attention back to Al.

"This is just a formality, but Agent Russell asked that we document everyone's whereabouts the night Walker was killed. It could end up helping Sam in the long run. So, if you saw or heard anything that might help . . .?"

"That makes sense. Let me think. We left the site a little after five, a couple of minutes behind the others. You and Pam were still there, wrapping up. Sam drove the LC van and I was up front. Susan was in the back."

"Did Sam say anything about his plans for the evening?

Al tapped her finger on her lips. "No, I don't think so. We talked a little about the bison skeleton he was working on, and how he thought they might have been moving the skulls to the edge of the kill during the butchering process. He mentioned some other kill sites where he saw similar patterns, but I don't remember their names."

"That's okay. Just whatever you can recall."

"It was about 5:30 when we got back here. The others were already back and had unloaded most of their stuff. We carried a few things over to Sam's room and that was it. Didn't see him again until the next morning."

"That's odd. When Pam dropped me off a few minutes later, Sam wasn't in the room. I assumed he walked over to the convenience store for more beer or a sandwich or something."

"Hmm . . . that is weird. Oh, wait a second! When we brought the stuff to your room, Sam was pulling a note off the door. Something from the front desk, I think, because I saw the hotel logo at the top. Maybe he went to talk to them after I left."

"Probably. I'll check with them next. How about after that?"

"Susan and I went into our room and took our turns in the shower. She went first. When I got out, she was sitting on her bed, watching the news. I checked my email and texts for a while, then decided to grab some dinner. That was a little after six. I asked Susan if she wanted to go along, but she said her daughter was going to call and she needed to stay put."

Al paused to look around the parking lot, as if trying to recall details from the night in question. "All of the vehicles were gone, I remember that. I decided to just run up to the sandwich shop up the street. Got my food and I was back twenty, maybe twenty-five minutes later."

"And Susan was still there when you got back?"

"Yeah, sure," Al said, a bit puzzled by Jake's question. "I ate in my room, and watched a movie and read until we turned in. Didn't leave the rest of the night."

"What about Susan? Didn't she need to get dinner, too?"

"No, she never left. I think she's trying to save her money," Al said. "She doesn't eat out much, just buys food at the grocery store and eats off that until it's gone. I brought her some coleslaw, said I ordered too much. She ate that, plus some leftovers from her lunch."

"And neither of you went anywhere after that? Didn't see anyone else?"

"Nope. Rob and Curt stopped by about the time I finished eating and asked if I wanted to hit the bar with them, but I was pretty wiped out and decided to pass. Other than that, we didn't see any of the crew until the next morning."

Jake thanked her for the info and headed toward the hotel lobby.

A SHORT TIME LATER, JAKE ALMOST COLLIDED with Pam as he exited the lobby door.

"There you are! I went in to talk to Susan and when I turn around you're gone."

"Sorry," Jake said, stepping back under the eave so they were both out of the rain. "Al remembered that Sam found a note on our door when they got back on Monday, and I wanted to check it out."

"So what did you find out?"

"According to the desk clerk, a man called about mid afternoon, asking for Sam Noggle. Said he had information on an important archaeological site nearby with a bunch of bones eroding out of the hillside. Said they were just like the ones at the Ghost Bog site, and he was worried they might get destroyed if someone didn't do something about them right away."

"Wow. I'll bet Sam was excited to hear about that."

"You have no idea. He'd have us working double-shifts at both sites, seven days a week."

"Anything else?"

Jake shook his head. "She remembered that he gave her a number for Sam to call, and to ask for Earl. She wrote it all down on the note, but she couldn't remember the number."

"Shoot. That would have been nice to follow up on. Maybe Agent Russell can get a list of the incoming calls and we can track him that way."

"She did say that Sam went to the far side of the lobby and made a call on his cell, which I presume was to this Earl character. It would explain the 'phantom collector' that Sam mentioned out at the site. Some people came to check in, so she didn't overhear anything that Sam said."

"So Sam should have more info on the caller and his site. I wonder if he told any of this to the sheriff?"

"Sam can be pretty damn stubborn sometimes," Jake said. "Anything he told the sheriff would likely be peppered with four-letter words, and not very helpful."

"He's not doing himself any favors with that attitude, that's for sure. We need to get in there and talk to him, find out what he knows and where he was on Monday night."

"What did you find out from Susan?"

"Not much. She wasn't very talkative, but that could be from Heather filling her in on my various shortcomings." Pam summarized what Susan told her, which mirrored what Al had said but with less detail. Jake relayed the additional information from Al's account, filling in the gaps.

Pam listened with interest, then wrote a few comments in her notebook. "Do you want to hit the jail again, see if we can sneak in to see Sam? I don't think we'll have much luck, but I don't know what else we can do."

"I don't think so. Let's face it, they're not going to let us in without a fight and I'd rather wait until the odds are in our favor," Jake said, shivering a bit from the cold air and increasing rain. All at once he felt exhausted, deep down in his bones. "Why don't we just get cleaned up, and meet later for dinner? We can compare notes on everyone's whereabouts and figure out what we want to tackle tomorrow afternoon."

"Good idea," Pam replied, stuffing her notebook into a jacket pocket. "Jake, I was thinking. If you want, I could drive down to Madison and track down Agent Russell. Maybe in person I can convince him to do something, right away, to fix all this."

Jake considered her idea, weighing the pros and cons, before coming to a decision. "No, I don't think so. At least not right now. You could chase all over looking for him, and we're not that certain of his current whereabouts. And even if Russell is around, you may not be able to get in to see him."

Pam looked a little disappointed, but Jake suspected it had more with to do with a sense of uncomfortable idleness, rather than a strong desire to follow up on her plan.

"Your call, I guess," Pam said. "I hope we hear from Agent Russell before things get any worse."

Jake gave her a knowing glance, not wanting to think too hard about that possibility. "Besides, I think I'd miss having you around."

"Really?" Pam gave him a big smile and leaned in close. "As a fellow detective, or otherwise?"

"Both, to be honest," he said, returning her smile. "But I think more of the latter, right now."

Pam gave him a long, ardent kiss. "I'll be back soon for dinner. And then we are definitely going to continue this conversation."

CHAPTER 31

Aꜰᴛᴇʀ ᴀɴ ɪɴᴛɪᴍᴀᴛᴇ ᴅɪɴɴᴇʀ, Jᴀᴋᴇ ᴀɴᴅ Pam lingered over coffee as iridescent snowflakes danced outside the restaurant
window. Despite the tranquility, the conversation soon turned to
Sam's dilemma and they began to compare notes. Before long, the
table was covered with sheets of paper that charted the location
of each member of the archaeology crew on the night of Walker's
murder. Everyone was accounted for and had an alibi in the form
of another crew person, except for Sam. Until they could speak
with him in person, a large red question mark would remain penciled next to his name.

Expanding their list of potential suspects proved somewhat helpful, but in the end it only opened up more questions.
Improbable suspects like Harold and Vera Emerson, with no
motive or connection to the victim, could be eliminated. Keith and
Agent Russell were also doubtful suspects, although Pam was a bit
concerned over Keith's recent behavior and lack of candor.

Any local resident might be a suspect, particularly if Walker
was killed by accident, say while trespassing. If that were the case,
it might be next to impossible to find the person responsible unless
they could trace Walker's movements that day of the murder. That
meant talking to his assistants, Ryan and Laura. It was also possible

that one or both of them held a long-standing grudge against their employer, which was worth checking out. Based on these concerns, a visit to Ryan and Laura was at the top of their list.

As they wrapped up their discussion, Pam took a sip of coffee and then set the cup off to one side. "Jake, can I ask you something about Sam?"

"Sure. What do you want to know?"

"How long have you known him?"

"Quite a few years now," Jake replied. "He has a temper, but Sam's more bluster than anything. I know he wouldn't have killed Walker, no matter how upset he was, if that's what you're getting at."

"It's not that," Pam said, avoiding his gaze for a moment. "I know you're the Ghost Bog project director, but you seem to almost . . . defer to Sam, a lot of times, even if you're not comfortable with his arguments. Is it because he knows more about bison sites?"

"No, it's not that," Jake said, chuckling. "It probably comes from some help he gave me, years back, when I was in graduate school. I was planning to analyze an old archaeology collection but couldn't drum up any professional support. I thought the collection had a lot of potential—lots of ceramics, lithics, faunal remains, some really interesting stuff—but without funding I couldn't hire anyone to do the specialized lab work."

"Like analyzing the animal bones?"

"Exactly. Running out of options, I took a chance and contacted Sam, thinking he might know of a student interested in taking on the project, maybe for their thesis. I had only met him once before that, at a conference, so it was kind of a shot in the dark."

"And he was able to help you out, I take it."

Jake nodded. "To my shock, Sam offered to analyze and report on the zooarchaeology assemblage himself, at no cost."

"That must have been a relief," Pam agreed. "I can see why you feel indebted to him."

"It's more than just that," Jake said. "I found out later that not only was Sam swamped with projects at the time, but he was also in the midst of his latest divorce. Not the best time for a casual acquaintance, and a student no less, to hit him up for a favor."

Jake took a sip of coffee before continuing. "But it paid off, big time. The site collection proved even more amazing than expected, and I managed to get a grant to do some more excavation at the site. Ended up forming a major part of my dissertation research."

Pam nodded, but she looked concerned. "I can see why you're reluctant to 'pull rank' on him at the dig, but we have to be objective as far as investigating Walker's murder."

"I understand," Jake replied. "And I can do that. You should probably know, Sam confessed that he's been feeling his years lately, concerned that his career is nearing its end. That's why he's so gung-ho about the Ghost Bog excavation. And I overheard Susan telling Heather that there's been talk at the Lewis and Clark Museum that Sam should start thinking about retirement."

"I can see why you're handling Sam with kid gloves," Pam said. "But we may have to ask him some tough questions, assuming we can ever get in to talk to him."

Jake nodded in agreement. "Understood. Let's see what we can find out from Walker's assistants. Maybe we'll uncover something that will help free Sam."

"Sounds like a plan, handsome," Pam replied with a smile, sliding her hand over Jake's. "For tonight, though, maybe we can head back to my room and think of something to take our minds off our troubles?"

Grinning, Jake called out for the check.

CHAPTER 32

THE FALLING SNOW OVERNIGHT LEFT A thin white blanket across Kohl County, but the winds shifted on Saturday morning and the moisture shifted to a steady, depressing drizzle. As instructed, the crew met in Jake's room and busied themselves over the next few hours updating maps, correcting paperwork, and cleaning artifacts. The archaeologists made short work of their tasks and by noon everyone was released. Jake and Pam excused themselves from a proposed group lunch and went to question Walker's assistants, Ryan and Laura.

"I didn't realize Walker and his team were staying in the same hotel as you," Jake said as they pulled into the parking lot.

"I spotted them one morning in the lobby," Pam said. "I'm pretty sure they're in the fancy new section, with the suites and kitchenettes. Bit pricier than my room, I'm sure."

"It would be nice if we could poke around in Walker's room, but I suppose that would be pushing our luck."

"I think so. The sheriff's office should have searched it already. Let's start with the assistants and see what we can find out from them."

Pam parked a short distance from the main entrance, and they made their way to the front desk. The clerk recognized Pam, and after a brief explanation was more than happy to provide them with the numbers of Ryan and Laura's adjoining rooms. After a quick elevator ride, they found the rooms. Jake rapped on the door, and the voices inside ceased.

"Hello? Oh, it's you," Ryan said. Laura mumbled something, and Ryan gestured for them to enter.

"What can we do for you?" Laura greeted them warmly, but her eyes looked wary. Ryan plopped down on the unoccupied bed and turned down the television. Two open, half-filled suitcases covered the second bed.

"We were sorry to hear about Professor Walker," Jake said, resulting in a derisive noise from Ryan, but he continued. "It must have been quite a shock."

"Yes, yes it was." Laura glanced at Jake and Pam but seemed ill at ease. "Um, the sheriff told us that Doctor Noggle has been charged with the crime, so I'm not sure if we should be talking to you . . ."

"That's why we're here," Pam said with authority. "Sheriff O'Neil has taken Sam into custody, but it isn't clear if he's actually responsible. The Wisconsin Bureau of Investigation has jurisdiction over the case, and Agent Russell isn't convinced that Sam was involved at all. We're helping him out."

Neither Ryan nor Laura replied, but Jake thought they looked more than a little nervous. He decided to shift the mood.

"You two are leaving?"

"Well, yes," Laura said. She picked up a shirt off the dresser and tossed it into the nearest suitcase. "The sheriff said we were free to leave at any time, although we might be called back later. The University paid in advance for the rooms but only through this coming Monday. They won't cover anything beyond that, so we're heading home."

"Before you leave, we'd like to ask you a few questions," Pam said.

"Why should we do anything to help you?"

"Shut up, Ryan!" Laura snapped, startling everyone present. "They're just doing their jobs, and your childish attitude isn't helping anything!"

Ryan slumped back against the headboard but didn't reply. Meek Laura held the authority now that Matt Walker was out of the picture.

"Did you ever come out to Ghost Bog? I mean, when we weren't there?" Jake asked.

Laura and Ryan glanced at each other.

"Yeah," Ryan said. "Once or twice, early on, after we first arrived."

"But we never disturbed or touched anything," Laura added. "We, well, Doctor Walker, was curious to see what you had found, and wanted to inspect the landscape so we could focus our own survey on similar areas. You know, low-elevation bogs, basin deposits, anything that could have served as a natural bison trap."

"Like that did us much good. The forests are thick with brushy undergrowth all over this area," Ryan said. "Found a few bogs, mostly small muck deposits, but the bugs were terrible, and we couldn't see anything. We could have walked right on top of mounds of bones and never would have known."

"You didn't dig anywhere? No shovel testing at all?"

Laura shrugged, refolding a pair of jeans before putting them back in place. "We couldn't dig without permits, at least on state and federal land."

Jake had trouble believing that someone as headstrong and arrogant as Matt Walker would worry too much about little things like regulations, but he kept his opinion to himself. "What about on private land?"

"I suppose we could have, but it was hard to tell where we were half the time," Ryan said, scrolling through messages on his phone. "And a lot of the forested land around here is owned by non-locals. I don't think he even knew who to contact if we did find something."

"I think Doctor Walker was hoping that we'd luck out and find something, anything, significant," Laura added. "He was very insistent, especially, um, after you told him to stay away."

"Look," Ryan said, growing more irritable. "We spent hours tramping through the woods, trailing behind him, usually lost. Never found anything, period. We talked to a few locals here and there, but that was a dead end too. Either they didn't know about any sites or bones, or they didn't want strangers tramping around on their land. We snuck on to a few places anyway, but never stayed long."

Laura was staring at Pam, who was jotting down their responses in her notebook. "Doctor Walker never had us on private property, as far as we knew," Laura said, voice rising. Ryan's remarks had upset her. "It wasn't our fault!"

"We're not interested in hitting you with trespassing charges," Pam said, softly but with authority. "Our only concern is tracking Walker's movements and finding out who really killed him."

Jake was impressed. Pam managed to make it sound as if they were conducting an official investigation, when in reality they were about as far from that as they could be. The term "obstruction of justice" kept floating around in the back of his mind. Neither Laura nor Ryan replied, but Laura seemed appeased by Pam's assurance.

Jake decided this was the best time to get to the heart of the matter. "What about the night Walker was killed?"

"We weren't with him," Laura said.

"I think he finally caught on that we were just about at our limit with him and his damn survey," Ryan said.

"Do you know why he was out at Ghost Bog?"

"I didn't think he was going out there," Laura said, focusing her attention on Pam. "That evening, before dinner, he said he had a good lead on a possible site. There was a jumble of bones eroding out of a stream bank, not far from a large rock outcrop."

"It did sound promising, I have to admit," Ryan said. "He mentioned there was limestone or dolomite in that particular area, and good bone preservation as a result."

"Do you know where this was?" Jake had studied the local land-forms in detail and was skeptical that anything of that description might be found nearby.

Ryan shook his head. "He didn't say. Kept it pretty close to the vest. Besides, he really didn't confine much in us underlings."

"He was very excited, though. It did sound perfect."

"How did he find out about this spot?" Pam said, watching them both. "Who told him about it?"

"Dunno. We never met the guy, and I honestly don't remember if Walker talked to him in person or over the phone."

"I think it was a phone call," Laura said. "Some guy who worked odd hours, which is why he was going over there in the evening."

"Why didn't one of you go with him?" Pam asked.

"Truth? We were exhausted!" Ryan's outburst made them all jump. "The odds of finding a site like yours are one in a million. Hell, I'm a lab tech. I don't want to be crashing through the woods, fighting off flies and ticks. I'm still covered with stings from the hornet nest we crashed into. Besides, we have a whole curation room full of bones to analyze and write up. Some of those speci-mens have been at Snelling College since the 1950s!"

This revelation puzzled Pam. "There's archaeological material sitting around like that and nobody's ever looked at it? How does that happen?"

"For decades it was standard practice to collect everything they could, figuring that there would be time and money to ana-lyze it later on," Jake replied. "Archaeologists and paleontologists would spend summer months in the field gathering showy items for displays, and the rest would be stashed away or traded to other museums."

Ryan nodded. "The public doesn't realize that some of the most exciting 'discoveries' in modern paleontology are from specimens collected before their grandparents were even born. Back then, they shipped railroad cars full of specimens to museums all over the country. Only a handful of bones ever make it into display cases for public viewing. The rest are stored in cabinets or stashed in basements, moldering in plaster jackets and dirt."

"So, you didn't go with Doctor Walker," Jake said, attempting to get the conversation back on track. "What did you two do the rest of the evening, after he left?"

Laura glanced at Ryan before she answered. "We ate dinner together at the place across the street, and then came back here. We were each in our rooms after that. Talked a few times through the adjoining door until it got late, then we each turned in."

"I shut the door during the news," Ryan added. "Skimmed through the channels after that, but there wasn't anything good on, so I crashed pretty quick."

"We didn't know anything was wrong until the next day," Laura said. "Doctor Walker didn't meet us in the lobby at the usual time, and nobody answered when I went to his room. We waited around for a while, and then ended up back here. After a few hours, the sheriff's deputy showed up and told us what happened."

CHAPTER 33

A S THEY REACH THE LOBBY, JAKE turned to Pam. "Well, what do you think?"

Pam shrugged. "It seemed like they were telling the truth, for the most part. I'll bet they did a lot more trespassing than they admitted, but most of the time they probably weren't even sure where they were."

"I think so too," Jake said. "They didn't exactly throw all the blame on Walker, but it was pretty obvious that he ran the show. I wish they knew more about this mystery meeting that he was supposed to have the night he was killed."

"I suppose if they were involved, they would have told us that Sam had been the one to contact Walker. Or at least they could claim that Walker told them it was Sam."

"That's true. It would throw suspicion back on Sam and keep them in the clear. Still, I'm not thrilled that those two are leaving town. Might be more that they could tell us."

"I agree. I suppose their mutual alibi clears them as possible suspects, but it seems like the sheriff just wants them out of the way so they can't cause any interference in her crusade to pin this on Sam."

"Maybe Frank Russell can do something," Jake said, taking his phone from his pocket. "He's running the investigation, right?"

"Worth a shot," Pam said. "While you call him, I'm going up to my room to change, and then let's grab some lunch. I'm starving."

Jake called Agent Russell and left a message on his voice mail. He explained the situation and stressed how he felt it would be a mistake to allow Ryan and Laura to leave the area. Without making it too obvious, he hoped, Jake insinuated there was a good chance that they knew much more about the night of the murder than they had admitted.

Pam returned as he was putting away his phone. After a brief exchange, they decided to eat at the supper club across from the hotel. Once inside, the hostess led them through the rather full bar area to the almost deserted dining room. She sat them in a cozy booth at the far side of the room, pointing out that the location should muffle the noise from the next room. The waitress appeared, took their drink orders, and left them to peruse the menus.

Jake and Pam chatted about their options and made small talk until the waitress returned with their drinks. After ordering, they both slumped back against the padded seat.

"Heck of a week, huh?"

"You said it," Jake said, setting down his drink and rubbing his hands together. "I hope Agent Russell can find a way to keep Ryan and Laura from leaving. I still think they know more than they're letting on."

"Me, too, but if you push them too much they might clam up. It'd be better if we had more to go on before we ask them more questions."

Jake nodded. "Maybe we can find out more about the meeting Walker had lined up. That could be key to solving this whole mystery."

"We can assume that Laura and Ryan told all this to Sheriff O'Neil," Pam said, nibbling on a breadstick. "She must think Sam was behind the call. In her eyes, he fits the bill to a tee. Past history with the victim, motive, and opportunity."

"I know. It seems like all the pieces fit together, but doesn't it feel just a little too perfect?"

"Maybe," Pam said, but she didn't sound enthusiastic. "Who else around here knows enough about the archaeology and geography to convince another scientist that the exact kind of site he's looking for is nearby?"

"Sure, Sam would know exactly what to say and how to phrase it. But still . . ." Jake trailed off as the waitress arrived with their soup and salad courses. They both ate in silence for a few moments, until Pam brought up another possibility.

"Could Sam have disguised his voice enough to fool Walker? Maybe he just wanted to draw him out to the site, and then get him arrested."

"I don't know. Maybe. But Sam isn't the devious type. He's more direct, like the proverbial bull in a china shop."

"No kidding," Pam said with a chuckle, and then paused, as if deciding how to proceed. "Well, maybe things got out of hand when Walker arrived. Suppose Walker, upset at getting dragged out there, started something and Sam felt the need to defend himself."

Jake shook his head. "I won't believe it. Not Sam. He has a temper, sure, but he's not violent. He's all bark and no bite."

"Okay, okay. Don't get mad at me. This is how I work. I like to look at problems from as many angles as possible."

"Sorry. Guess this has me more frazzled than I thought." Jake pushed his soup aside and took a few halfhearted bites of his salad. His brows were furrowed in concentration. "You have a point, though. The person who called Walker had to know the local archaeology and geology well enough to convince him it was the real thing."

"So, who here could do something like that? I mean, other than Sam?"

"Well, I could, and Heather. To be honest, anyone on the WSU dig crew could describe a plausible scenario," Jake said.

"What about Ryan and Laura? They're scientists like you." Pam pulled a notebook from her bag and started a list.

Jake nodded. "Yeah, his assistants would definitely know what to say to get him excited. But that's a bit extreme, don't you think? I mean, draw your boss out to the woods, shoot him, and frame someone else?"

"Don't be naïve, partner. I've seen and read about a lot worse. Besides, killing your boss is almost trite in this day and age."

"You have a devious mind, Deputy Hauser," Jake said, slipping his hand over hers. "All hidden in such a gorgeous package."

She returned his smile and snuggled against him in the booth. "It's all true, I'm afraid. You're lucky I'm on the side of law and order. I would have made a spectacular criminal mastermind."

Jake raised one eyebrow in mock concern. "Hmm. Not sure about that. I'm pretty certain super villains don't wear pink Supergirl panties."

Pam let out a cry and elbowed him in the ribs. "Ooh, I knew that was going to come back to haunt me! Look, I didn't plan that . . . I mean when we . . ."

"When you planned your nefarious seduction of a mild-mannered college professor?"

"What, so now I'm a bad girl, rotten to the core? As I recall, mild-mannered professor, you weren't exactly an innocent bystander." Pam smiled, showing her dimples.

"Fine. I'll accept my share of the responsibility, but I think having you around is a corrupting influence," Jake said. "But I think we're getting off the subject."

"Hmm. Nice cover, Professor Caine. Okay, back to the case. Laura and Ryan are possible suspects. Who else?"

Jake rubbed his chin. "I suppose we need to include Al and Susan, too, if you want to make the list complete."

"What do you know about those two?"

"Not much. This is the first time I met either of them. Susan has been Sam's assistant for years, but he never talked much about her. I got the impression that she helped out with basic identifications and data entry in the lab, but not much else. Don't think she wrote any reports or presented papers, or anything like that."

"Not to be mean since I'm a rookie myself, but she's not really a digger, is she?"

"No, she isn't. Maybe Sam browbeat her into coming out. He is a bit overzealous about making sure the excavation is finished on time."

"What about Al?"

Jake shrugged his shoulders. "She has more field experience, so I imagine she would know what to say to interest Walker."

There was a pause in the conversation as their entrees arrived. Both tucked in and ate in silence for a few minutes until their hunger pangs ebbed.

"I can't believe anyone from the University crew is involved in this," Jake said at last. "I've known most of them for at least a couple of years. And other than Heather, they've never met Sam before this. What reason could they have for framing him? Or for killing Walker, either?"

"I think you're right," Pam said, dabbing at the corner of her mouth with a napkin. None of them make sense as a suspect. That leaves Walker's assistants, Sam himself, Susan, and maybe Al as our best suspects."

"I don't think we can rule out the locals," Jake said, pushing his plate to the side. "And it could be a coincidence that Sam is accused of the murder. We don't know for a fact that someone is trying to frame him for the crime."

"I suppose, but O'Neil is sure gung-ho about pinning it on him." Pam took a last bite of her meal, then tossed her napkin over her plate. "The local angle seems unlikely, if you ask me. This feels like something within the archaeology community. Have you heard Al or Susan say anything, even indirectly, that might be construed as negative about Sam?"

Jake rubbed his chin, deep in thought. "Nothing comes to mind, to be honest. Susan and Sam snapped at each other when they first got here, but it wasn't anything out of the ordinary."

Pam scribbled something in her notebook, causing Jake to

frown. "Don't read too much into that, Pam. I think they were just tired from the trip."

"Maybe," she said, closing the book. "But when people are tired or stressed out, they tend to reveal things that might not otherwise."

After paying the bill, Jake and Pam stood just inside the door-way, bundling up against the falling rain. Pam was asking about their plans for the rest of the day when Jake's phone rang. After a brief but choppy conversation, Jake turned back to Pam, smiling.

"That was Keith Emerson. He's going to get us in to see Sam, tonight!"

CHAPTER 34

JAKE AND PAM SPENT THE REST of the afternoon in Pam's hotel room, arguing over semantics and hidden meanings in Keith's message. Most of the disagreements arose from unanswered questions and the incomplete information provided. Jake felt like a suspect himself, repeating the limited information from Keith: He could get them in, quietly, to see Sam for a brief visit; show up just before 8 pm at the side entrance. Don't draw any attention or raise a fuss, and don't tell anyone else. Keith was working on getting Sam released, but things were more complicated than he had anticipated. Frank was on board and would be acting soon.

Their conversation grew heated at times, but Jake and Pam realized they were both venting their frustration over the entire situation. After a while, they realized they were going in circles and that some time apart would be a good idea. Pam drove Jake back to his hotel, and then returned to her room for a long nap.

Jake paced in his room. He tried to busy himself with paperwork but his mind kept wandering, so he soon abandoned the attempt. He ran into Heather and Michelle in the lobby while getting some ice, but decided not to say anything to them about visiting Sam in case something went awry. He declined their offer to join them for dinner, telling them he and Pam had planned to see a movie. Michelle's face lit up with that news, while Heather didn't even bother to hide her disgust.

"DID YOU EAT ANYTHING?" PAM SAID as she pulled her car into the municipal parking lot, a few minutes before eight. "My stomach was doing flip-flops when I got up. I ate some crackers and club soda just to settle it down, but it hasn't helped."

"No. Well, a few pretzels about an hour ago. Too keyed up," Jake said, squinting into the darkness. "There's the door, over there."

Leaving the car, they crept toward the side door. It swung open, showering them with light.

"Over here," Keith called out needlessly. He ushered them inside, secured the door, and shook their hands.

"So, are we going to be able get Sam out of here?"

Keith shook his head. "Not yet, I'm afraid. I'm working on it, but . . ."

"Did you explain the ramifications of an improper arrest to the sheriff?" Pam voiced echoed in the corridor, and Keith raised his hands to caution her.

"I have, and I explained the situation to the mayor. Told him how an improper arrest could open up the town to a lawsuit. I think he is concerned, but he's afraid to do anything. O'Neil has gotten to him, made him think that if Sam is let loose there's going to be a killing spree in Scenic, with the news spread across the country."

"That's ridiculous," Jake and Pam said in unison.

"I agree. The problem is, for all his boasting and bluster, Lucky Mike is a ditherer. He won't make a move unless he's sure that everyone else agrees. Or those making the most noise are solidly in his corner."

"So, Sam is stuck here? There's nothing we can do?"

"Frank is pretty mad. He's tied up with a case in Eau Claire right now, but he did call O'Neil to complain and he said he'd be here in person to deal with the situation by the end of next week."

"Another week?" Jake let out a long sigh. This was not the news he had hoped for.

"It's the best we can do, I'm afraid. I'll keep working on it from my end, but I don't have the leverage that Frank can muster," Keith said, and then he brightened. "But I can get you in to see Sam, at least for a few minutes. Follow me."

The trio walked down the deserted hallways, making a couple of odd detours. Jake assumed they were using a route not accessible to the general public.

"Have you talked to Sam already?"

"I did see him this morning, and explained what's going on. He's doing okay, under the circumstances," Keith said, as he stopped to insert his keycard at a security door. He chuckled to himself. "He seemed more concerned about the dig and how much ground you've opened up, rather than the fact that he's behind bars and facing a murder charge."

"That does sound like the old Sam, I have to admit," Jake said.

"I'm not sure he was that . . . comfortable with me," Keith said. "I suppose he sees me as one of the 'establishment.' Guess I can't blame him for that. Wait here one second."

Keith stepped around a corner and walked up to the same desk where Jake and Pam had been halted a few days before. After speaking with the guard for a few moments, Keith returned, smiling.

"All set."

Jake and Pam exchanged glances but followed without comment. They weren't about to question a good thing.

Keith stepped behind the deserted desk and buzzed them in. "I'll wait here," Keith said. "Uh, try not to take too long."

Jake and Pam walk down hallway, eerie shadows dancing in time with the flickering overhead lights. All of the cells were unoccupied, except for the end.

"Sam?" Jake said, voice cracking. "How are you doing?"

"Jake! How are things going at Ghost Bog? Did Al and Susan finish their unit? Because they need to expand to the east, after that. That's where that rib cage was oriented, and we need . . ."

"Sam, Sam! The site is fine. Everything is way ahead of schedule. It's all good."

Sam halted, staring at Jake as if oblivious to the bars separating them. His hands gripped the bars so tightly that his knuckles were white. Seconds passed, and Sam relaxed and nodded his head.

"Okay, good. Just been worried, that's all. Not much else to do in here," Sam said. He looked over and noticed that Jake was not alone. "It's, uh, good to see you, Pam."

"Hi, Sam. How are you?"

"We're trying to get you released," Jake blurted out.

"I'll bet that's going nowhere fast," Sam grumbled. "Damn sheriff comes by a few times a day, tries playing that good cop-bad cop crap on me."

"Have you told her anything?" Pam asked.

"Nothing. Well, the first couple of times I asked for a lawyer, but she just ignored me. Now I tell her to go to hell, if I answer her at all."

Jake winced, just imaging the scene. A shadow fell over him as Keith walked up.

"We need to get moving," he cautioned. "Technically we're not doing anything illegal, but if we want to defuse the situation, we shouldn't give the sheriff anything to use against us."

Jake asked for a few more minutes, in private, while Sam stared daggers at Keith. The attorney shrugged and stepped back toward the entryway.

"Don't trust that man," Sam said. "Something about him just rubs me the wrong way."

"Look, we don't have much time," Jake said. "Sam, in as much detail as you can, tell us what happened the night Walker was killed. Where were you?"

Pam pulled out her trusty notebook as Sam ran his hand through his hair, gathering his thoughts.

"Well, when I got back to the hotel, I found a note from the desk pinned to our door. Said a collector named Earl had bones from Ghost Bog and from another site that he wanted to return. There was a phone number, but I went to the office to see if I could get some more info before I called him. Gal at the desk said the caller was worried about bones eroding out of a hillside, bones like the ones from Ghost Bog. Wanted me to call him back."

"That's it?"

Sam nodded. "Couple of folks walked in, so she had to check them in. I moved away from the desk and called this Earl. He described the find spot, a big bog deposit near an eroding slope, less than a mile from Ghost Bog. Wouldn't give me the exact location over the phone, said it was too hard to find. Wanted me to come over to his place to see the bones, and some chert tools he found with the bones."

"Anything unusual about his voice?" Pam asked. "Any background noises that stood out?"

"No, sorry. Hard to hear him, to be honest. Figured he was an older guy. I think he was outside, 'cause it sounded windy."

"Would you recognize his voice if you heard it again?"

Sam shrugged. "Maybe. I'm sure it wasn't Walker, if that's what you're driving at."

Keith, standing in the doorway, cleared his throat. Jake waved his hand in reply, before urging Sam to continue.

"I wrote down the guy's directions on the back of the note. Didn't make much sense, even then. Lots of 'turn here' and 'turn there' and 'first road past the brown barn' kind of stuff that don't mean nothing unless you've lived there your whole life. Anyway, drove all over the county looking for the address and never did find him. Got back to the hotel late so I just turned in."

"Do you still have the note?" Jake inquired.

Sam looked at the floor. "Nope. Tossed it away on the drive back. I was pretty pissed, by then."

"Did you tell the sheriff or anybody else about this?" Pam asked.

"No. Well, not the specifics. Said I was out meeting with a

collector when they first started interrogating me, but it was obvious that they thought I was making it all up. So, I stopped talking after that."

"What about your cell phone?" Pam asked.

"Sheriff took that, too, but not before I locked the screen. I don't think they can get into it."

"Which means Earl's number should still be in the history," Pam said. "That could be a big break for us, if we can get hold of it."

"Okay folks, we've got to go," Keith announced. "We're pushing our luck as it is."

"One more thing," Sam said, turning his attention back to Jake and Pam. "On my way back to town I drove by the site, so I stopped in for just a second. You know, to make sure everything was secure. The Emersons must have seen me, because they told the sheriff I was out there. O'Neil made a big deal out of it when they arrested me."

CHAPTER 35

Having gathered all the information they could with the time available, Jake and Pam said goodbye and promised to do all they could to get Sam released as soon as possible. Keith was guardedly optimistic, confident that Frank would be able to expedite things once he was able to return to Scenic. After seeing them out, Keith walked to his own vehicle, parked not far away. The desperate, scared look in Sam's eyes haunted Jake as they returned to Pam's car.

"So, is it a big deal that Sam was spotted at Ghost Bog the night of the murder?"

Pam stared back at Jake, a troubled look in her big blue eyes. "It could be. It puts Sam at the scene, and with his history with Walker it could be enough to convince a jury. Or at least a judge, in order to keep him locked up."

"But we know Walker wasn't killed at the site."

"Right, but O'Neil could argue that when the Emersons saw Sam he was moving the body to the spot where it was found, maybe with a plan to dispose of it properly later on."

"I wonder why they didn't mention that they saw Sam when we talked to them?"

"I don't know. Maybe they misunderstood what we were asking,"

Pam offered. "Seeing Sam at Ghost Bog wouldn't be unusual, so they didn't think we would care. Or, it's possible O'Neil ordered them not to saying anything."

"I suppose we should get something to eat," Pam said, as she started the engine. "I'm feeling pretty low. We could talk things over for a while, decide what to tackle next, tomorrow."

"To be honest, I'm too keyed up to discuss this right now," Jake said, slumping back in his seat. "And I'm exhausted. All I want is a stiff drink. Maybe we should sleep on it for tonight."

Pam grinned back at him, eyebrows raised. It took a second for Jake to realize how his comment might be interpreted.

"Um, I wasn't implying anything by that . . . I mean about us . . . you know."

Pam let out a little laugh, and then shifted the car into drive. "Let's start with some dinner and that drink."

After a late dinner and several drinks, Jake and Pam purchased a bottle of wine and returned to Pam's hotel. They had agreed from the onset not to discuss anything to do with the crime or the dig until the next day. Instead, they rented a comedy movie and ended up falling asleep next to each other, exhausted by the day's events.

In the morning, after a good laugh at the results of their less-than-romantic but relaxed evening, Jake and Pam walked to a nearby diner for breakfast. Feeling refreshed, they decided to plan out the rest of their day and how best to use the information obtained from Sam the night before.

"You're right," Jake said, sipping his orange juice. "The evidence that they do have is all circumstantial. While it doesn't paint Sam in a good light, it isn't conclusive."

"Agent Russell should be able to get it cleared up, once he gets here," Pam said, nibbling on a slice of melon. "If he ever gets here. But I still think we should keep at it from our end. If we can narrow down some suspects, that should make it easier to get Sam out of jail."

"So now we have everyone's story as to where they were on the night of the murder. Except for any locals who might be involved."

Pam rolled her eyes. "I don't think that's going to lead anywhere, Jake. No way to narrow down a vague group of potential suspects like that. We should focus on the people directly involved with the dig, if you ask me."

Jake looked around the crowded diner, filled with Scenic residents and a few late-season tourists. It would be akin to finding a needle in a haystack. Then a thought occurred.

"What if we were able to track down Matt Walker's movements on the day he was killed? That might help us narrow down who he might have spoken with. It would be easy enough from there to come up with a list of local suspects."

Pam frowned at him, pushed her plate aside, and reached across the table to take his hand. "Jake, don't take this wrong, but you seem fixated that Walker's death was part of some local conspiracy."

"I'm not fixated," Jake countered. "There's just something in the back of my head, a feeling that we're missing something important."

"You know, stranger killings are less common than you'd think. Most often the victim knows their assailant."

Jake shrugged and nodded, without enthusiasm.

"Could it be that you just don't want to consider that this might have been an 'inside' job?"

Jake withdrew his hand from hers and thought it over. "I suppose I am reluctant to think that it could be another archaeologist," he said. "Scientists can be . . . quirky, I'll admit. And there are more inflated egos and nasty characters in this field than you might find in other professions, but murder? That's stretching it a bit."

Pam smiled, a thin grim smile that made Jake feel like he had stepped right into her trap. "Exhibit one for the defense: Jacklyn Wardell and Maggie Devlin."

Jake slumped back against the booth as the jaws of the trap snapped shut. Years earlier, Maggie Devlin killed fellow archaeologist Jacklyn Wardell, and then killed again in an attempt to cover up her crime when Jake started looking into the Wardell cold case.

"Touché, Deputy Hauser."

"Sorry. Sometimes it's tough to see the whole picture when you're too close, you know?"

"You're right. No apologies necessary."

Pam smiled. "I will admit that confirming his movements that day would be a good idea. It can't hurt, and to be honest I don't know what else we can do right now."

Jake nodded, happy at least to have one avenue to pursue. "Back to Ryan and Laura?"

"You got it."

As Jake paid the bill, Pam exited the diner and called the hotel. The old man at the counter, nattily dressed in crisp white shirt and bow tie, handed him his change with a big smile. Jake's attention was drawn to the large silver watch on the man's wrist, emblazoned with a red, stylized S on the face.

It was similar to the watches found at Ghost Bog, but not identical. Glancing at the wall behind the counter, covered with ads for local shops, Jake was struck by the variety of "S" logos that seemed to be associated with every business in Scenic.

With Jake rooted in place, the counterman engaged him in some small talk. "You folks visitin' in the area, or just passing through?"

"A little of both, I guess. We're with the archaeology crew, working on a dig nearby."

"Oh, yeah. Seems I read something about that in the paper. Finding lots of dinosaur bones and stuff?"

Jake nodded but didn't bother to correct him. "We've had quite a few interesting finds. We'll be finishing up soon, and then it's back to the University for us. But we have enjoyed our stay in Scenic."

The counterman beamed at his last remark. "Wonderful little town, that's what it is. I'm fourth generation myself. My kids are all here yet, and the grandkids, of course."

He pointed to a series of framed family photos behind the

register, rambling off names and ages. Jake zoned out on the details, staring instead as the man's watch danced through the air. In the uproar following Walker's murder, Jake had almost forgotten about the human remains from the dig, and more importantly, the recent skeleton with two watches.

"That's a nice watch," Jake said, during a lull in the counterman's monologue. "Is it made locally?"

"Sure is. Well, they used to be, I guess," he replied, chuckling. "Thompson's Jewelers, back when Howard senior was running the place, started making special watches as graduation gifts. Caught on fast with the fellows, and pretty soon it was tradition for all the graduating seniors."

"Sort of like a class ring."

"Exactly. Most of the guys in this part of the state don't have much use for rings, and the watches are a lot more practical. Each one had the owner's initials on the back and the year they graduated."

Jake wondered how closely they kept their records, as a means of identifying the body in the bog. "Do they still make those watches?"

"Hmm? No, Thompson's shut down about ten years ago. After Howard junior died, one of the nephews took over but then the economy tanked. He sold out his stock and moved down to Arizona."

Jake left the diner, mind racing with this new information. Pam was finishing up her call, frowning, when he reached her in the parking lot.

"Uh, oh. I recognize that look," Jake said. "Bad news?"

"Could be better. Ryan and Laura didn't answer, so we're stalled on talking to them again."

"They didn't check out, did they?"

"No. I'm on good terms with the desk clerk, and she told me that they extended their stay for 'at least another week.' According to her, someone from Snelling College called them, and a few minutes later Laura called down to hold their rooms."

"Good. Sounds like my message to Agent Russell got through. He probably called the college and explained the situation."

"Sounds about right," Pam said, looking despondent. "But with them gone, we won't be able to ask them about Walker's movements. I suppose we could wait in the lobby for them, but—say, what are you grinning about?"

Jake told her what he had learned about the watches. She listened closely but didn't appear too excited by the news.

"I wanted to ask him about the store records but thought that might come across as pretty odd. Plus, what are the chances he would know about those, right? Still, it's something that we should look in to."

Pam nodded but had a puzzled look on her face. "I guess so, but what does this have to do with Walker's movements? Or with Sam, for that matter?"

"Assuming, just for the sake of argument, that Walker's murder has a local motive. What's the only thing at Ghost Bog that has a recent, local connection? Our John Doe with the watches!"

Pam's eyes widened, and she smiled. "I have to admit, it does make some sense. I'm not saying there's a connection, mind you, but it is an avenue we haven't explored. What do you have in mind?"

"Tracking down the store records would be a long shot, at least with the time we have, but what about checking out some of the antique or resale shops in town? I'll send some photos of the watches to your phone, and you can tell them you're looking for a replacement or want to buy something similar."

"Okay. Something to do while we wait for Ryan and Laura to reappear. What are you going to be doing while I'm chasing all over town?"

"I'm going to pull and clean the watches, as best I can. I bought some cleaning supplies a while back but kind of forgot about it," Jake admitted. "Maybe I can decipher the owner's initials and the graduation year. I also want to take a closer look at John Doe's skeletal remains. I can take some measurements and get a better idea of his height and age."

Pam nodded. "It might not help Sam, but at least it'll put us one step closer to solving the *other* Ghost Bog mystery."

CHAPTER 36

Back in his room, Jake sat hunched over his desk, staring at the back of one of the watches. He paused to adjust the magnifying loupe in his right eye, and then continued to scrape at the back with a fine dental pick. Frowning, he set the pick aside and reached for a cotton swab sitting in a glass containing a clear, oily liquid. He dabbed the watch with it, then replaced the swab, almost upsetting the desk lamp in the process.

Fortunately, the first desk lamp bounced up against the second lamp, as both were set precariously close on the small desk. The rest of the surface was covered with brushes, dental tools, and a menagerie of household cleaners. The second watch sat on top of a small box on one side, a small area glistening in a sea of black tarnish. The throaty rumble of a car engine drifted through the open window, and then fell silent.

"Knock, knock. Okay to come in?"

"Sure, Pam. C'mon on in. You'll have to excuse the smell."

"Wow, you're not kidding! I think you have too much chlorine in your pool."

"No pool, just cleaning chemicals," Jake said. He set aside his tools and removed the loupe from his eye. "Trying different combinations in various strengths, just to see what works best. Don't want to use anything too harsh, so I don't make it worse."

"That explains the open door and window," Pam said, eyes settling on the second bed, covered with bags containing human bones. "I realize the smell is pretty strong, but it's probably not a good idea to have all these bones sitting out. Somebody walking by might get the wrong idea."

"Oh, yeah, I suppose so." Jake walked to the window and drew the shade, leaving a small gap at the sill. He leaned in and gave Pam a kiss. "How did you make out?"

"Pretty good. Hit gold on my first stop."

"Which was?"

"The Scenic Antique Mall. There was a big display counter right by the door, and they had about two dozen Scenic watches. The owner, Peggy McKenna, told me all about them."

"You didn't tell her why we're interested in them, did you?"

Pam cocked her head, frowning. "No, Professor Caine. I *am* a deputy sheriff and have done things like this before, you know."

"Sorry. Just nervous, I guess. So . . .?"

"I told her I saw the watches around town and wanted to get one for my boyfriend, 'Stan.' Unlike you, Stan is a wonderful guy who lavishes me with gifts."

She was grinning, so Jake realized he wasn't in too much trouble. "He does sound like a great fellow. I wish you two all the happiness in the world."

Pam gave Jake a playful shove, then continued with her story. "Peggy explained how the style of the 'S' changed over time and showed me some examples. I let her look at the picture and said that 'Stan' liked this one the most. She said it was kind of hard to tell, but she thought it looked like the type popular in the late 1980s and early 1990s."

Jake did some quick mental calculations. "So about forty years old, give or take. Subtract eighteen years for the typical age of a graduating senior, and we're looking for someone born in the early to mid 1970s."

"Sounds about right. Of course, we don't know when they ended up in the bog, though."

"Actually, it probably happened right around graduation or soon thereafter, based on the bones."

"Really?"

"Sure. I did a lot more than inhale toxic chemicals while you were gone, you know. John Doe's third molars—the wisdom teeth—have erupted but show only minimal amounts of surface wear. That fits with someone about eighteen years old. Same for the degree of fusion of the long bones; all consistent with someone about seventeen to twenty years of age."

"Impressive. I didn't realize you could be that specific from just the bones."

"Well, most of the traits give you an approximate age range, so it's best to look at more than one characteristic," Jake said. "One of the best measures is the fusion of the two halves of the pelvis, at the pubic symphysis. The John Doe skeleton is a perfect match for a male eighteen or nineteen years old."

"So, you're sure he's a he, right?"

"Almost without a doubt. For sex, there are a number of quantitative and qualitative traits, for both the cranium and post-cranial elements."

"Um, I think I got that, but how about a repeat in English?"

"Sorry, occupational hazard. Basically, you can look at different features of the skull, the pelvis, and the long bones to see if they show typical male patterns or female patterns." Jake picked up several different elements and pointed out the various traits that were indicative of an adult male. He explained that there was some degree of overlap for some characteristics, so it was again a good idea to look at all of the bony structures rather than just one or two.

"With the right tools, you can also take measurements that you can use to calculate height. Our friend here was about 5-foot-11, and pretty muscular, based on the muscle attachment points I examined."

"Probably an athlete, then."

"Likely, although he could have done a lot of manual labor, like a farm kid."

"Interesting. It should help us narrow down his identity," Pam said.

"This is probably the most important thing," Jake said, removing the cranium from a nearby padded box. He rotated it so that the back of the skull was facing up. "See these cracks, the little breaks radiating out from this depressed area? It's an impact fracture. It looks like someone struck John a pretty good blow from behind, with something heavy."

"Is that the cause of death?"

"Maybe. Not sure if it would have been enough to kill him, but I'll bet it would have knocked him unconscious. And then if he were face down in the wet bog . . ."

Pam nodded, following the implication. "Are you sure it was from a blow? Couldn't he have gotten those injuries if he fell and hit his head?"

"I don't think so. Keep in mind I'm not a forensics expert. But from what I've read, he would have had to fall from a good height *and* land on something pretty solid in order to cause fractures like this."

Pam watched as he placed the skull back into the box. "Oh, I called the hotel again, but Ryan and Laura still weren't back."

"Maybe they drove back home or to the college, to get more stuff for their 'extended' visit."

"I asked my friend at the desk to call me when they come back. Until we hear from her, we'll just have to wait. Speaking of killing time," Pam paused to rummage through her backpack. "Brought you a present." She handed him a book.

"*A Reef of Heads* by Kevin Corbett Nelson. That's a weird title."

"It's a mystery novel, according to the blurb on the back. I wanted to buy something to thank Peggy for all her help. Besides, I thought it might sharpen your detective skills."

"Ha, ha. I'll stick with Agatha Christie, thank you. Or Raymond Chandler."

"Both excellent choices, hon," Pam said, squinting her eyes at him. "You could really rock a fedora, now that I think about it."

Jake gave her a quick kiss on the cheek. "Thanks for the book. Should be a nice break from the archaeology journals I usually read."

"You're welcome. Let me borrow it when you're done. I was paging through it and it looks like a pretty good read."

"Maybe I'll start on it today, after I finish with these watches."

"How's that going?"

"Kind of slow, but I'm making progress." Jake sat down at the desk and waved her over. "On this one, from John Doe's wrist, you can make out 'Cl—s of 199-.'"

"That's not all that helpful, you know," she said playfully.

Jake frowned. "This last number was either a 2 or a 7. Based on what you found out, I'm going with a 2. And some of the initials are almost visible. The first one is a C, I think, or maybe a G. The last one could be a B or an R. Maybe an H."

"Could be a K, or even an A. If I squint, it could be a P." Pam moved behind him, leaned over, and rested her arms across Jake's shoulders. "If you ask me, I think you could see just about half the alphabet on the back of that watch."

"Thanks a lot. Are you trying to be difficult?"

"Ooh, somebody is getting grouchy," Pam said in a sing-song voice. She began to rub his shoulders. "I think you've been working too hard. Maybe a little break would clear your head."

Jake started to protest, but he was starting to appreciate Pam's efforts as a multitude of knots began to dissolve. He tilted his head to one side and caught an enticing whiff of her perfume.

"I think you may be on to something, after all," Jake said, grinning. "Maybe we should . . ."

A sharp rap at the door caught his attention, and Pam released him from her grip. He shrugged and went over to the door.

"Hey, Al. Come in. What's up?"

"Hi, Jake. Oh, hi Pam," Al said, as she looked around the room. "Hope I'm not interrupting anything."

"No, we're just doing a little research on the bog skeletons. What can we do for you?"

"I, I have something I need to tell you. It could be important. About Susan."

CHAPTER 37

A L'S VOICE CRACKED AS SHE SPOKE, and Jake realized she was genuinely upset. He cleared off a chair for her and offered her a beverage, which she refused. Pam sat across from Al on the bed, and she and Jake waited for her to begin.

Al took a deep breath and let it out slowly. "It's about Monday night, when Doctor Walker was killed. You asked about all of our whereabouts that evening, and I realized that what I told you wasn't accurate."

She paused, looking between Jake and Pam.

"Susan wasn't in the room the whole night. I mean, she wasn't gone for long, but she did leave for a little while. At least, I think it was only a little while."

Jake had a confused look on his face. Al noticed and let out a little laugh. "Sorry, I must sound like an idiot."

"It's okay," Pam said in a soothing voice. "Just take your time."

Al returned her smile and continued. "It was getting late, maybe close to ten, and I was starting to doze while laying on my bed. You know, kind of drifting in and out as I skimmed through my phone. Susan said she was going to the desk to post some letters to her family. She left and I fell asleep. I woke up with a start when Susan came back in. I glanced at the clock and it was after 10:30."

"So, she was gone for about a half-hour, maybe longer?" Jake asked.

"Yeah, at least that long. But it just didn't register at the time," Al said. "And she was acting nervous. She apologized for waking me and said it took a while to get her tea in the lobby. I only half heard her because I was so out of it. I went into the bathroom and got ready for bed, then crashed."

"Could she have come back earlier, then left again?" Pam asked.

"No, I sleep pretty light. I'm sure I would have heard her. Anyway, her response kind of nagged at me the next day, but it didn't click until I went to the lobby myself today to get some tea."

"Why didn't you tell us this the other day, when we asked if either of you had gone out that night?"

Al looked Jake straight in the eye. "It didn't occur to me, to be honest. It's not like she drove off somewhere. I just blanked, I guess. I am sorry, that's why I came here now."

Pam stood up from the bed and took a few steps away from Al. "Could Susan have driven anywhere during that time? I mean, you were asleep."

"I don't know, but I don't think so. I'm not sure our van was even in the parking lot then." Al looked flustered, trying to fill in the gaps as best she could. "But Susan didn't have her purse with her, only her room key and a handful of envelopes."

"It could be nothing," Jake said, trying to diffuse the situation. "Maybe Susan mailed her letters and decided to make some tea, and it took longer than she planned. Then she woke you up by accident when she got back and felt bad about it."

"It's unlikely that she would have been able to drive anywhere in such a short time anyway," Pam said, although she gave Jake a knowing look. "But Agent Russell will want us to be as accurate as we can. Is Susan in your room now?"

"No, she took the van about an hour ago. Said something about meeting her family in the Twin Cities for dinner. I think they were driving up to see her. I told her I didn't mind, that I wasn't planning to go anywhere."

"Nothing that can't wait, I think," Jake said, following Pam's lead.

"I am sorry," Al said, wiping at the corner of her eye. "I've been going back and forth about this, if it was even worth bringing up. I like Susan. I don't want to get her in any trouble, but I don't want to make things any harder for Sam, either."

"I'm sure it won't amount to anything serious," Pam said, patting Al on the shoulder. "Say, since you're on your own tonight, why don't we head out to the Scenic Bar for dinner and drinks? See if anyone else wants to join us, and we'll meet out front around six."

Al was thrilled with the suggestion and agreed to contact the rest of the crew. As she left, she apologized again for not remembering Susan's mysterious absence. Pam put a finger to her lips and cocked her head, listening, until she heard Al's retreating footsteps.

"So, what do you think?"

"I don't know, Pam. It's probably nothing. Like you said, there's no way Susan could have driven out to the site and back during that short amount of time."

"I didn't say that. She couldn't have gone far or done much during that time, but it's still possible she was up to something that she doesn't want us to know about. Remember, Susan didn't mention this to us, either."

"If it was so minor, maybe she just overlooked it. We were all pretty stressed out at the time."

"We're talking about alibis for a murder investigation, Jake. Minor details are important. And Susan wasn't very forthcoming when I talked to her, if you recall."

Jake nodded. "True, but do you really think she was up to something related to Walker's murder?"

"Maybe. Maybe not. She could be involved in something else that she doesn't want the rest of us to know about." Pam paused as she sat back down on the bed. "And not to go too far out, but let's say she is involved in the murder. Maybe she has an accomplice, or more than one, who was more directly involved. Her side trip to the lobby could have been to contact them without Al finding out."

"Okay, now I think you're reaching."

"Maybe. But it's not impossible, you know."

"For the sake of argument, I suppose. But then she frames Sam on top of it?"

"That might not have been part of her plan. You know, just an accident thanks to Scenic's less than stellar police force."

Jake chuckled. "Well, I suppose we should start out small and at least ask her about that missing half hour. Just to be thorough."

Pam stood up with a smile, pleased to have made her case. "Good. We can take care of it tomorrow, right after work. So, any thoughts on how we should spend the rest of our afternoon?"

Jake glanced at his watch. "Since we have a few hours before we go out, I guess I'll keep cleaning these watches. I think with a little more work I can get those letters to show up better."

The smile on Pam's face faded, but Jake didn't notice as he resumed his place at the desk.

"I still think there's a connection between Walker's death and the John Doe skeleton we found with the watches. Just need to figure out what it is."

Pam sighed, then picked up her bag and keys. "Sure, go ahead. I'm going to head back to my hotel and take it easy for a while. I'll see you later."

Jake's attention was already focused on one of the watches, as he scraped at the back plate with a dental pick.

Pam looked back at him from the doorway and shook her head sadly. She took a step back, leaned over, and gave him a quick kiss on the cheek. "Jake, honey, I have to say this, just once. Despite what happened at Waconah, not every cold case ties into a modern crime. Don't get so wrapped up with John Doe that you miss something important that might help Sam in the Walker case."

CHAPTER 38

"**I**S THAT *REALLY* ALL YOU CAN tell us?"

Jake would have preferred to ignore the harsh tone of Heather's question, but a quick look at his assembled crew revealed that everyone else also wanted more information than he was prepared to share.

This hadn't gone as planned, he thought to himself as he let out a long, heavy sigh. Jake kicked at the ground with his boot and then repeated what he had already told them—twice—that morning after they had arrived at the dig site.

Dinner with the crew on Sunday evening had gone well. Everyone came, save Susan, and they were able to put their recent troubles behind them for the most part. Conversation was light and upbeat, with only a few references make to Sam's continued absence. Underneath it all, Jake could sense the crew's growing unease with the situation, and by the end of the night he had decided it was important to give them at least a little info on Sam's predicament, even if it put Keith Emerson in a difficult situation. Pam convinced him to wait until the next day, at Ghost Bog, arguing that any mention in a public setting was asking for trouble. Privately, she hoped Jake would abandon the idea by morning, but no such luck.

After reaching the site and unloading their equipment, Jake called a brief meeting and thanked them all for their great work. He pointed out that they only had a week or two left and might finish before then, depending on how many bones and artifacts were present in the unopened excavation units.

Jake then announced that he had spoken with Keith Emerson, briefly, late last night and that things were looking up. Keith had talked with Sam, who was in good spirits under the circumstances. Keith was also in contact with Agent Russell, who would be back in town soon, and between them they were confident that Sam would be let out soon. Pam stood off to one side, watching their reactions, and hoping that Jake wouldn't take things too far.

The onslaught of follow-up questions caught Jake off guard. He had hoped a revised version of the truth would be sufficient to keep their spirits up and temper any growing thoughts about taking more direct action. If anything, his speech seemed to have the opposite effect.

After another half-hour of questions and clipped responses, the crew grudgingly returned to work. With the end in sight, they tackled the remaining excavation blocks with renewed vigor, hoping to finish before the cold weather worsened.

"Well, I guess that could have gone better," Jake said to Pam, as they removed the tarp covering their half-finished unit at the eastern edge of the site.

"I could say I warned you, but that's not my style," she said, pausing to move Jake's backpack off to one side. She reached in and pulled out a small box wrapped with bright red ribbon, tied in a bow. "Say, what's this? Finally get around to buying a present for your new girlfriend?"

Jake took the box from her with a wry smile. "Sorry, not this time. These are the two watches from the burial. I was thinking that we could stop by that antique shop after work and see if the woman there might be able to narrow down the time frame if she saw them in person."

"Good idea, but poor timing. The shop is closed on Mondays."

"Oh. Well, maybe we can go there tomorrow."

"We can try, but Peggy did make a point of saying that the pattern only changed every seven or eight years. It might not be possible to narrow it down much."

"Hmm. Guess I need to decipher the dates on the back, then, if we're going to make real progress. Maybe I can find some ideas on the Internet that might help."

"Or you could just leave it up to Agent Russell and the Bureau. I'm sure they have techniques designed for stuff like this."

"I suppose. It's just that I hate to not know . . ."

"Besides, we have other priorities. We need to talk with Susan about her mysterious half-hour absence, remember?"

"Right. Sorry, guess I've been fixated on the watch angle."

"No problem, that's what partners are for." She looked across the site, as if to confirm that Susan was out of earshot. "I was watching her when you made your announcement about Sam."

"She was about the only one who didn't ask a bunch of questions, I noticed."

Pam nodded. "Her whole demeanor was . . . nervous, I guess, but then she always comes across that way. While you were talking, though, she seemed numb, as if she were shielding herself from the whole thing."

"Do you think she was trying *not* to react?"

"Maybe. It could just be that she's so traumatized by the whole situation that her brain doesn't know how to react. Some people get pretty keyed up when they're under stress."

Jake agreed that they should proceed with caution when they spoke to Susan at the end of the day. With that settled, they continued excavating their unit, carefully removing mapped bison bones and associated artifacts. The remainder of the day proceeded without incident. The archaeologists cleared more units than they had anticipated, primarily along the edge of the "kill zone" where fewer bison had been dispatched and butchered.

On the drive back to Scenic, not too far from the hotel, Jake asked Pam her thoughts on how best to approach Susan with their concerns.

"I took Al aside after lunch and said we were going to talk to Susan right away when we got back, so she's going to duck over to the convenience store first thing. If we give it a few minutes, we should be able to catch Susan in her room before she gets settled in. We don't want to start interrogating her in the parking lot."

"Good thinking. I'll drop my backpack in my room, and we can head over right away."

Pam pulled to a stop in the parking spot outside Jake's door. She waved to Al as she walked past. The rest of the crew was near their vehicles or heading toward their own rooms.

Jake walked around the front of the car only to stop short a few feet from the entrance. The door to his room was ajar.

"What the hell?"

"Forget to lock up this morning?" Pam asked as she joined him.

"No, never. I'm always careful about that. I lock it and check the knob twice; it's a ritual."

"Maybe the maid left it open?"

"I hope that's all it is," Jake said, reaching forward to push the door open. The fading evening light filled the room, revealing a debris field of scattered papers, clothes, and boxes strewn across the beds and floor.

Michelle and Heather were a few yards away, but well within earshot of Jake's cuss-filled tirade. They dashed over, eyes wide with concern, to see what had happened.

"Somebody got into my room and ransacked the place!"

"Is anything missing?" Heather asked, craning her neck to look over Jake's shoulders.

"Not sure." He reached in and switched on the light. It was worse than his first glimpse had indicated. The desk and dresser drawers were opened and overturned, and most of the boxes were open and the contents dumped out. Jake spotted his coffee mug perched neatly in the center of the desk, just as he had left it that morning. The oddness of the undisturbed mug distressed him more than anything at that exact moment.

"I'm going to check with the front desk," Pam announced, heading toward the lobby.

Jake took a deep breath and stepped into the room. After a quick scan, he started searching in earnest. Michelle and Heather stood nervously inside the doorway. Jake wandered around the room and then went into the bathroom. When he emerged, he was shaking his head.

"Nothing seems to be missing. My laptop is still locked in its case, and the bathroom wasn't touched at all. Most of the project files are together, too," he said, pointing to an undisturbed pile of binders next to the desk.

"Weird," Heather said, as she and Michelle moved into the room. "What about the artifacts?"

"It looks like that's what they were most interested in, but nothing appears to be missing." Jake gestured to Sam's bed, now strewn with a large number of plastic bags, each with its own artifact.

"You're right. All of the big spearpoints are right here. These are the two Al and I found, and Heather, these are the four you pulled from that big unit in the center."

"Uh-huh," Heather said, as she picked up a few stray bags that had fallen onto the floor. "Same with these stone knives that Sam found. He was excited about this one, because it's made of Knife River flint."

"I remember that," Michelle said. "Just like the big Kirk spearpoint I found."

"The bone tools are here, too," Jake said, sifting through a small pile of bags littered over a chair. "And all the special bones we pulled, like these teeth Sam wanted set aside for isotope analysis."

Heather was about to comment when Pam appeared in the doorway. Jake explained the situation, twice pointing out that nothing was taken.

"But they spent enough time looking, it seems," Pam said. "And they focused on the artifacts and stuff in the boxes, right?"

Michelle stopped, dropping the bags in her hands back onto the bed. "Should we not be touching this stuff? I mean, won't the police want to check them for fingerprints?"

Jake and Pam looked at each other, and he shrugged. "It might not be a good idea to get the Scenic Police involved, given everything that's going on. And it doesn't look like anything was actually stolen."

Pam nodded. "I spoke with the desk clerk, and he called the maid. She told him that her cart moved while she was cleaning this row of rooms. She didn't make anything out of it, just thought she was having a senior moment."

"Could she have been in on it?" Heather asked.

"I don't think so. Both she and the clerk apologized and seemed pretty upset. After some prodding, I did get her to admit that she left her passkeys on the cart. They're attached to a big wood paddle, so it's hard to carry them in her pocket. Someone could have moved the cart, swiped the keys, and used them to unlock your door."

"Did anyone else have any problems?" Jake asked, addressing Michelle and Heather. They both responded that their room was secure and undisturbed when they got back but went to check with Rob and Curt. Pam replied that she would speak to Susan soon.

Pam turned to Jake after the two girls had left. "Easier for us to talk to Susan, since it gives us an excuse to ask her about the other night."

"Good thinking," Jake agreed, frowning as he scanned the room, as if hoping that a significant clue might appear.

"I did tell them that nothing seemed to be missing, but that we'd appreciate it if they kept their eyes open for any strangers lurking around in the future."

"I suppose you're right," Jake said. "No real harm done, after all. I do wonder what they were after, though."

"Artifacts to sell?"

"I suppose. Seems like a lot of effort for a few spearpoints, most of which are broken. And they didn't take anything."

"Maybe they were scared off."

"I guess. They were here long enough to make a huge mess, at least."

"I'll help you clean up, but we should go and talk to Susan first."

Jake agreed, and after making sure the door was secure, they walked toward Susan's room. Heather and Michelle caught up to them and passed along the news that Rob and Curt's room was not disturbed, before returning to their own room.

Jake rapped on the door and Susan appeared, still dressed in her field clothes, munching on a granola bar. With a quizzical look, she invited them both inside.

Pam spoke first. "Someone broke into Jake's room while we were out at the site today, Susan."

"Oh, my goodness! That's terrible! Was anything taken?"

"No," Jake said, with a grim smile. "They made a heck of a mess, though, but everything seems to be there. We're thinking that they got scared off."

"Did you call the police?"

"No," Pam said. "It wouldn't do any good, considering how they feel about us. And nothing was missing, so . . ."

"We wanted to make sure everything was okay in here," Jake said, making a show of glancing around the room. "Obviously they didn't bother in here. Same with the guys, and Heather and Michelle."

Susan shivered. "I'm going to be extra careful with the lock from now on. If anything had happened in here, I don't think I could handle it."

Jake nodded, then leaned against the dresser. "We did have a couple of quick questions for you, though, if you have a second."

Susan stiffened, then sat down on the bed. "Well, I suppose. I need to wash up . . ."

"This won't take long," Pam said with a smile, taking a chair by the desk. "We just need to clarify a few things for Agent Russell. You know, doing what we can to help out Sam."

She agreed, but Jake noticed a cloud of doubt on the older woman's face as Pam continued.

"On the night Walker was murdered, you told me you never left the hotel room."

"That's right. I was in all evening. Didn't go anywhere."

"Hmm. The desk clerk remembered seeing you in the lobby for a while that night, though, around ten."

Susan sat for a moment, eyes wide. "Oh, that!" she said, regaining her composure. "I must have forgotten. Yes, I went to the lobby to put some letters in the box, and then I made some tea. Took forever for the water to heat up, so I just waited around. Sorry I didn't mention it. I guess it slipped my mind."

Pam glanced at Jake, but he was deep in thought. She pulled out her notepad and entered a few lines. "No harm done. I'll just make that correction."

Susan smiled and nodded, seemingly at ease. She talked a bit about hotel living and being so far from her family, just random small talk.

At the mention of her family, something clicked in Jake's mind, a problem he had with Susan's absence at dinner the night before.

"At least you were able to see them last evening, for dinner," he said, mulling over his words carefully.

"Um, yes. Yes, it was so good of them to come up. And dinner was just lovely."

"Did they stay in a hotel in the Twin Cities? Some of them can be pretty expensive."

"Well, no. We can't afford anything like that."

"Oh, I know what you mean," Jake said with a laugh. "I had to stay there for a conference a few years back and it put a huge hole in my bank account!"

"I believe it," Susan said, relaxing. "No, David and Angela drove back home after dinner."

Jake stopped and stared hard at her. "Drove all the way back?"

"Yes," Susan replied, a bit sharp. "It took a little while, but David didn't mind."

"That's hard to believe," Jake remarked. "That's at least an eight-hour drive."

Susan opened her mouth to reply, only to close it without a reply. Her shoulders dropped, and she shook her head.

"You didn't meet your family yesterday, did you?"

"No. No, I didn't." Susan exhaled loudly, and when she tilted her head back her eyes were rimmed with tears. "I suppose now I have to tell you the whole story."

CHAPTER 39

"I WAS MEETING WITH AN ATTORNEY," SUSAN announced, wringing her hands. "I didn't want to speak with anyone from the area, so our family lawyer got in touch with a colleague in St. Paul who agreed to see me."

She paused, but only for a moment. "I, I was concerned how what I've done might affect me, now that Matt is dead."

Jake and Pam stared back in shock, both about to unleash a flood of questions. Susan noticed their reaction and continued.

"No, it isn't like *that*. I didn't have anything to do with . . . with the murder. Or with Sam getting arrested, if you were thinking that. I'm sure he didn't have anything to do with the murder, either."

"So, what were you concerned about?" Jake inquired, trying to keep his voice even. He was tired after a long day in the field, upset about the invasion of his room, and losing patience.

Susan dropped her eyes, avoiding Jake's glare. "I . . . I'm the one who told Matt about the Ghost Bog site. I gave him all the information about the bones, what the deposit was like, pretty much anything he asked for."

"Where did you get this info?"

"Mostly from the preliminary reports, and from emails that passed back and forth between you and Sam. Sam kept everything and was always showing it to us. I didn't see the harm in sharing the news with Matt."

"Why do it in the first place? You had to know how much Sam disliked him."

"Yes, but that's part of the reason why I did it." Susan raised a hand, hoping to continue without interruption. "Matt told me how interested he was in the discovery and how much he wanted to help, but Sam wouldn't even acknowledge his emails. It was very frustrating. He pointed out how much he could help Sam, given his experience and expertise. At first, I only passed on general news, but the more I gave him, the sillier Sam's attitude seemed to be. So, I started giving him more detailed information. Matt has always been very persuasive."

"You knew him? From before this?"

"He was my advisor when I was an undergrad at Snelling University. He was a new professor in the department but already one of their shining stars. He took me under his wing, as they say."

"Is that all?" Pam asked.

Susan's face turned bright red. "It's hardly any of your business. But, yes, we had a brief . . . relationship. But that was over a long time ago."

"Did you keep in touch over the years?"

"No. Not really. I think we crossed paths at a few conferences but never spoke at length."

Susan waited a moment, as if in anticipation that Pam might pursue her line of questions. When none came, she continued.

"Finally, Matt's requests got to be too much, especially when the start of the field work got closer. He wanted detailed copies of the maps and access to the artifact inventory. And information on the permits, who was the principal investigator, stuff like that. I didn't have most of it, and I realized I shouldn't share that information without checking with Sam first."

"And you knew how he'd react," Jake said.

Susan nodded. "Then, Matt gave me a choice. Well, an ultimatum,

I suppose. Provide him with all the information he wanted, and he would set me up with a lab supervisor position at Snelling College. More money, more security; everything I didn't have at the Lewis and Clark Museum."

"But you've been there for years," Pam said. "Don't you already have those things?"

"For most of those years I was only an hourly employee, with no benefits and a meager salary. Even with the salaried appointment I have now, I've gotten furloughed twice in the past six years. Every time there's a budget shortfall or some other problem, I get tagged because I have low seniority. And I don't have my graduate degree, so that works against me. I left grad school once Angela was born. Always meant to go back, but it was never the right time.

"Matt told me that I was already in too deep, that Sam wouldn't look too kindly on me helping him behind his back. Sam does have a temper and isn't one to let grudges go."

"But if you had gone to Sam," Pam argued, "and explained the situation, he might have understood."

Susan shrugged her shoulders. "If I had approached him the right way, I might have smoothed things over. I did stall Matt, by telling him that only Jake had the information he wanted. About a week before we arrived here, Matt asked about my husband, how he was doing, and commented that he 'should really give him a call.'"

"So, at the time of your relationship . . ."

"Yes. David and I had been married for little over a year when Matt and I . . . were together. It was a stressful time for both of us, trying to set up a life together. I was in school and David was working his way up the corporate ladder. When we did see each other, we spent most of our time arguing or fighting about stupid things.

"With Matt, though, it was paradise. He helped me with my research work and was always positive and supportive. Made me think I could conquer the world! Matt was brilliant, so charming in those days."

Jake was about to speak when Pam cleared her throat and shot him a withering look. She wanted him to let Susan continue without interruption.

Lost in her reverie, Susan didn't notice their silent exchange. "Looking back, I was deluding myself, but the attention was flattering. Our . . . affair . . . didn't last all that long. Matt's attention waned after a few months, as he got involved in more and bigger projects. And he was soon surrounded by a flock of enthusiastic undergrads and grad students. His 'followers' as he liked to call them."

She paused to take a sip from her water bottle. "Things between David and I improved after that. He got a promotion, so the pressure at his job eased up. I got my degree—with honors—and went right on to grad school. Then I got pregnant, and Angela became the focus of our lives."

Jake couldn't keep quiet any longer. "But if it was all in the past . . ."

"That's just it. I never told David, and even now I don't know how he'd react! I, I couldn't take a chance on him finding out. So, the day before we left St. Louis, I sent him all the information I could pull together, hoping that would be enough. I never thought Matt would show up here, expecting to join the excavation. And the way Sam reacted—it was a nightmare!"

Pam spoke up, frustrated by Susan's lengthy explanation. "But why were you meeting with a lawyer? I'm not seeing the connection."

Susan began rubbing her hands together again. "I tried to avoid Matt while he was here, as much as I could. He did call a few times, but I didn't tell him anything. I knew he was talking to the mayor and some other government people, but I don't know what about. Honestly."

"That still doesn't explain about the lawyer."

"I'm getting to that. After he was . . . killed, I panicked, started to think that they would track me down, find out we had talked. I was worried that it would all come out in the open. What if David found out?"

"I still don't see how . . ."

"The Scenic Police might think it was my fault that Matt came out here in the first place! That would make me liable for his death!"

Pam shook her head. "I don't think it works that way."

Susan wasn't hearing her at all. "Don't you see? If they found about us, they'd realize Matt came out here because of me. If he hadn't come to Scenic, he would still be alive!"

CHAPTER 40

A L RETURNED JUST AS SUSAN WAS finishing her explanation-slash-confession, having delayed her return as much as she could. Jake and Pam reassured Susan that they couldn't anticipate how she might be considered responsible. Susan acknowledged that her attorney had told her the same thing, but nonetheless advised her to contact her immediately if the Scenic sheriff or district attorney tried to question her about their relationship. Susan also added that having Sam caught up in all of this was making her sick with worry, but she was glad to hear that Agent Russell was working to have him released.

Jake and Pam returned to his room and began cleaning up the mess left by the intruder. Jake pulled two beers from his fridge and they discussed what to make of Susan's confession.

"These bags go in this box, right?" Jake nodded in assent, and Pam continued with her task. "I just don't see it. Why would she think that she could be held liable for Walker's death, just because she knew him beforehand? It's not like she forced him to come up here."

"I agree, it seems weird. It makes more sense that she was afraid of saying anything in case her husband found out about their old affair, but how would that even come up? And why call a lawyer?"

"I don't think she's telling us the whole story," Pam said, shifting one full box to the side and starting in on another. "It could be that she's more involved than she admits."

Jake shook his head as he cleared the last scattered papers from the floor near the door. "So, Susan killed Walker and dragged his body through a couple hundred yards of thick brush? Having trouble picturing that."

"She has a pretty strong motive, if Matt Walker was blackmailing her about the inside information and threatening to reveal their affair."

"Which was decades ago," Jake said, pausing to sip his beer.

"It doesn't matter. It was still a concern for Susan, and that's what matters," Pam said, sitting down on a cleared spot on the bed. "And there is a financial motive. Walker was promising her a secure, better-paying job. Maybe she accepted, and he reneged on the deal once he got up here."

"I'll grant you the motive angle, but the timeline doesn't fit. According to Al, Susan was gone for 30 or 40 minutes, tops, not enough time to drive out to Ghost Bog, kill Walker, move his body, and drive back to the hotel."

"She could have had help."

"Who? Al? That seems even less likely."

"Unlikely doesn't mean impossible, partner. But what about Ryan and Laura?"

"I don't know if they even knew each other before this," Jake replied.

"If they did, and likewise held a grudge against Walker, it would be easy for the three of them to cover their movements the night of the murder."

Jake hadn't considered that. Ryan didn't seem to have a very high opinion of his now-deceased boss, either, based on his earlier behavior. "You have a point. I guess we'd better talk to Ryan and Laura again as soon as possible."

Pam raised her beer in mock triumph and then drained the rest of the bottle. She glanced at the clock on the nightstand between the beds. "Not anymore tonight, I think. It's getting pretty late and we still haven't eaten."

"Ouch, you're right. Do you want to grab some carry out, or . . .?"

"I'm too beat to go out, and I'm still a mess from today. Why don't you order a pizza and salad from the place down the road?"

Jake nodded in agreement, scanned the takeout menu from his last order, and made the call.

"Going to be about an hour. Guess they're busy tonight."

"No problem," Pam said as she grabbed her backpack and headed for the bathroom. "You don't mind if I use your shower, do you? I've got some clean clothes in my pack."

"Sure, go right ahead."

"Oh, I won't be locking the door, Jake. I assume you'll be a gentleman," Pam purred as she paused in the doorway. She turned and flashed him a sly, dimpled smile, batting her eyelashes over her bright blue eyes. "But then again, I won't mind if you aren't."

CHAPTER 41

"**N**ONE OF THE TARPS WERE DISTURBED, Jake," Heather said, in a loud voice that carried across the brisk morning air.

"So, just the shed, then," Jake said, tugging at a loose splinter of wood from the damaged doorframe.

Upon arriving at Ghost Bog, the archaeologists were surprised to see the shed door hanging open, which led to some good-natured bickering over the identity of the person responsible for failing to secure the door. Closer inspection, however, revealed that the padlock had been forcibly removed, along with a substantial portion of the adjacent frame. The damage was not confined to the entrance, as open boxes and equipment were strewn about the interior of the shed.

Jake took charge at once. He ordered Heather, Curt, and Rob to check on the excavation units to see if any of the dig site had been disturbed. Michelle and Susan were sent to inform the Emersons about the break-in and damage to the shed. After taking photographs of the interior and the door, Jake, Pam, and Al began removing the equipment and repacking the boxes. Fortunately, Jake had insisted on maintaining a detailed tracking inventory from the start of the project, which made their job easier.

A short time later, Michelle and Susan returned, each carrying a blueberry muffin, courtesy of Mrs. Emerson.

"Mr. Emerson said he'd be over later to fix the door," Michelle said, in between bites. "Neither of them seemed too upset. They didn't hear anything, but Mrs. Emerson said Gypsy and Shadow were howling like mad late last night. They figured it was deer or maybe a bear passing through, so they didn't make much of it."

"No car noises or anything like that?"

"They didn't mention any," Susan said, peeking into the building. "How bad is it?"

"Bit of a mess, but nothing seems to be missing," Jake replied. "All the boxes are accounted for, according to the master inventory."

"I don't think any of the tools or other equipment are missing, either, Jake," Al said, wiping her brow as she exited the building.

"And the units haven't been touched," Heather said as she, Curt, and Rob joined the group. "Whoever was out here, they weren't interested in the dig."

"Just like my hotel room," Jake whispered to himself.

"Should we call the police?" Susan asked, eyes wide.

Jake rubbed his chin, thinking. "I don't know if we should bother. Nothing was taken and the sheriff isn't thrilled with us to begin with."

"Maybe we should post guards, you know, overnight," Heather suggested. "The Emersons can't keep an eye on the site 24 hours a day."

"I don't want to lose half my evening sitting out here, freezing in the car," Rob said, shaking his head. From the looks on their faces, the crew wasn't in favor of overnight sentry duty on top of a full day of digging.

"But we need to fix the lock, at least," Heather said, voice rising.

"Mr. Emerson will take care of that," Jake said with authority, attempting to calm the situation. "It was probably just kids messing around. But we should make sure all of the more valuable stuff is taken back to the hotel from now on."

"We can't fit all the bones and artifacts in our rooms. There's just too much of it."

"What if Curt and I started taking some of the artifacts back to campus?" Rob said. "We could load up the van on Friday, drive back late and unload Saturday morning. Then we could meet you guys back up here on Monday."

Jake considered the idea, as the crew chimed in with their opinions. "We are way ahead of schedule, and we'd be hard pressed to fit everything in the vehicles when we're ready to wrap up. Heather, what do you think?"

Jake noticed Heather hanging back, not commenting on Rob and Curt's idea. He was concerned that she might harbor ill feelings from the previous day, when he chastised her over her comments about Pam.

"It sounds like a good plan to me, boss," Heather said, perking up. "If there's room, I'd be willing to go along, and we can split the driving time. I could stand to check on my apartment, anyway."

Jake started the rest of the crew on their units while Heather, Curt, and Rob worked out their plans. With the details in order, the trio joined the others and before long the excavation was progressing steadily. As they worked, Jake continued to minimize the impact of the vandalism any time the topic arose. He was helping Pam clean her unit floor at the far end of the site when she called him on it.

"You know, Jake, you're pushing the 'innocent vandalism' theory a bit much."

"Think so?" He paused to brush some loose soil into a dustpan. "Do you think they're on to me?"

"Maybe," she said, tucking a stray lock of hair behind her ear. "I think they'd *like* it to be that simple. Everyone is pretty worn out after everything that's happened so far."

Jake nodded. "Unfortunately, I think we both figure that whoever broke in here . . ."

". . . Was the same person who ransacked your room," Pam said. "Somebody or multiple somebodies are not happy that we're here."

"So, are they just trying to scare us off, or are they looking for something specific?"

Pam shrugged her shoulders, and then glanced back at the rest of the crew. "You ought to know, though, that some guy in a big truck cut off Michelle and Al when they were driving back from the grocery store on Sunday."

"Why didn't they tell me?"

"They said it was no big deal," Pam said. "It was intentional, from the way they described it. To be honest, I think they didn't want to upset you. You do have a lot on your plate, you know."

"Still, I wish they had said something. They weren't hurt, right?"

"Just scared, I think. I think the whole town is starting to wonder about us and some of the more belligerent ones are acting up."

"Great," Jake said, shaking his head. He tapped his fingers together, deep in thought. "We need to get to the bottom of this, right away. I don't want to waste any more time, if things are coming to a head."

"Sounds good to me. What do you want to do?"

"We need to clear Sam, period. To do that, we need to figure out who really killed Matt Walker."

"That's a tall order, hon," Pam said, brushing away a final bit of soil from a bison rib. "And how are we going to do that?"

"We'll track his movements, during the last day or so before the murder. If we figure out where he was, we might discover where he was killed. And that might provide the clue we need to identify the killer."

Pam nodded her head, following his line of reasoning. "So, back to Ryan and Laura?"

"Yeah. Can you call your friend at the hotel and have her check to see if they are around?"

"Sure. I don't think she can do anything to keep them there, though, if that's what you're thinking," Pam said, retrieving her phone. "There is a chance they could be involved, you know. And Susan's behavior is still a concern."

"If Ryan and Laura are involved, maybe we can trip them up somehow. Let's see how solid their alibi is for the night of the murder. If anything seems amiss, we'll follow up on that. But my main concern is finding out what we can about Walker's movements."

Nodding, Pam walked away from the dig area and dialed the hotel. Jake finished brushing the unit floor and began mapping the bones. After a few minutes, Pam returned.

"They're in. She agreed to call me if they leave, so unless we hear otherwise, we are good to go." Pam knelt next to him and took out a tape measure to help with the mapping.

After a few minutes, Pam spoke again. "You know, if Ryan and Laura are involved, they might just send us off on a wild goose chase."

"They might," Jake agreed. "But right I don't see any other options. I still think there's a local connection behind all this, and they're our only lead."

"I'll admit I'm starting to come around to that idea. Not much else to go on, to be honest," Pam said, stopping to read off some measurements. "Do you want to tell Agent Russell about the break-ins, or the incident with the truck?"

"I suppose we should, but I don't think it would make much difference. He might just think we're being paranoid." Jake paused to connect some points on the map. "Now that I think about it, maybe we shouldn't say anything. I'd rather he and Keith were focusing their efforts on getting Sam out of jail."

Pam nodded and was about to reply when Gypsy and Shadow burst through the tall grass at the edge of the clearing, several hundred feet ahead of Harold and Vera Emerson. Harold was loaded down with boards, tools, and a shiny new padlock, while Vera contributed a basketful of freshly baked cookies and muffins. With Jake's assistance, Harold repaired the splintered doorframe and replaced the lock. They each offered to cover the cost of the repair, but after much debate agreed to split the cost. Vera made a remark about the stubborn foolishness of men in general, leading to considerable amusement among the female members of the crew.

Jake took the good-natured ribbing in stride, happy to see the crew smiling and laughing again. He hoped the mood would last. Deep down, he had his doubts.

CHAPTER 42

"I NOTICED HEATHER WASN'T QUITE ON BOARD with us leaving early," Pam said as she guided her Camaro out of the gravel drive and onto the highway.

"Maybe not at first," Jake said. "Right after I said we were closing up—and she started to complain—I took her aside and said we were going to the Scenic municipal building. I told her that Harold mentioned that Keith was in town, so you and I decided to hit him with a 'surprise' visit, maybe spur him into action."

"What are you going to do tomorrow, when she finds out we didn't see Keith?"

Jake shrugged. "I'll just tell her that we couldn't find him, that he was in court or with a client or something. I did say we wanted to keep it quiet, in case nothing came of it, and that's why we weren't announcing it to everyone."

"Pretty sneaky stuff, Professor."

"Your deviousness is starting to rub off on me, I'm afraid. Probably will end up sinking my dreams of tenure."

Without taking her eyes off the road, Pam punched him playfully in the shoulder. Rather than risk further onslaught, Jake changed the subject.

"The crew will be busy enough taking the artifact boxes back to the hotel, for the run down to campus this weekend. The Emersons said they would keep a closer eye on the dig from now on, but I'd rather err on the side of caution and start moving things now."

"Makes sense. I called the hotel again before we left, and Ryan and Laura are still there," Pam said. "We should be there in about fifteen minutes. Let's hope this works."

A short time later, Jake and Pam stood outside Laura's door. A small tray of empty hotel dishes sat just outside, awaiting pickup. Jake put his head near the door and picked up voices within. He took a step back and knocked.

"Oh, it's you," Laura said with surprise after opening the door. "I, um, didn't expect to see you again."

"We have some follow-up questions," Jake said. "May we come in?"

She ushered them inside, calling out to Ryan as she did. He emerged, frowning, from the door leading to the adjoining room.

"What is it this time?"

"Not happy to see us?" Pam asked, smiling.

Ryan sighed as he sat down in one of the two available chairs. "Not really, if you must know. It's because of you and that Bureau agent that we're still stuck in this one-horse town."

"Nothing to do with us, I'm afraid," Pam said. "That's all on Agent Russell. We just follow orders."

Jake cringed inwardly, reminded once again that he and Pam were acting solely as amateur detectives, without any real association with the authorities. If anyone called Agent Russell or his superiors to complain, they could be in big trouble.

Ryan rolled his eyes as he leaned back in the chair but didn't reply. Laura, sitting next to him, spoke up. "So, what do you want to know?"

"The night of the murder," Jake said, while Pam pulled out her trusty notepad and pen. "You ate dinner at the restaurant across the street and then came back here, correct?"

They both nodded.

"You didn't leave the hotel, at all, for any reason? Even for just a few minutes?"

They both answered in the negative, without any hesitation.

"What about phone calls?" Pam asked. "Either incoming or outgoing?"

This time Ryan and Laura exchanged glances before answering.

"Not me. Laura?"

She looked at the floor, but only for a second. "I texted with my fiancé for a bit after I climbed into bed. You can check with him, if you need to. But what we talked about is private."

Laura turned a rosy shade of red, not comfortable with going into details. Pam looked at Jake and nodded.

"We don't need to hear personal details," Pam said. "About what time was that?"

Laura told her the approximate time, and Pam wrote down the information. She turned to Jake and shook her head. The time didn't overlap with Susan's visit to the hotel lobby.

"We need a bit more detail on the day Walker died," Jake said.

"We weren't with him that night," Laura said.

"But what about during the day?"

"Yeah, we went to check out two areas, but we didn't find anything," Ryan said. "One spot was on some state land in the far northeastern corner of the county. The second one . . . was way west of that, I think."

Laura nodded. "It was at the west edge of the county. I think we were over the state border, or at least we crossed it while driving. I remember seeing a sign for rental cottages along the St. Croix River."

"Was that also state-owned land?"

They both shrugged. "I think so," Laura said. "I never got a chance to record the locations on the map."

The mention of a map caught Jake's attention. "You have a map, showing all the locations you visited?"

"Well, sure. Doctor Walker had copies we used in the field, and then each night I would recopy the pertinent data onto a clean master copy."

"May we see it?"

Laura agreed and went to a large plastic file box perched on the edge of her dresser. She flipped through it and pulled out a folded map, which she opened and laid out on the bed.

Jake examined it with interest. It was a large topographic map covering all of Kohl County and portions of the adjacent counties. In addition to the towns and roads, the map showed all the major landform features including rivers, wetlands, high and low elevation spots, and glacial deposits. Scattered across the page were red circles and ovals of various sizes, some filled in with hatched or crossed lines. All of the filled areas had dates written next to them, and some also had a short description of the landform or vegetation. All of the marked areas had a red "X" next to it, except for one with a blue "+" sign: Ghost Bog.

"Nearly all the spots we looked at are displayed as bogs or lowlands, or something similar," Laura said. "There are also a few river cuts. But we never found anything."

Jake followed a few of the elevation contours between the marked spots, noting the dates as he did. Walker's approach could be politely described as haphazard; finding any archaeological or paleontological sites in this manner was close to zero, on a good day.

"The dates are scattered around quite a bit," Jake remarked.

"We did move around a lot each day. Well, at least at first."

"I think he was hoping to get lucky and hit a hot spot," Ryan said. "If nothing panned out, we'd shoot across the county and try a few 'promising locales' somewhere else. And once in a while he'd want to track down a landowner to see if they had any leads. That was a real waste of time."

"I don't see the dates for the day of the murder, or the day before that."

Laura leaned in. "Oh, yeah. When we got back to the hotel that afternoon, he kept all the paperwork. He must have taken it with him when he left again that evening."

"Do you have it now?" Jake said.

"No, not here. It wasn't with the stuff we took out of his room," Laura explained. "After the police looked through his suite, the hotel people wanted it cleared out so they could rent it again. We packed up his luggage and papers and brought them down here."

"So, it must have been with him, in your SUV," Pam said.

"I guess. Ryan, you grabbed his briefcase out of there, right?"

"It's in my room. I'll go get it."

"Wait a second," Jake said to Laura. "Where was the SUV parked when it was found?"

"I don't know. They never told us."

"So how did you get it back?"

"A couple of days after . . . it happened, the sheriff's deputy called and told us we had to come and pick it up."

"At the impound lot?" Pam asked.

"No, it was in the parking lot in front of the city building."

"I had to walk over there to get it, too," Ryan said as he returned. He set a thick leather briefcase on the chair. "They said it wasn't their problem if I didn't have a ride. When I got there, the receptionist had me sign a release or something, and then she gave me the keys. That was it."

Pam pressed him for details. "Was the vehicle processed? I mean, did they remove anything that you could see, or tore it apart in any way?

"No, not that I could tell. The briefcase was between the front seats, where it always was. It was open, but he usually left it like that."

Eyebrows arched, Pam started writing furiously in her notepad.

Laura reached into the briefcase and pulled out several folded topographic maps, a small tourist map of Kohl County, and a battered county plat book. She sorted through a few of the dirt-stained topographic maps until she found the ones she wanted.

"Okay, here's the one showing the spot we checked in the northeast." Laura pointed to a small red circle with a large black X over it.

"Right," Ryan said, glancing at the sheet. "We only walked in about a hundred yards before he wrote it off. 'A pointless endeavor' were his exact words, if I remember."

Laura nodded and then pointed to a penciled-in area on another map. This location straddled the county line. "We were about here for the second trip. It was in the woods, off this twisty forest road. It wasn't clear where we were, so we were going to figure out the specific spot later on."

Pam looked up from her notebook. "How do you know which areas are state land and which are privately owned?"

"The county plat book lists the landowners," Laura replied, handing her their copy. "The book and the topographic maps are at different scales, so you have to adjust between them to figure out who owns what."

Pam paged through the small booklet and then glanced at the cover. "This is almost 15 years old. Is it even accurate anymore?"

"In the past, county plat books were only published on an irregular basis. Too expensive to do a new one each year," Jake said. "But for historic research, and genealogy, they can be useful. I think now most of the information is available online."

Jake took the book from her and soon found the two pages showing the locations. "Both areas seem to be state land. And there aren't any private properties anywhere close to either one."

"We did stay off of private land, as much as we could," Laura said. "Well, we tried to, at least."

Ryan led out a harsh, "Yeah, right," in response but didn't elaborate.

Jake inquired about the areas investigated by Walker and his team in the days prior to his murder. With Laura's assistance, he checked the location of each area visited against the owner listed in the plat map. The book was worn, with several loose and reversed pages, which frustrated his efforts. But after a few minutes, they had tracked down each of them. All but a few were situated on land owned by the state, county, or federal government.

Discouraged, Jake shook his head, trying to puzzle out what might be missing, some pattern that would reveal itself. He looked back and forth between the field maps and the master copy.

"So much for a local connection," Pam murmured.

Jake frowned at her, and then he noticed one spot, not too far from Ghost Bog, circled crudely in blue ink rather than the red marker used everywhere else. It had no hatched lines through it, and no date was attached.

"What's the significance of this spot?"

Laura peered at it with interest. "Hmm. I don't recognize that one. It isn't one of our original survey spots. Maybe he added it later." She turned her attention back to the master copy.

"You did check a bunch of spots near there," Pam said. She pointed to a half-dozen red-hatched circles in close proximity to the location marked in pen. "But it looks like nothing turned up."

Ryan leaned over to look. "Oh, yeah. That was the first week. Walker thought he had a series of hot spots, all similar to your Ghost Bog, and not that far away. He was really excited about those. Couple of bogs, some deep gullies, but he still thought they were 'promising,' as he put it."

"He did think those had some potential," Laura remarked, thinking back. "I think he was going to ask someone local if there were more areas like that in the county."

"Maybe that's where he got the idea to survey this spot," Jake said.

"Could be," Laura said. "In any case, it's not on the big map, so I don't think Doctor Walker ever bothered with it. He may even have scratched it in while we were out there but decided against it after those other spots turned up negative."

Jake rubbed his finger on the edge of the pen mark and a small bit of ink stuck to his finger. "Do you know who his 'local source' might have been?"

Ryan laughed again. "Walker made it clear from the onset that *he* would make the big decisions and we were just there to follow orders. Let's just say that questions were not appreciated."

"Well, let's see who owns that parcel," Jake said. "Maybe the owner or a neighbor put your boss on to this spot."

Jake picked up the plat book, checked some landmarks on the topographic map, and used that information to find the corresponding page in the index. He flipped to the correct page, only to find the stubby remnant of the page. The torn edge was white and crisp, still jagged against his fingertip.

"Someone ripped this page out. Recently."

CHAPTER 43

"I**T MAY NOT MEAN ANYTHING, JAKE**," Pam said, sitting back on her bed. After their meeting with Ryan and Laura, Jake and Pam had walked down to her room to discuss their options.

"That was a fresh tear," Jake said as he paced back and forth. "The rest of the plat book is ragged and worn, practically falling apart. But not that page. And they both swore they didn't remove it, so who did?"

"I don't know. Walker could have done it himself, you know."

"Or the killer, trying to hide his tracks," Jake said. "It could even have been the sheriff, if she's involved."

"Now I think you're reaching. O'Neil is incompetent, sure, but that doesn't make her a criminal."

"Well, someone deliberately removed that page. I think finding out who is key to all of this."

"Even if they did, how are we going to track it down?"

Jake stopped pacing and scratched his goatee. "There's sure to be a copy at the Scenic municipal building, in the deed or tax offices. We can check there in the morning."

Before Pam could reply, Jake's phone beeped. "Text from Heather," he said, scanning the display. "They got the artifact boxes safely stashed in their rooms. And my room was locked when they arrived, so no problems there. Oh, and they're all heading over to the sports bar for dinner, if we're interested."

"Fine by me, but I want to get cleaned up first."

"Okay, I'll tell her we're in but won't be there for a while," Jake said, tapping the keyboard.

Pam sat up and rubbed a knot on her shoulder. "Jake, do you really want to bother with the city offices? I mean, can't we just go out there ourselves and look around?"

"We will, but I'd like to see who owns it before we trespass. And if it's state land, I'm curious to see who lives nearby."

"You know, we're only assuming this is the location where Walker was killed. We don't know where they found the van."

"Want me to call the sheriff?" Jake asked with a smirk.

"Ha, ha. No, but what about Agent Russell? He should know."

Jake nodded his head, then glanced at his watch. "Pretty late now. I doubt he's in the office."

"Call him anyway and leave a message. It can't hurt," Pam said, rising off the bed. "While you do that, I'm going to get cleaned up and then I'll run you back to your hotel. On the way, you can figure out what lie you're going to tell the crew when we get to the bar."

A SHORT TIME LATER, PAM EASED HER Camaro out of the parking lot and onto Main Street, in the direction of Jake's motel. The evening sky was already dark, with only a few wisps of fading sunlight visible in the western sky.

They had driven less than a mile when Pam abruptly changed lanes and turned left at the next cross street.

Jake looked at her. "Did you leave something at your hotel?"

"No," Pam said, staring at her rearview mirror. "I think someone is following us."

Jake spun his head around, only to groan and squint his eyes at the glaring headlights of the trunk positioned about seventy-five feet behind them. "Are you sure?"

"Pretty sure," Pam said, making another quick left turn, this time without signaling first. "They pulled out of the parking lot right after we did, from the entrance by the restaurant. I was going slow enough that they should have passed us, but they didn't."

Pam drove straight for about a half mile, and then made another left turn. She accelerated, then decreased her speed as she neared the junction with Main Street. Looking back, they both recognized the front of the large black truck getting closer and closer.

"From their description, I think this was the same vehicle that was hassling Michelle and Al the other day," Pam said, assessing the approaching traffic before she turned right on Main Street. She gunned the engine and the Camaro soon exceeded the posted speed limit.

Jake continued to monitor the movements of the pursuing truck.

"I think you're right," Jake said. "He just cut somebody off pulling onto Main Street, and now he's coming up fast."

Pam grunted in response, focusing her attention on the road and surrounding vehicles. She maneuvered the car with confidence through the crowded street, increasing the distance between them and their pursuer.

"Okay, this should do the trick," she said, slowing as they neared a traffic light. The black truck was still behind them, separated by three or four cars. "Hang on."

As the light turned yellow, Pam jammed on the brakes, causing the cars following to do the same. The light turned red and Pam stomped on the gas and shot through the intersection, a chorus of horns blaring in her wake. The Camaro roared to the next intersection where Pam turned off the lights and made a quick left, pulling into a crowded parking lot on the opposite side of the street.

As Jake and Pam watched, the black pickup zoomed down Main Street, swerving and honking in a desperate attempt to get to the front of the pack. Clearing the other cars, the truck increased its speed and rocketed down the road. It was soon out of sight.

"Nicely done, gorgeous," Jake said as he leaned over and kissed Pam on the cheek.

"Piece of cake," Pam replied, smiling. "With a little effort, I could have come up right behind him before he even made it to the next light. But I'd rather not chase some stranger all over the county without backup."

"Think it's safe enough to head back to the hotel? Or should we hunker down here for a while?"

"I think we're good," Pam said, as she turned on the headlights and shifted into gear. "They know we're on to them now, so they ought to keep their distance. For a while, at least."

CHAPTER 44

A FTER ACCOMPANYING THE CREW TO GHOST Bog and helping them set up for the day, Jake and Pam drove back to
Scenic. Their cover story, of hoping to ambush Keith Emerson,
was starting to wear thin, but Jake hoped it might last at least one
more day.

Perched in her usual spot at the reception desk, Nora greeted
Jake and Pam when they arrived. He asked if Keith Emerson was
available but was informed that once again, he was out of town.

"Is there anyone else you'd like to talk to?" Nora inquired, smiling. "Most of the staff are out today, but I think a few folks are here."

Jake glanced down the hallway, seeing mostly closed doors and
dark offices. "Do you happen to have a copy of the Kohl County
plat book?"

"Well, now there I can help you," she said, rummaging through
the shelves next to her desk. "We have a copy right here . . . somewhere. Are you looking for more places to find your dinosaur
bones?"

"Sort of. There's a property we'd like to investigate . . ."

"Aha! Here we are," Nora said as she handed the book to Jake.
It was also battered and dog-eared from heavy use but it seemed
to be in better condition than the one used by Walker and his

team. Jake set it on the edge of Nora's desk and opened it to the desired page.

"Okay, here we are," he said to Pam. Jake took the copy of Walker's map out of his pocket and set the two pages side by side. Tracing the relative locations on each map, he soon found the spot indicated.

"State-owned land, but there are some private parcels nearby." Jake pointed to a series of small square and rectangular sections. He drew a sketch map of the property lines on his copy of Walker's field map and penciled in the landowner information. "Let's see. Boschke . . . R & J W. . . . BN et al . . . Meyer . . . P & E H . . . KE . . . and LF. Rest is state land."

"Why are some just initials?" Pam asked, peering over his shoulder.

"Space limitations, that's all. If there isn't enough room on the map for the full name, they include the initials and put the full listing in the index. See, like they did here, for the Emersons." Jake pointed to an irregular-shaped parcel not too far away that was marked H & V E. "That's their property, and this is about where Ghost Bog is located."

"I get it. Let's check the index and find out who's who."

Jake nodded and flipped to the back of the book. "That's odd. All of the index pages are gone."

"This is starting to be familiar. Are there any *intact* copies of this book around?"

Jake turned to Nora, who had going back to her filing after giving them the plat book. "Nora, is there another copy of this around? This one has a few pages missing."

"Oh, I'm sorry. There should be one in Peter's office, the official copy, but I can't let you in there without permission."

"I understand. What time do you expect him in today?"

She shook her head. "He's out of the office all day. He and the mayor and a few others are in Superior for some regional planning meeting. I think he might be back tomorrow afternoon."

"Any chance we could look at the tax records? Just for these properties . . ."

"Peter handles all that," Nora replied, shaking her head. "You'll have to wait until he gets back."

"It's not important anyway," Jake said. "The location we want is on state land."

"We must get some new copies," Nora said, taking the book back from Jake. "Everyone seems interested in this old thing lately."

That caught Jake's attention. "Really? Like who?"

"Well, that other scientist, the poor man who got murdered. Terrible thing to happen, just terrible."

"Doctor Walker was here, checking out the plat book entries? When?"

"I, I'm not sure," Nora said, a confused look on her face. "I don't know, but it was a few times, before he got killed. Peter said he was surveying the county, to find more dinosaur bones like you found at the Emerson's place."

"Bison, not dinosaur," Jake corrected, growing somewhat frustrated. "There aren't any dinosaur fossils in Wisconsin . . ."

"Such a nice man," Nora said, oblivious. "Always so charming when he visited."

"Could I borrow that book one more time?" Jake said. When she complied, Jake opened the book to the appropriate page and took some quick photos with his phone. "If we take this county road to this point," he said to Pam, "we can drive down this forest road to about here, where the road curves, and then head over on foot. That should be the easiest way to get out there."

Pam studied the map and nodded. "Do you want to go out there right away?"

Jake paused, thinking it over. "Let's go back to the site first. We don't know how long it will take and I don't want the crew to wonder where we are. Heather might get it in her head to drive into Scenic to 'rescue' us."

"That would definitely lead to more trouble," Pam said as they returned the plat book to the receptionist. They thanked her again for her help and began walking down the hallway toward the side entrance.

Without warning, a voice boomed out from behind them. "Alright, you two. That's far enough!"

CHAPTER 45

"I THOUGHT I HEARD TWO UNWELCOME VOICES," Sheriff O'Neil said, sneering, as she caught up to Jake and Pam. "I suppose you're here to cause more problems?"

As they turned to face her, Pam adjusted her backpack, jabbing Jake with the corner. She murmured an apology while reaching into one of the small pouches on the side. Perhaps a warning for him to behave?

"Just a quick visit with Nora," Jake said, smiling.

Sheriff O'Neil turned her head toward the receptionist, who waved at the mention of her name. O'Neil rolled her eyes as she focused her attention back on the archaeologists.

"Fine. Just keep your distance from the cells. There's no reason for either of you, any of your group, to be anywhere near them." She crossed her arms, a smug look on her face.

If she was trying to bait him, Jake thought it was a pretty clumsy attempt. He stood for a moment, his best polite smile on his face, before he replied.

"Well, we should be on our way. If you'll excuse us."

"Just a minute," Sheriff O'Neil said, her shrill voice echoing in the empty hallway. "This saves me the trouble of tracking you down."

Jake and Pam waited for her to continue.

"It's been brought to my attention that you people are planning to flee the jurisdiction. I know what you're up to, so don't try anything."

"I don't know what you're talking about," Jake said, frowning. "We still have a week or two to go, and . . ."

"Don't give me that," she snapped. "You're planning to sneak out of town this weekend!"

That statement caught Jake by surprise, but he soon regained his composure when he realized what she meant.

"Oh, that," he said, shaking his head. "We're overloaded with artifact boxes, so we need to transfer some of them back to the University. Some of the crew are going to run a van-load there this weekend, and be back to work here on Monday."

"A likely story," the sheriff said. "Don't think you're going to pull any funny business while I'm in charge."

"It's the truth. Besides, it seems safer to move the boxes now, especially in light of the break-ins."

"What break-ins? I don't know anything about that."

Jake started to explain about the recent incidents at the hotel and at Ghost Bog, but the sheriff cut him off.

"Doesn't mean a thing. Sounds like an excuse so you can slink out of town in the middle of the night!"

"We're not going anywhere," Jake replied, frustration mounting. "Call the hotel if you want. We're still booked there for two more weeks."

"And since we haven't done anything and aren't under arrest," Pam said, "there isn't anything to prevent us from coming and going as we please. Unless you have a signed court order stating otherwise?"

Sheriff O'Neil sputtered, growing angrier by the second. "I don't need any damn court order if *I say* you can't leave town! Don't forget who's the law in Scenic. Bad things can happen to people who don't follow the rules around here!"

"Is that a threat?" Now Jake's temper was starting to rise.

"Call it what you like. I'm just stating the facts. Don't think that I'm not keeping an eye on you, either."

"Well, we'll just continue to behave ourselves then," Pam said, putting her hand on Jake's shoulder. "C'mon, Jake, time to go."

They were a few steps away when Pam stopped and turned back to Sheriff O'Neil, who stood glaring at them, a satisfied smile on her face. "Oops," Pam said, reaching into her backpack. "Almost forgot to turn off my phone."

She pulled out the phone, holding it just over her head. "Wouldn't want to run down the battery, after recording this conversation."

The smile on O'Neil's face disappeared and her eyes bulged. She took a half step toward them but then stopped. Pivoting, she stomped down the hallway in the opposite direction, muttering to herself.

CHAPTER 46

As THEY DROVE TO THE SITE, Jake and Pam discussed their unpleasant encounter with Sheriff O'Neil. Their biggest concern was how she had found out about their planned trip to the University, even if she did have some of the details wrong. Jake wouldn't accept that any of the crew had told her, but Pam made a convincing argument that Susan might be involved, perhaps in a misguided attempt to help Sam or out of fear that she might be accused of complicity in Walker's death.

At Ghost Bog, Jake was forced to admit another failure in their attempt to see Keith Emerson. Heather denounced it as a colossal waste of time, hinting that Pam's influence was behind the fiasco. Her attitude did little to improve the morale of the tired, dispirited crew.

With most of the site excavated, the archaeologists were now down to the last dozen or so units. If the weather held, Jake announced, they might finish in a few days. Unfortunately, a quick check of an online weather app revealed dropping temperatures, flurries that evening, and a major snowstorm developing to the northwest. With the incoming storm, however, Jake had an excuse to end the day early and investigate the location marked on Walker's map.

During the mid-afternoon break, Jake ordered the crew to close up for the day and start loading additional artifact boxes into the van. Curt and Rob would drive down to Wisconsin State University on Thursday, instead of waiting for the weekend. If the weather stayed good, they could drive back up to the site on Friday and rejoin the others, who would stay behind and work on the remaining units. If necessary, Heather and Michelle could make a follow-up trip over the weekend.

The archaeologists, a bit concerned at first over the abrupt change in plans, quickly agreed with the new proposal. Jake did not mention Sheriff O'Neil's veiled threat, but Pam studied Susan's face as Jake outlined his new strategy. If she was upset about the change, it didn't show.

AN HOUR LATER, JAKE AND PAM were driving slowly down the forest road in the direction of the mysterious spot marked on Walker's map. The road was little more than a two-track path in some spots. As they rounded a small bend, they stopped short in front of a washed-out gully, blocked by fallen trees.

"End of the line," Jake said. "Guess we walk."

"These trees look like they were dropped on purpose. Like a barricade."

"Maybe. Someone could have pushed them over to keep people from driving into the washout." Jake gestured beyond the barricade, where a large portion of the dirt and gravel road had slumped into the ditch.

After adjusting their packs, Jake and Pam hiked down the road, now overgrown with brush and tall grass. There were no signs of recent human activity. After another twenty minutes, they reached the approximate location of the curve shown on the map.

"This should be the spot." Jake pulled a compass from his pocket, took a bearing, and studied the map. Nodding, he removed some bright green flagging tape from his pack and tied it to an overhanging branch.

"What's that for?"

"Just being cautious. If we get lost or have to double back, we can find this spot again and start over."

"Very clever, Daniel Boone. Any more wilderness tricks to show off?"

"No, that's it. If we get into real trouble, I'll dig out my copy of the Junior Woodchucks guidebook. Ready to go?"

Pam nodded and the duo pushed forward into the thick brush lining the edge of the road. The tangled vegetation and low-hanging branches slowed their progress, compounded by the uneven terrain. Jake rechecked his compass every thirty yards or so, and as they moved north the ground rose and leveled out. They soon came across an old trail heading more or less in the direction of the spot marked on Walker's map. Picking up speed, they were not too far from their destination when Jake spotted a pile of rusted cans and metal scrap along the edge of the trail. A few steps beyond, the trail opened into a small clearing, encircling the framework of a dilapidated shack. Only two walls were standing, and mounds of building debris and other rubbish were scattered about.

Jake knelt and examined some pieces of broken crockery while Pam walked to the far side of the structure.

"This isn't what Walker was looking for, was it?"

"No, we're still a little south of the area marked on the map," Jake said, tossing the sherds back to the ground. "This is probably an old hunting camp or maybe a squatter's cabin. Dates to the late nineteenth century, based on the artifacts scattered around."

"You can figure that out just from this junk?" Pam asked, kicking a bullet-ridden piece of tin out of her path as she wandered away from the cabin.

"Sure. Historic artifacts are great temporal markers. Lots of records on when they were first developed, how long they lasted on the market, and when they started to get replaced," Jake said, circling back in her direction. "Hey! Hold it, don't move any further!"

Pam stopped, startled, one boot resting on top of an innocent looking pile of lumber. "What? What is it?"

"Just stay put. Trust me." Keeping his eyes on Pam, Jake trotted back to the edge of the cabin and then strode toward her, counting his steps.

"Yeah, just about where it should be," Jake said as he drew up beside her.

"What, this?" Pam pushed down with her foot and the board cracked in protest.

Jake put his hand on her arm. "Careful. This is the privy pit for the cabin. They're always about thirty or forty feet from the house. The wood is from the outhouse, all collapsed and rotten. It's probably not too deep, but it's full of rusted junk and broken glass. Don't want to fall in and break your ankle."

Pam took a few steps away, still scanning the nearby ground. "This is new, though. Look!"

She bent down and retrieved a cigarette butt, somewhat crushed but still intact. "This hasn't been here long. And the grass is tramped down over here, too."

"Couple more spots over here," Jake said, moving to the far side of the privy pit. "Looks like a fresh path, leading that way."

Moving in tandem on opposite sides, Pam and Jake followed the trail to the north edge of the clearing. After a brief search, they discovered a narrow gap in the brush and a sinewy trail beyond, littered with fallen orange and red leaves.

"Looks like it heads north and west," Jake said, glancing at the map. "Should put us right in the vicinity of the spot he marked."

Pam nodded. "We need to check this out."

They moved forward with caution, pushing smaller branches aside and avoiding the thicker limbs. The level terrain turned into a gradual incline, and then a much steeper drop, until they found themselves at the edge of a large shallow basin, bathed in sunlight, surrounded by old growth forest.

"Huh. Looks like the remnants of an old kettle pond," Jake said, scanning the area. "This could be what Walker was looking for."

Pam knelt to inspect the waist-high vegetation that carpeted the area. Most of the plants were stripped bare, while others appeared to have been trimmed or pruned. Nearly all were curled over and brown, killed by the recent cold weather.

Along the edges of the basin, Jake noticed some larger trees with cut branches, interspersed with strung camouflage netting. Plastic pails and metal cans were strewn about, and distinct paths were visible cutting across the landscape. Unlike the old cabin, this spot looked well maintained and visited on a regular basis.

"Oh, crap," Pam said suddenly, rising to her feet. "Jake, this is a . . ."

The loud snap of a cracking branch echoed across the clearing, drawing their attention as figure in a brown camouflage coat emerged from the brush.

Eric Holcombe stepped into view, brandishing a shotgun.

CHAPTER 47

"**O**KAY, YOU TWO. DON'T YOU MOVE, not one inch."

Jake and Pam froze, about a dozen yards apart. Eric pointed his gun at one of them, then the other.

"Stumbled across my crop, did ya?" he asked, face twisted into a sneer.

"Crop?" Jake replied, looking anew at the dead vegetation dotting the landscape.

"Man, for a big-city egghead you sure don't know nothing. Pot, genius. Got my own grass plantation here. Just a little side business but it brings in some decent cash. Not as much as the lab, but it ain't bad."

Eric tilted his head as he spoke. Jake looked past him and could just discern a small mobile trailer, decked out in camouflage paint and netting, just beyond the edge of the trees.

"Good thing I was out here dropping off supplies," Eric said. "Having a heck of a time keeping out the trespassers lately."

"Trespassers," Jake said, as the extent of Eric's drug operation dawned on him. "Like Matt Walker?"

The smirking smile on Eric's face disappeared. "My . . . partners . . . aren't keen on advertising what we're doing. As long as I keep things under wraps, they don't much care how I handle problems.

Found out that nosy bone guy was planning to snoop around out here, so I had to . . . deal with him."

"That was pretty clever, I must admit," Jake said, keeping his voice level. "How did you draw him out here?"

Eric frowned, trying to figure out if he was being insulted. After a moment, he shrugged. "Wasn't all that hard. You college boys think you're so damned smart, but you wouldn't last an hour in the woods. No street smarts, that's it. Hey! What are you doing?"

Pam had shifted, transferring her backpack to one shoulder. "Nothing. My bag is getting heavy, that's all."

Eric narrowed his eyes but soon decided she was telling the truth. He turned back to Jake. "The bone guy bought the story we gave him, so I met him just off the highway, that way." He gestured to the southeast, in the general direction of the smaller private parcels that bordered the state property. "Walked him the long way 'round, and then when I couldn't deal with his yapping anymore, I shot him."

Jake couldn't believe how nonchalantly Eric dismissed taking a human life. "You killed him, just like that, right here?"

"Nah, back by the old cabin. Man, you should have seen the look on his face! Never saw it coming."

"How did his body end up at the dig site?"

"Man, you *are* stupid, aren't ya? I carted him over there with my deer frame. Lots of trails out here and some lead right to the bog if you know what you're doing."

Eric looked rather pleased with himself. Then he seemed to realize that he was a bit too talkative with his audience.

"Okay, that's enough with the third degree." He gestured with the shotgun. "You two start heading back the way you came. Not too fast, and don't try nothing."

Jake and Pam walked with difficulty over the narrow trail. Eric followed close behind, growling unhelpful suggestions to hurry up and then to slow down.

Jake began pushing small branches aside and letting them

whip back against Eric's face and chest. Eric began to grow more annoyed, muttering and cursing under his breath. Jake made sure Pam noticed his efforts, and she responded with an almost imperceptible nod.

Pam feigned a stumble, while Jake took a step forward and pretended to trip on an exposed root. Eric was not happy.

"C'mon, keep it moving. I should just shoot you here and let the bears deal with you." He fished a cigarette from his pocket, lit it, and took a long drag.

Looking ahead, Jake spotted a thick branch at shoulder level a few yards ahead. He rubbed his "injured" ankle and leaned toward Pam. "Get ready," he whispered.

The captives regained their footing and dashed forward, causing Eric to curse and speed up in pursuit. Jake grasped the targeted branch with both hands and pushed it with all his might, straining against the building tension. At the same moment, Pam pretended to stumble again, crashing into the brush on the opposite side of the trail.

"Stupid broad! What the . . ."

At that moment, Jake spun to his right and let the branch snap back at Eric, who attempted to block it with his left arm. Caught off-balance, the force of the impact knocked Eric on his back. He crashed backwards, the shotgun blasting over their heads as he fell.

Jake grabbed Pam's wrist and they bolted forward, crashing through the brush-choked trail as fast as they could. The old cabin was soon in sight.

As they reached the clearing, Pam pulled free of Jake's grasp and twisted her backpack off her shoulder. Avoiding the old privy pit, Jake ran to the right side and Pam moved to the left.

"This way, quick," Jake said, pointing toward the trail at the opposite side of the clearing, in the direction of the old forest road.

"No, over here," Pam said, struggling with the zipper on her pack. "Behind the cabin!"

Jake shook his head. "He'll see us!"

The sound of Eric crashing through the brush was growing closer. There wasn't time for a debate. Cursing, Jake backtracked toward the sagging cabin wall where Pam was already kneeling, backpack at her side.

In his haste, Jake stepped on a fallen board and yelped as a long nail pushed through his boot into the sole of his foot. He doubled over in pain as his momentum carried him to the ground, a few yards shy of the cabin.

Eric burst through the underbrush into the clearing. He grinned maliciously at the sight of Jake in the open, resting on his backside. He shouldered the shotgun and took aim.

Pam leaned out from behind the opposite side of the abandoned cabin, her service weapon in her hand.

"Hey! Freeze!"

Eric twisted toward her, shotgun raised.

A single shot echoed across the clearing.

CHAPTER 48

"JAKE, ARE YOU ALRIGHT?"

"Yeah. Stepped on a damn nail. I'm okay."

Eyes focused, Pam cautiously approached Eric's body. Reaching him, she kicked the shotgun aside and then nudged him with her boot. A large red circle of blood stained his chest.

She knelt, keeping her gun hand off to one side, and put her left hand on his neck.

"He's dead."

"I don't think you had much choice," Jake said, removing his boot. He took the first aid kit out of his pack before gingerly pulling off his sock.

Pam walked over to Jake as he began to clean and treat his injury. She was shaking and breathing in short, quick gasps. "It was a good shoot," she muttered to herself. "Good shoot."

"Are you okay?"

"Yeah, just the adrenaline rush. Whew." She sat down opposite Jake. "I, I never shot anyone before."

"Really?"

"Being a cop isn't like you see on TV," Pam snapped, eyes wide. "You hardly ever need to pull you gun, let alone use it on someone."

"Sorry. Guess I'm not thinking too clear."

"It's okay. Me neither." Pam put the safety on and returned the gun to the holster in her backpack.

"Have you had that with you the whole time?"

"Of course. I'm still a cop, even when I'm not on duty." She looked around the clearing as Jake finished bandaging his foot. "Can you walk?"

"Sure. I might need a tetanus shot, maybe a stitch or two, but I'm fine."

Pam pulled her cell phone from her bag. "Good. Where are we?"

"I can point it out on a map, but I don't know if I can describe it to anyone over the phone."

"No, I mean are we on state land or private property?"

"Definitely state land. I think his entire operation is hidden out in the forest, with a trail leading south to one of the private parcels along the highway."

"Good. I have to call this in, but I'd rather not deal with Sheriff O'Neil again. I'll call Agent Russell. This is going to fall under his jurisdiction anyway."

"I hope you can get through," Jake said, wincing as he slid his boot back on over his injured foot.

"If I get voice mail, I'll contact the front office. When I explain the circumstances, they'll be able to reach him no matter what he's doing."

"Good," Jake said, standing up with Pam's help. "I have a feeling it's all going to hit the fan now."

MIRACULOUSLY, PAM WAS ABLE TO REACH Agent Russell immediately. He had just finished a meeting in nearby Eau Claire and could be there within an hour. After confirming their location based on Jake's description, he ordered them to remain by their vehicle until "his people" were on the scene.

Within an hour, the area was swarming with Bureau agents, lab technicians, and state troopers. Agent Russell was an anchor amidst the hurricane of activity, a calm commanding presence in a sea of chaos. Keith Emerson arrived just as darkness fell, followed soon thereafter by an irate Sheriff O'Neil. Agent Russell intercepted her before she reached the command area. Jake and Pam, sitting in the back of an ambulance, didn't hear any of their conversation, but within moments Sheriff O'Neil had returned to her vehicle, where she sat without speaking for the rest of the night. At some point, she drove away, unnoticed.

Most of the evening passed in a blur. The paramedics treated Jake's injured foot, assuring him that no stitches were necessary and that his recent tetanus vaccine was sufficient. Jake and Pam made a series of phone calls to Heather and Sheriff Rostlund, respectively, attempting to explain the situation and deal with the anticipated fallout. Pam had more success with her boss than Jake did with his assistant, but Heather was mollified by the news that Sam would soon be released. As midnight approached, Agent Russell sent Jake and Pam back to their respective hotels, with a friendly warning that he'd be calling on them tomorrow—early—for more information.

Any hope of a stealthy return to his room and collapsing into bed was dashed when Jake arrived at the hotel. He had just stepped out of the patrol car before he was mobbed by the anxious crew. Jake answered the rapid onslaught of overlapping questions as well as he could but soon lapsed into clipped responses of "I don't know" and "I'm not sure" until the tumult died down. Recognizing at last how exhausted he was, mentally and physically, the crew allowed him a reprieve. Jake made his escape but not before informing them all to take the morning off. They might be out later in the day, but he'd let them know for sure tomorrow.

The throbbing of his injured foot woke him moments before the shrill ring of the hotel phone echoed across the room. A quick squint at the clock showed that he had slept for nearly nine hours, but it didn't feel like it. Cursing, Jake staggered over to the desk and answered with a gruff "Hello?".

"Good, you're awake," Agent Russell said. Jake was tempted to argue but couldn't gather the energy.

"Mmm."

"I'll be finishing with Deputy Hauser soon, then I'll need to talk to you. One of my agents will be there in fifteen minutes to collect you."

"Mmm . . . fine." Jake's befogged thoughts were focused on locating the correct button to start the in-room coffee maker.

Once he realized that he was listening to the dial tone, Jake placed the phone back on the receiver and scanned the room for his cell phone. He spotted it on the floor near his discarded trousers. Two new text messages were indicated on the screen.

The most recent was from Heather, asking about their plans for the day. The second was from Pam, sent over an hour prior. "U OK? Meeting with Agent R in a few minutes. Wish me luck. VERY nervous . . . LUV U." Jake raised his finger to type out a response when he noticed that her profile photo had a red circle beside it, showing that her phone was turned off. Probably still with Agent Russell, he thought. He jumped up from the bed, now very much aware that he had less than fifteen minutes before the car would arrive for his own meeting.

Jake sent a quick text to Heather, asking her to meet him outside in ten minutes. He gulped down some bitter coffee as he dashed into the shower. After the fastest shower on record, in his estimation, Jake was dressed and ready to go with almost thirty seconds to spare. He opened his door to find Heather and Michelle waiting anxiously outside.

"Finally," Heather snapped. "So, what's the plan? Are we going to pick up Sam first or . . ."

"Good morning to you, too," Jake said, ignoring the barrage of questions. He noticed Al standing a few feet away, looking pensive. "Agent Russell wants to meet with me."

"When?"

"Now, more or less." He pointed to the dark-colored sedan with government plates that had just pulled into the lot. "Everything will be figured out by the time I get back."

"How long will you be gone?" Michelle asked.

"Not sure." The driver, a grim-faced young man in a dark suit, stepped out of the car, glanced at Jake, and then pointed to his wristwatch.

"What do you want us to do in the meantime?"

Jake thought for a moment. "As soon as you're ready, head out to the site. Make sure everything is secure in the shed, and then start packing up all the bone and artifact boxes that you can fit in the University van. Keep all the paperwork here, though. If Agent Russell is cool with it, we'll send Curt and Rob back to town with a load later today."

Heather nodded. "What about the rest of us?"

The agent cleared his throat. Jake raised his hand as he double-checked that his door was locked.

"After that, just continue with whatever units are open and try to finish as much as you can. Don't open any new areas, just in case."

"That won't be a problem. There's not much left to open anyway."

"But what about Sam?" Al asked, glancing with suspicion at the agent, who was now tapping his fingers on the roof of the car.

"I'll let you know as soon as I find out," Jake said, walking toward the waiting vehicle. "Don't worry, I think the worst is all behind us now."

CHAPTER 49

"SHE YELLED AT HIM TO FREEZE, but Eric kept moving. He had his gun raised to shoot when she shot him."

Agent Russell leaned forward in his chair, eyes locked on Jake. "She told him to freeze. Those were her exact words?"

Jake was confused. "Yeah, I guess. I wasn't thinking about it at the time."

"Are you certain she didn't say, 'Police, freeze!'?" Agent Russell nodded slowly as he spoke. "Remember, you weren't focusing on what she said at the time."

"Yes, I remember now," Jake said. "Pam identified herself as the police and told him to freeze. He turned toward her, gun at his shoulder, and she shot him in self-defense."

Agent Russell smiled as he entered the information into his notebook. "Fine. That corresponds with my statement from Deputy Hauser." He shifted some of the documents spread out in front of him, then added some additional notes while Jake waited for him to continue. Their meeting was now into its second hour, and Jake's mind was starting to fog from the repeating pattern of questions-responses-notes-more questions. He shifted in the uncomfortable plastic chair, wincing as he massaged his leg.

"How's the foot?"

"Fine. I've had worse," Jake said. It stung a bit more than Jake let on, but he blamed that on the haphazard bandaging he had done while rushing to get ready. Agent Russell didn't look up, instead focusing on his paperwork.

Jake stole a glance at the vintage wall clock mounted on an adjacent wall. The Bureau had commandeered a dozen offices and meeting rooms in the Scenic municipal building following the shooting, including the conference room in which he now sat. The table in front of Agent Russell was awash with maps, photos, and paperwork. It was only a bit more organized than Jake's own office back at Wisconsin State University, which reminded him that he needed to notify his department head about their recent troubles. Professor Chang had supported him during the Wardell affair, but he wasn't sure how she'd react to yet another incident.

There was a light tap at the door, and Nora entered with a pot of coffee and a plate of muffins. The receptionist smiled at Jake, still bewildered by the flurry of activity after the Wisconsin Bureau of Investigation agents arrived. Both men refilled their mugs, and Jake took an extra muffin, grateful for the first food he had all morning. She left a few moments later.

"It shouldn't be much longer," Agent Russell said, his attention once again focused on his paperwork. "Anything you'd like to add to your statement? Any questions?"

Jake sipped his coffee, giving it some thought. "Nothing I can think of, I guess. I do appreciate how quick you arrived last night."

"It was fortunate that I was nearby, but we did have a number of agents on stand-by, ready to move it if necessary."

"Why was that?"

"Well, there's been a major increase in drug trafficking in the area, tied to some spikes around the Twin Cities. The Bureau had a pretty solid line on some of the locals involved. Our next step was to locate the processing facility and identify the ringleaders."

"Which we stumbled onto yesterday."

"Right. And Matt Walker blundered into it earlier, leading to his death." Agent Russell leaned back in his chair, in the mood to chat. "We found some papers under a floorboard in the trailer that will tie in some additional suspects, and my agents are executing search warrants on Eric's residence as we speak."

"Sounds like a big operation. I wouldn't think Eric could handle all that himself."

"He couldn't," Agent Russell said. "He was just a small cog in the machine. But what we uncover should lead us farther up the food chain."

Jake nodded, and then took another bite of his muffin. "So, what about Sam? When can we get him out of jail?"

"It's already underway. Two of my agents corralled the judge early this morning, who reversed his previous orders 'in light of new evidence' and signed the forms for his release."

"Will the sheriff comply? I mean, she hasn't been all that helpful in the past."

"Two part-time deputies we had our eyes on were implicated by evidence found in Eric's trailer and have been placed under arrest. Based on that, I was able to convince the Scenic authorities to stay clear. If they impeded our investigation, in any way, I told them we'd put the town government into receivership and the state would take charge."

"Can you really do that?"

Agent Russell tilted his head, a sly smile on his face. "Probably not, but they're not going to take the chance. To make sure they played ball, I had Keith tell them that a special codicil allows the Bureau to take command of local governments in time of crisis, so that was enough to keep them quiet. Remember that, Professor. A good threat can go a long way, especially if people have something to hide."

Jake found that remark a bit unsettling. "Can I go get Sam, then, once we've finished here?"

"Keith is with him now. Sam will need to provide statements to my agents regarding his knowledge of past events, his arrest, and his treatment while incarcerated. Your friend will have a pretty substantial civil suit against Scenic when this is all over."

"I'm sure he's more interested in getting back to Ghost Bog, and then leaving Scenic for good."

"Yeah, he did mention getting back out to your site as soon as possible, in somewhat colorful language. I'll text Keith about driving him back to the hotel, and then out to your dig later today."

Agent Russell paused, reaching across his makeshift desk to a stray folder at the far edge. He pulled it over, glanced inside, and turned his attention back to Jake.

"On an unrelated topic, have you made any progress with the John Doe?"

Jake slumped back in his chair. "Sorry, not much. To be honest, it really hasn't been high on my list."

"I know. You've been too busy playing amateur detective. Again."

Agent Russell's demeanor suggested there wasn't any malice behind the remark. Working from memory, Jake summarized what little data he had gathered, noting the sex, age, and height of the individual and the presence of the skull fracture that likely led to his death.

"All in all, that sounds like a good amount of information, if you ask me."

"The watches we recovered might prove more definitive, but they are in pretty bad shape." Jake recapped what he and Pam had learned about the Scenic watches. Agent Russell listened with interest but didn't appear overly enthused.

"You don't have an idea of when this event occurred, do you?"

"Not yet. The first watch, the one he was wearing, has the initials CB or GB. Maybe CR or GR. The graduation year is definitely 1990, so we have a *terminus post quem* of 1990.

"Excuse me?"

"Sorry, archaeology jargon. It means the earliest date something could have ended up in the ground."

"I see. You know the burial occurred no earlier than 1990, assuming John Doe got his watch at graduation in late spring."

"Right. But we don't know how long after his graduation his death occurred. Six months, one year, but likely not more than that, based on the estimated age of the skeleton," Jake said. "Assuming he graduated at 18, he would have been born around 1971 or 1972."

"Interesting," Agent Russell said, rubbing his fingertips together. He suddenly looked very tired, as if the events of the last 24 hours had caught up to him. "And the second watch?"

Jake shook his head. "It's damaged, so we're having more trouble with it. The style of the 'S' suggests it is from about the same time period. I couldn't make out the initials, but I can work on it some more."

Agent Russell nodded, stifling a yawn. He seemed inclined to let the matter drop.

"I wonder if the two cases could be related somehow," Jake said. "You know, the killing of John Doe and Walker's murder."

Agent Russell frowned. "I don't see how. Walker trespassed onto Eric's growing operation while looking for his own archaeology site. Eric wasn't even alive when the first death took place."

"I don't mean that he was *directly* responsible. It's just an odd coincidence, with the bodies found in such close proximity."

"But three decades apart, give or take." Agent Russell shrugged his shoulders and began collecting his papers. "He probably didn't want to take the chance that someone might stumble across Walker near his property, so he moved him over by your dig. In case you haven't noticed, strangers aren't always well thought of in Scenic."

Jake had to admit that was true. Beneath that veneer of touristy hospitality, there was an undercurrent of tension that seemed to permeate the community. Before he could continue, Agent Russell stood up. The interview was over.

"I wouldn't look too much into it, Professor Caine. Just one of those things. That bog does have a bad reputation, you know."

CHAPTER 50

OUTSIDE THE MUNICIPAL BUILDING, JAKE PAUSED to zip up his jacket, shivering in response to the driving wind and biting cold. It was much colder than when he had arrived. He watched the beehive of activity with a bemused expression, as Bureau agents entered and departed with brisk efficiency. Few locals were visible, and Jake supposed most were hiding out in their offices, attempting to stay clear of the madness.

At the end of their meeting, Agent Russell had offered Jake the use of a Bureau car and driver to return him to the hotel or take him out to the dig, at his convenience. Jake demurred, at first, mentioning that he had some calls to make, but Agent Russell pressed a card into his hand with a name and number, telling him the offer was good for the next few days, should he change his mind.

His first call was to Heather, whom he assumed was tearing her hair out waiting for news. She answered on the first ring. As soon as he could get a word in, Jake summarized the results of his meeting and the slight delay in Sam's return. She wasn't thrilled but seemed to accept his explanation.

"Well, if it was me, I'd sue them for every penny they've got," Heather said. "It would serve them right. So, what do you want us to do with the rest of the day?"

"Is the van loaded?"

"Just about. Maybe another hour. We've been rechecking the box inventories while we pack, just so we don't lose anything during the move. Plus, the cold is slowing us down."

"Good thinking," Jake said. "As soon as they're ready, have Curt and Rob head back to WSU. I'll call the department to let them know they're on the way."

"It might be tough for them to get back, you know. There are snow flurries expected up here, but a big front is supposed to dump a load of snow south of us."

"Tell them to play it safe. If they have to stay home for a day or two, that's fine. We should be wrapping things up early next week, regardless." He paused, mentally sorting through additional tasks requiring attention. "Everyone else can work on finishing the open units, but if this cold keeps up, we may just wrap up early today."

"That might be for the best. If it stays like this the open ground is going to start freezing up."

"If Pam isn't too busy, ask her if she could drive into town and pick me up."

"She isn't here," Heather replied, somewhat smugly. "I figured she was with you."

"Huh. No, she isn't with me. I thought she'd head out to Ghost Bog as soon as she was done with Agent Russell."

"Do you want me to send someone, maybe Michelle?"

"Hmm. No, I need to make some calls first, now that I think about it. I'll get one of the Bureau guys to drive me out, since they offered."

"Suit yourself. See you later."

Jake checked his messages, expecting to see one from Pam, but nothing appeared on the screen. Her profile icon was still red, so calling her wasn't an option. He sent a short text, asking her to give him a ring as soon as she could.

He then called the Archaeology Department at Wisconsin State University and spoke with a curator about the incoming load of artifacts. Jake arranged for a temporary storage area in the lab and then texted the information to Heather, Curt, and Rob. That task completed, he called the University again, planning to speak with Professor Chang, the department chair, about their recent problems. He was not looking forward to this conversation.

Fortunately, Professor Chang wasn't available. Jake left a lengthy message, explaining the situation as best he could: The discovery of the two skeletons; Walker's intrusion and subsequent murder; Sam's arrest; Pam's arrival, the discovery of the meth lab, and the self-defense shooting of Eric Holcombe; and finally, Agent Russell and the Bureau's involvement. He rambled on occasion, overdoing it on some things while trying to smooth over other parts. In truth, the story didn't cast him in a very favorable light. Professor Chang had backed him up before, but would she maintain that level of commitment again? Repeated association with murder could hardly be good for the University's image. Jake knew he would have a lot of additional explaining to do once he got back to the University. Hopefully, it would be sufficient to keep him employed.

Jake was about to contact the Bureau agent about a ride when he paused, lost in thought. After reviewing everything that had happened, he was more convinced than ever that the two crimes were connected. The passage of time didn't matter. No one had thought the Wardell and Droessler killings were related, either.

Maybe Eric did plant Walker's body near the dig to implicate the archaeologists in the crime, but would he? He could have hidden the body somewhere—anywhere—in the forest. Walker's remains might not have been found for months, maybe longer, if they were buried elsewhere. After all, the John Doe from Ghost Bog was there for decades, undiscovered until the archaeologists came along. There had to be a connection. The first step in finding that connection was to identify John Doe.

Jake looked across the municipal parking lot to the Scenic Library, tucked away at the edge of the government offices. With a determined nod, he made a beeline for the library entrance.

"CAN I HELP YOU?"

The young woman behind the counter was inconsistent with Jake's expectation for a small-town library. She looked to be about Heather's age, with reddish-orange hair, cropped short, and dark blue mascara. Several piercings and at least one arm tattoo were evident, partly obscured by her Miskatonic University Literature Department sweatshirt. She looked more goth than librarian, but her greeting was pleasant.

"I'm doing some research on some local families and events, from the early 1990s," Jake said, trying to maintain an academic façade without going into too much detail.

She gave him a curious look. "You're one of the archaeologists, working out at Ghost Bog, right?" Jake nodded and introduced himself, and she continued. "Thought so. I saw your photo in the paper. I'm Mallory, by the way, but everyone calls me Mal. Does this have something to do with the ancient bison you found?"

"Not directly. I want to track down some people who may have been out there at one time, might know something about the history of the property. The Emersons gave me a list of names to track down."

Mal nodded. "Well, we have copies of the *Scenic Sentinel* on microfilm, but the index only covers the late 1880s into the 1930s. The *Scenic Sentinel* office may have an index themselves, but I don't think it is available online. I could call over there . . ."

"No, that isn't necessary," Jake said. "What about high school yearbooks? I could use those to track down the full names of the people I'm interested in."

"Those we do have," Mal said. She guided Jake across the reading area, occupied at present by a small number of older local residents perusing various magazines, to a series of shelves against the far wall. "All the yearbooks are here in the Reference section, except for the older pre-war volumes. Most of those are over at the Historical Society. Let me know if you need anything else, okay?"

Jake thanked Mal for her help and then found the shelf with

the years he sought. He pulled seven volumes, bracketing the late 1980s through the mid 1990s. From the dust and stiff spines, Jake surmised that no one had looked at these books in quite some time.

Setting himself at a nearby table, Jake spread out the books and pulled three sheets of paper from his backpack. On the first sheet, he wrote down the names of every male with the initials CB, GB, CR, and GR, along with the year they graduated. On the second sheet, he listed all males with the initials CH and GH. The third sheet contained the names of any boys with initials similar to those he sought, such as CK or GK, CA or GA, and CP and GP. The classes were small, so it was easy to search each senior class and record the names that fit into each group. Each sheet contained about a dozen names.

With that initial step completed, Jake began tracking down the names listed on the sheets using online phone records. He found several boys—now men, he corrected—of about the right age living in or near Scenic. A couple more were living in nearby cities and towns in northwestern Wisconsin, and about a half-dozen resided in the metro Twin Cities area. He also located a Scenic High School alumni page that included another six individuals living outside the Midwest, and two more who died after graduating. As each person was recognized, Jake crossed his name off the list.

After an hour of searching, Jake was left with seven names, four of which were on his first list. He recopied the list of "probable IDs" onto a new sheet of paper:

Carl Ballinger
George Barham
Cal Benton
Gerald Rogers

One name seemed more familiar than the others: George Barham. Jake opened the yearbook from George Barham's senior year and leafed through the candid group pictures of various clubs, activities, and events. George was present in many photos, mostly involving sports. That would fit with the skeletal analysis, Jake thought. Cal Benton appeared in some of the same photographs, too, suggesting he might fit the skeletal profile.

Many of the photos contained the same group of kids, over and over. Jake recognized some familiar faces, including Mayor Mike Greene, Peter Holcombe, Sheriff O'Neil, and several of the Scenic civic and business leaders who were present on the Ghost Bog tour. It looked like George Barham and Cal Benton were part of the old gang, too. Bit of an odd coincidence that so many current business and political leaders of Scenic were in the same graduating class.

Using his phone, Jake took photos of the senior portraits of all four individuals, as well as of the candid group shots in which Barham and Benton were present. Carl Ballinger and Gerald Rogers had kept low profiles, as few pictures of either boy appeared in their yearbooks. To be thorough, Jake also took photos of the three boys recorded on the second sheet.

A quick recheck of online phone records revealed no families named Barham or Benton in Scenic, or at least none with listed phone numbers. Maybe he would ask Harold and Vera Emerson if they knew anyone from either family.

Noticing the time, Jake decided he had better finish his work and contact the crew before heading over to join them. Sam was probably out at the site by now, and Jake's absence wouldn't improve his mood. He was a bit surprised that Sam hadn't called already, trying to track him down.

Jake placed the yearbooks on a small cart to be shelved and walked to the front desk to thank Mal for her assistance. As he neared, his phone let out an angry buzz that seemed to echo across the room. Avoiding the dirty looks from the patrons seated nearby, Jake waved to the librarian and whispered a quick thank you as he rushed for the lobby door.

"Hello?"

"Hi, Jake. This is Keith Emerson. Did I catch you in the middle of something? You sound out of breath."

"No, no. Just dashing out of the library." Jake paused to push the door closed behind him, to block out his conversation. "What can I do for you? Is Sam ready to head back out to the site? Because of the cold we're going to wrap up early and —"

"That's why I'm calling. About Sam, I mean. He, well, um, Sam is in the hospital."

CHAPTER 51

"WHAT HAPPENED?" JAKE YELLED INTO HIS phone, causing a few gray-topped heads to pop up inside the library. He could almost feel the tsk-tsk sounds pointed in his direction, but under the circumstances he didn't care.

"He wasn't feeling good, well, he didn't look too good," Keith said. "We decided it would be best if he went to the hospital for a once-over."

"What do you mean, he didn't look good? Don't play around with me."

"It's nothing serious. Well, probably nothing. The doctors are going to run some more tests, you know, to be sure."

Jake exhaled, forcing himself to relax. "Look, Keith, just tell me what happened, from the beginning."

"We were finishing the deposition, and Sam's cough started getting worse. I mean, he had been coughing all morning, but by then it was getting pretty harsh . . ."

"Coughing, got worse. Can you be more specific?"

"Sorry. He looked pale throughout the deposition, but I figured it was from being locked up for so long. Anyway, he had this dry raspy cough that he couldn't seem to shake. Then he started coughing up blood."

Jake shuddered. Not a good sign, under any circumstances.

"It wasn't a lot of blood, not really," Keith said. "Just some spatters on his handkerchief. But still, something you don't want to ignore."

"Right."

"And his breathing seemed labored to me. I called Frank and he brought in the paramedics. They didn't think it was too serious but suggested that he get checked out at the hospital, just in case. You know, because of his age."

"That makes sense. So, then . . ."

"Sam wasn't thrilled with the idea at first, but he started coughing again, and then he looked a little spooked. He agreed, and Frank got him shuttled over there quick before he could change his mind. I think it was just after your interview ended."

Keith paused, and Jake heard a noise in the background. He was about to interject when Keith spoke again.

"I'm at the hospital now. Been here for over an hour."

"You've been there over an hour and this is the first I'm hearing about it? Are you kidding me?"

"I'm sorry. But I was waiting to hear from the doctor, you know, before I did anything."

Jake was attempting, with little success, to zip up his jacket with one hand while simultaneously juggling his phone and backpack. "Okay, okay. I'm heading over there right now."

"That might not work. The doctor said it could just be a cold, maybe a chest infection, aggravated by exhaustion. She ran a bunch of tests and then gave him a sedative so he could rest. He's kind of out of it right now."

"I understand, but I'm still coming over." Jake paused to fish the Agent Russell's "free ride" card from his pocket. "I want to talk to the doctor, even if Sam is asleep. And I can take over so you can head home or back to work."

"That's okay. I don't mind hanging around. I still feel bad about mentioning the site to Walker, so maybe I can make it up to you guys this way."

"I understand. It's not necessary, but I won't turn down any help," Jake said as he started to relax. Sam probably just picked up a virus. They'll just keep him overnight, let him out tomorrow, and by next week they would all be back home. "I'm going to make a few calls and I'll be there soon."

After Keith hung up, Jake dialed the number and arranged for transport to the Scenic Hospital. He had a few minutes, so he rang Heather.

"Hey, boss. Are you still planning to come out? The snow flurries are getting worse, and the wind is freezing."

"I know. Go ahead and close up for the day."

"What about Sam? Is he going to want to see the site before we close up?"

"That's the reason I'm calling. I heard from Keith and Sam is over at Scenic Hospital."

It was several minutes before Jake could interject. He described Sam's cough, leaving out the details. "It sounds like he picked up a bug, so to play it safe they want to run some tests and keep him overnight."

"Ha! As if we can trust anyone in this weirdo town!"

"I'm going over there right now, so I should have more information soon."

"I want to come, too. We can all be there in about twenty minutes . . ."

"No, there's no need for a mob scene at the hospital," Jake said, cutting off her protest. "Let me talk to the doctors and see what they say, and then we can plan out our strategy. I don't even know what the visiting hours are over there."

Heather grumbled something that Jake couldn't make out. After a drawn-out sigh, she spoke. "Fine. But let me know right away, or I swear I'm coming over."

"Agreed. Just get everyone back to the hotel and let them know what's going on. I'll call you within the hour, no matter what."

The Bureau agent drove Jake to the Scenic Hospital, and after a short delay at the registration desk, Jake located Sam's room. As

Keith had predicted, Sam was asleep, but Keith and the doctor were conversing in a nearby waiting area. The doctor greeted Jake and explained the situation. Her prognosis was exhaustion, aggravated by his recent visit to the Scenic jail, topped off with a nasty cold. Bronchitis was a possibility but unlikely. She recommended that Sam stay in the hospital for a day or two, and if he did have a bacterial infection, they could put him on a course of antibiotics before his release.

Jake didn't imagine Sam would be too keen to remain away from the site any longer than necessary, but as the fieldwork was wrapping up he hoped Sam would be willing to listen to the doctor. He spoke with Keith after the doctor left, and then accompanied him to the cafeteria where they shared some coffee and a late lunch.

Jake called Heather and informed her of the situation. She was happy to hear that his illness was minor, but likewise doubted that Sam would be willing to sit out any of the remaining days at Ghost Bog. With Sam asleep, Jake convinced her not to drive over, but agreed that she and the crew could take turns staying with Sam during the rest of his stay. Heather promised to have a schedule ready by the time Jake was back at the motel and planned to bring maps and photos to bring Sam up to speed.

The next few hours dragged by. Jake and Keith made small talk in the waiting area, with most of the conversation revolving around the recent finds at the site. Very little was said about Walker's murder or the encounter with Eric Holcombe. Sam woke just before visiting hours ended but was still quite groggy. He asked a few questions about the excavation but seemed confused, so Jake kept his answers simple. A bedraggled nurse ejected them from the room a short time later, and Jake promised to give Sam a full report in the morning.

Keith dropped Jake off at his hotel, and which point he was set upon by Heather, Michelle, Susan, and Al. After a brief recap of the afternoon's events, they worked out a schedule so that Heather, Michelle, and Al would take turns sitting with Sam throughout the day, until he was released. The other two would accompany Jake to the site, where he would supervise the final stages of fieldwork.

"This works for me," Heather said, glancing at the visitation scheduled penciled in her notebook. "Curt texted just before you got here. They made it to the University without any problems, but it was too late to unload. They're going to do that tomorrow and drive back up on Saturday. If that's cool with you."

Jake nodded as he glanced over her shoulder at the schedule. "That sounds fine. Ask them to text when they're on their way. The rest of us can handle what we have left to do at Ghost Bog."

He frowned, noticing a name missing on the schedule. Jake turned to Susan, standing mutely at the edge of the group. "Susan, what about you? Do you want to take a spot at the hospital tomorrow?"

The group fell silent. Michelle's eyes went wide, and Al shook her head. Heather turned away, texting into her phone.

"I, I'm not feeling all that well," Susan said, sniffling and clearing her throat. "I think I'm coming down with something. It might be best if I stay clear of the hospital. For now, at least."

"That makes sense," Jake said, sensing her discomfort at seeing Sam again. "No sense risking anyone's health. I'm sure he'll be on the mend soon."

Susan nodded. She shivered a bit as a gust of cold air swirled around the parking lot. "Do you think . . . I mean, would it be alright if I stayed behind tomorrow? Rather than go out to the site? I don't want this cold to get any worse."

"I understand. No problem. The rest of us can handle things until you're feeling better, and Curt and Rob will be back Saturday."

"And there's Pam, too." Michelle added.

"If she bothers to show up," Heather said peevishly. "Wasn't there at all today."

CHAPTER 52

WHAT HAD HAPPENED TO PAM? Sitting on his bed, Jake sipped rye whisky and water from a plastic cup and tried to decompress after the stressful events of the last twenty-four hours.

Again, he checked his phone messages. No messages from Pam, and his mood sank even further. Her profile icon still showed the same harsh red color. The annoying crimson glow seemed to haunt his vision as he closed his eyes and rubbed the bridge of his nose.

Where could she be? It wasn't like her to vanish, not without a call or text. And why wasn't she answering her phone? Jake thought about sending yet another message, then decided against it. What was the point?

Jake glanced at the open bottle, which he had kept hidden as a surprise for Sam, to celebrate the end of a successful excavation. Didn't seem as important now, with Sam in the hospital and multiple dead bodies tied to the Ghost Bog dig. They had discovered and excavated an amazing site, almost unique in Midwest archaeology, but he was as anxious and depressed as he had ever been.

Pam's vanishing act had been the final straw. Given everything that happened, should he be worried? Maybe it was something minor, a glitch with her phone or just part of the spotty service in the area. He checked his phone again. Nothing.

Did something happen to her? Eric was dead. He was probably the one behind the break-in at the site, the incident with the black truck, and their other troubles. But Jake couldn't picture him acting alone. Maybe his accomplices were involved, tracking them down to exact revenge.

Jake shook his head. Unlikely. Guess he'd been watching too many crime shows on TV lately. If they were smart, Eric's pals were laying low or had scattered to avoid Agent Russell and his troops. Still, if they weren't that smart . . .

Walking to the window, Jake pushed aside the curtain and peered through the blinds into the darkness. A few scattered snowflakes were visible, dancing in the breeze before settling to the ground in the parking lot. He didn't know what he expected to see—maybe a lurking stranger in a black hat and trench coat? Should he be concerned? He could call Agent Russell, but what did he expect him to do? As far as the Bureau was concerned, the main event was over and now it was just a matter of cleaning up.

Jake considered driving over to Pam's hotel, but the girls had taken the Lewis and Clark Museum van to go to dinner, with plans to pick up some gifts for Sam afterward. Curt and Rob had the Wisconsin State University van. He thought about borrowing Curt's car, using the emergency key he left behind, but wasn't sure the situation warranted it. Plus, the roads were a bit of a mess and Jake wasn't feeling all that sure of himself.

With a sigh, he sat back down on the bed and reached for his phone. Jake scrolled through the contact list for Agent Russell's number when his gaze landed on the hotel phone on the side table. It then dawned on him to call Pam's hotel rather than her cell phone. The front desk answered on the second ring and rang her room. No answer.

Stomach in his throat, Jake asked to leave a message, imploring Pam to call him back as soon as possible, regardless of the time.

His mind raced through a hundred different scenarios of Pam in danger. He took a final sip of his drink, now resolved to call Agent Russell and demand action.

Jake had entered two numbers when his phone buzzed, and it was only with the greatest of effort that he didn't fling it across the room like a venomous snake.

"Hi, hon," Pam said. It was the sweetest, most welcome sound Jake could imagine. He almost sobbed with relief but soon gained his composure.

"Hi yourself," Jake said, voice cracking. "Been trying to get ahold of you for quite a while. Everything okay?"

"Yeah, I'm doing good now. I'm sorry I didn't get back to you sooner. I shut my phone off before my interview and didn't realize I never turned it back on. I guess I was more frazzled than I thought."

"It's okay," Jake said. "It's been one heck of a day. For all of us."

"I crashed when I got back and only woke up a little while ago," she explained. "I was getting out of the shower when the room phone rang. When I checked the message, I realized my phone had been off all this time."

"I was getting worried. A little, at least."

"Don't worry, I can take care of myself," Pam said. "But I do appreciate the thought. I think," she said in a playful tone, "someone is falling for me pretty hard."

"I know better than to argue with you. But I am relieved you're okay."

"So, how did you make out with Russell? Was Sam happy to be back out at the site?"

With a heavy sigh, Jake summarized the results of his day. Pam interrupted with questions a few times, but for the most part listened with rapt attention until he finished.

"Wow, you must be exhausted. But it doesn't sound like Sam's illness is anything serious. He should be released in a day or two."

"That's what I'm hoping. Just in time to wrap things up at Ghost Bog," Jake said, stifling a yawn as he glanced at the alarm clock.

"Are you going to come out tomorrow?"

There was a slight pause. "I think I'm going to stay in tomorrow, if that's okay. To be honest, I'm worn out. I'm going to need a vacation to recover from this vacation."

"I understand. We're about done anyway, so we'll be fine."

"What do you plan to do with the info you collected on John Doe? Some of the students you couldn't track down sound like viable prospects."

"I don't know. Turn it all over to Agent Russell, I guess, when I give him the bones and the watches."

"Are you sure that's a good idea? I mean, he doesn't seem all that interested in following up on the crime. It might just get filed away and forgotten about."

"I won't be up here much longer. Not enough time to follow up on anything, at least not anything substantial. Plus, it's not really my responsibility."

"Seems to me we've had this conversation before. At least keep copies of everything for yourself. Might be something we need later on."

"We?"

"Sure. You're not getting rid of me that easy. Our time together has been the best part of this whole trip."

"Are you heading back to Donovan soon?"

"Yeah, afraid so. My vacation days are about spent. I'll come out for a few hours on Saturday, just to wrap things up and say good-bye to Michelle, Al, and the guys. And Sam, of course."

"Sure," Jake said. "It was great having you here. You were a lot of help . . ."

"Is that all? Just another shovel bum, slaving away in the cold, frozen dirt?"

"Hardly, and you know it." Jake paused, recalling some of the problems in this previous long-distance relationship with Amanda. "I suppose we'll have some things to work out, you know, about the future."

"You've got that right, Professor. This isn't some holiday romance, you know."

"Never thought otherwise. We can discuss the details once we're settled back home."

"We could get started on that tomorrow night, if you're interested," Pam said. "After you finish for the day, get cleaned up and then grab a pizza, maybe some salads, and bring them over for dinner. I'll be in the mood for company by then. Oh, a bottle of nice wine might be a good touch. Maybe two bottles, now that I think about it."

Jake agreed to her brilliant suggestion, and after some additional flirtatious small talk, hung and up and prepared to turn in. Yawning, he made a mental note to include a dozen roses to his shopping list. Maybe two dozen, after giving it some further thought.

CHAPTER 53

"Q UIET OUT HERE TODAY," JAKE SAID, as he scraped the last bit of loose soil from the floor of his unit.

"Not to be mean, but without Heather around, that's not a surprise," Al said, dumping some soil into a nearby screen. Michelle, giggling, began kneading the moist dirt through the metal mesh.

"Looks like this unit is played out. Guess I'll call this one."

The sun was shining down on the Ghost Bog dig, but there was still a chill in the air. Michelle and Al were working on one of the remaining units along the edge of the excavation area. Jake was nearby, removing the last tiny pieces of bison bone from another square.

"Well, I'm sure Sam appreciates her company today," Jake said. He sat on an overturned pail and began to complete the rest of his unit paperwork. "I hope she doesn't get him too worked up. There's not going to be much left for Sam to do when he gets out here."

"How many more days left, do you think?" Michelle said.

"With the guys back this afternoon, we should be able to finish sometime tomorrow. It'll take a day or two to clean up and pack away all the equipment and artifacts. Might send one van load back on Sunday. I'll let Harold know he can start backfilling soon."

"Do think you'll need Susan for any of that?" Al asked, resting her arms on her shovel. "I mean, I'm not saying she can't stay, but . . . well, she was tossing and turning a lot last night. Lots of sniffling. I figured it was her cold, but I think she was crying, too."

Jake nodded. "I think we could spare her," he said. "I'll mention it to her this afternoon. She might have to arrange a ride . . ."

"She was talking to her husband yesterday," Al said. "I think she's already planning to have him come and pick her up. I don't think she wants to ride all the way back to the museum . . . with Sam."

Jake nodded. Her hidden involvement with Matt Walker, however unintended it may have been, would definitely set Sam off on a tirade. Best to break it to him slowly, with Susan far out of range.

"Heather was on a bit of a tear at dinner last night," Al said, resuming her work.

"It wasn't that bad, Jake," Michelle interjected. "Mostly about being glad to be out of here. I think she's ready to head home."

"It's more than that, if you ask me." Al turned to Jake. "Heather got it in her head that Sam was poisoned by the jail staff."

"She was just blowing off steam, that's all," Michelle said, rising to her friend's defense.

"Heather thinks the whole town has it in for us. They're going to take us out, one by one."

Jake rolled his eyes. "Can I assume large quantities of alcohol were involved?"

"Moderately large, yes," Al replied, smiling. "She may have been venting, but I picked up a few hostile looks from the bar crowd while we were there."

"I'll ask her to keep her conspiracy theories to herself from now on," Jake said, shaking his head. "I hope she doesn't say anything more. I'd hate for Sam's doctor to get wind of this."

"She's just been worried about Sam, that's all," Michelle offered. "We all were. She'll be fine once she spends some time with Sam, sees that he's doing okay."

The crunch of tires on gravel cut through their conversation.

Jake looked up, thinking that perhaps Pam had changed her mind and decided to join them. But the dark blue sedan was not her sporty vintage Camaro, and the slim man who exited the vehicle was definitely not a shapely blonde police officer.

PETER HOLCOMBE WAS ABOUT THE LAST person Jake had expected to see at Ghost Bog, given all that had happened in the past few days. He was uneasy, but Peter seemed as cordial as ever.

"Hello, Professor. You've made great progress here. And just in time, I think. Winter is right around the corner."

"Un, hello, Peter. Thanks. It was a big job but we're just about finished. Not much time left."

Peter nodded as glanced around the excavation area. Jake noticed the old-fashioned black mourning band on his left arm.

"I..I'm very sorry about your son."

"Eric was always a wayward youth. Mixed up with the wrong crowd, and they led him astray."

"That's too bad."

"In all honesty, we've been estranged for years. I've been trying to reconnect with him for months—that night in the diner, for example, was another of my futile attempts to bond with the boy. I would plead my case, and Eric would roll his eyes and snort derisively. He thought he knew better."

"I imagine that was very stressful."

"Too little, too late, I'm afraid." Peter paused as he watched Al and Michelle working a few yards away. "Is your friend, the deputy, here?"

"No, she isn't. She, uh, had some things to deal with in town, so she decided to take the day off. Can't make her dig since she's a volunteer." The joke fell flat. Peter's cool demeanor, only days after the violent death of his son, was making Jake anxious.

"Professor, might we talk somewhere a bit more private?" He tilted his head toward the girls. "Won't take but a second."

"Sure, I guess. Maybe up the trail?"

"I'm not dressed for hiking," Peter said, with a somewhat condescending smile. "How about your storage facility? That would suit me fine."

Jake agreed, leading the way. Peter was acting a little peculiar, but he didn't appear angry or upset. Maybe he just wanted some closure.

"Eric showed considerable potential when he was a lad, but he got tied up with a bad element," Peter said as the pair stepped into the shed. It took a moment for their eyes to adjust to the dim interior light. "I'm certain someone else was behind this insane scheme to manufacture and sell drugs."

Jake nodded, but he was puzzled. In his brief conversation with Eric, it felt like Eric was responsible for the growing operation. Not a criminal mastermind by any means, but smart and sneaky enough to grow his own stash. But could he plan a murder?

"I hope the authorities will be able to track down his employers."

"Perhaps," Peter said, stepping off to one side, placing himself in partial shadow. "I endeavored to interest Eric in the sciences, history, geology, all of my favorite fields of study, but he never had any aptitude for it."

Another incongruity. "Eric had no knowledge about archaeology or paleontology, I suppose?"

"Ho, ho! No, not a wit. Decidedly not. I guess a perchance for natural history and sciences skips a generation."

"Huh. Kind of surprising that he was able to fabricate a story with sufficient detail to entice Matt Walker to come out. From what his assistants said, the description he gave of the site was quite elaborate. A very cunning trap."

Peter did not respond. He slid his hands into the pockets of his jacket.

"I think you're right, Peter. Eric was led astray, just a pawn for someone else. I think the police should start looking for . . ."

Peter casually withdrew his left hand, holding a small, shiny automatic pistol.

"No sudden movements, if you please, Professor Caine."

CHAPTER 54

J AKE FROWNED AT PETER. "I AM sorry about what happened to your son. Threatening me isn't going to solve anything."

Peter chuckled. "I'm quite unconcerned about Eric's demise. To be honest, it makes things a bit easier for me in the long run. I'll need to acquire some new help, but with luck I'll be able to line up someone with more on the ball, so to speak."

"You set this up, didn't you?" Jake asked, the pieces falling into place. "With your background, you'd know exactly what to tell Walker in order to set him up! And enough to tempt Sam into driving around all night looking for a collector who didn't exist."

"Correct. Your temperamental partner's behavior neatly filled in the minor gaps in my plan. For someone who complains so much about 'public interference' he doesn't mind talking and talking once you get him started."

"But why?"

"Doctor Walker came to me, in my capacity as the county registrar, with his maps, all enthused about his planned survey. After studying the locations, I realized the arrogant fool would blunder right into my facility. Obviously, I couldn't let that happen."

"So, you were in it together."

"In truth, Eric was more of a junior partner in my operation, dealing with the heavy lifting and such. My expertise centered on planning, and of course handling the commercial end of the enterprise."

"Of course."

"Having him on guard duty, while for the most part unnecessary, did have the benefit of keeping him from getting in trouble in town."

Jake couldn't stop staring at the gun, glinting in the low light. "Shooting me isn't going to bring him back."

Peter shook his head. "You misunderstand, Professor Caine. This has nothing to do with Eric. I'm here for the watch."

"Huh? The watch from the skeleton?"

"The second watch, Caine. The second watch."

"How do you know about—?"

"One of your crew mentioned its discovery while I was nearby. I knew immediately it was mine."

"Yours?"

"Yes. Lost in the struggle with George. I always suspected I lost it that night, but never imagined it would turn up." Peter held up his right arm, and even in the low light Jake could see a faded, jagged scar along the inner side of his wrist. "It was simple enough to purchase a replacement."

"George. George Barham, I presume?"

"Very good. I thought you might be a bit closer to the truth than you let on. Been doing a bit of investigating on your own, have you?"

"A little," Jake admitted, realizing he wasn't helping his situation. "Haven't gotten anywhere beyond a cursory look at the bones."

Peter clucked his tongue, not fooled by Jake's efforts. "A futile effort, but unnecessary at this point. The watch, please. Now."

Jake started to move through the boxes on a nearby table. It wouldn't help matters if Peter realized that both watches, the human remains, and all his notes were locked in the footlocker back in his hotel room.

"Mind telling me what happened?" Jake scanned the shadows for anything that might serve as a weapon, but he didn't hold out much hope.

"I don't see why not, since this never took place," Peter said, leaning back against the doorframe. "A story as old as time, two young men fighting over the affections of a young lady. George was an athlete and a bully, using his brute strength to get what he wanted. I was the brain in our clique. I tutored Emilia for four years, and we were quite fond of each other. George didn't like that situation and forced his way into Emilia's heart. The summer after graduation, as we all made our plans for the future, I arranged a meeting at Ghost Bog with George so that we might . . . discuss . . . our difficulties. He grew violent, naturally, and overpowered me after a brief struggle. That's when he tore off my watch. As luck would have it, he threw me down next to a lead pipe I had secreted in that spot before his arrival. As he stomped off, I brought the pipe down hard on his fat head, and that was that."

Jake was half-listening, more intent on figuring a way out of the situation. Soon, Peter would realize that Jake was wasting time. And then he might realize that the watch wasn't there. "Sounds like you had it all planned out. I'm surprised no one realized he was missing."

"After making sure the body was well buried, I drove his car to the Twin Cities, left it in a bad part of town, and took the bus back. Then out went the letters."

"Letters?"

"Oh yes, all beautifully forged and incredibly caustic to his friends and family. George, you see, had decided to strike out on his own and see the world. He was cutting his ties to the rustic backwater of Scenic and didn't want anything to do with any of them from that point forward. His note to Emilia was particularly hurtful."

"Very clever," Jake said. His hand brushed against an unused can of mosquito repellant, put aside once the cold weather arrived.

It might work like pepper spray, he thought, but Peter might still shoot him during the struggle.

"It was, it really was. His family disowned him, and Emilia was heartbroken. Fortunately, I was there to pick up the pieces."

"Hmm. Wait—you said this 'never took place.' What do you mean?"

"It's very simple, Professor. Oh, and keep your hands clear of that hatchet, if you don't mind."

Jake pulled one hand back from the hatchet while simultaneously pulling the insect spray closer with the other hand.

"As I was saying. Once I have the watch, I'm going to dispose of it for good. You won't say a word. No one will believe you anyway."

"They won't?" Jake shifted so that the can was now firmly in his grasp but hidden from Peter's view. He was running out of small boxes to examine. Soon, Peter would realize that the watch wasn't there.

"Without the watch, there's nothing to tie me to George Barham's death. You never told Sheriff O'Neil about the second watch, so they'll think you made it all up. Angry with me about the actions of my poor misguided boy, shot by your girlfriend while trespassing. No one will believe kindly old Peter, dedicated public servant and widower, now bereft of any family thanks to the machinations of outsiders, had anything to do with any of this."

"How do you know that I haven't told the sheriff about the second watch?" Jake wasn't really interested in his reply but felt the need to keep Peter talking. He wasn't sure how Peter would react once he knew the watch was missing. Would he force Jake to go back to the hotel? Michelle and Al were in potential danger, too, and he couldn't let anything happen to them. He would have to act soon.

"You forget what a small community Scenic is, Professor. We work in close quarters, and I often check the sheriff's messages. And I have access to all her files. Grace may not be the finest peace officer in the world, but she is rather meticulous when it comes to her notes."

Jake turned, about to respond, when a subtle movement caught his eye. Peter noticed it as well.

Gypsy stood just outside the doorway, head cocked, studying the scene within. Focusing on Peter, the dog let out a low growl but did not advance.

Apprehension clouded Peter's face as his eyes darted between Jake and Gypsy, but he kept the gun trained on Jake. Jake slid his hand toward the top of the can, feeling blindly for the spray trigger.

Shadow suddenly crashed against the door, howling as he joined his sister. In the confusion, Peter lost his composure. He started to swing the gun away from Jake and toward the dogs, unsure of the greater threat.

Jake stepped forward and blasted the noxious spray into Peter's eyes. His glasses provided little protection from the onslaught; he began screaming and clawing at his face in a vain effort to gain some relief.

Gypsy and Shadow let out a chorus of barks and howls, snapping at Peter's legs as he tried to avoid the poisonous stream. In the chaos, the gun dropped to the floor. Jake kicked the weapon aside. He moved closer to Peter, maintaining the pressure, as his finger grew numb on the trigger.

Futilely attempting to shield his eyes with his arm, Peter broke away and staggered through the doorway. The spray can sputtered and spit as it emptied, but the beagles maintained their assault on Peter's legs. The besieged man stumbled three, maybe four, steps before he collapsed into the arms of Agent Russell.

CHAPTER 55

"**Y**OU'RE GOING TO SPOIL THOSE DOGS, feeding them salmon like that," Sam said, shaking his head.

"They've earned it," Jake said. "Besides, it's just some leftovers from dinner last night."

Jake didn't dare tell him that he had ordered the fish specifically for Gypsy and Shadow. Only Pam knew about that, and she was sworn to secrecy. Well, bribed to keep quiet, to be honest.

"Harold and Vera will never get them back on dry dog chow after this."

"Are you pretty much packed?"

"Yeah. I want to take some more photos of the site area before Harold starts to backfill, and then we're going to head out. Going to be a long haul, but if Al and I split the driving it won't be too bad."

Jake nodded, tossing the last bits of fish to the ecstatic beagles. He glanced across the meadow, watching as Harold warmed up the backhoe. "He should have most of it done today, but Michelle and I will check the backfill in the morning before we drive back to the University."

"Heather's riding back with the guys?"

"Yes. Our van is packed to the brim. There's more room in Curt's car, and I think she's in a hurry to get home anyway." Jake paused, looking around the bog as the crew finished closing down the site. Al and Pam were saying their goodbyes to the rest of the crew.

"I'm thinking of asking Al is she'd like to transfer to the Zooarchaeology Division on a permanent basis," Sam said. "She'd need some training to get up to speed, but I think she has potential."

"I agree, I think she'd be a perfect fit. Did you get a chance to talk to Susan before she left?"

"No. Not sure what I'd say, to be honest. I guess I understand where she's coming from, with money worries and all that, but I'm not sure I can let it go."

"It's a tough spot. Maybe give it some time."

Sam kicked at the frost-covered soil. "Maybe. I'm thinking, just thinking at this point, that I might see if she'd want to switch to another lab, maybe in the Zoology or Bioarchaeology sections. She could stay on at the museum but not have to put up with me. Might be easier for her to lock onto something with more job security. Hell, I don't know. Might make things easier all the way around."

Jake nodded. It was a difficult situation, with no clear way out. He decided to change the subject. "We got a lot accomplished here, that's for sure. Going to take years to analyze it all."

"That's a fact, Jake. Definitely a feather in our caps," Sam said, smiling. "Despite it all. And I must admit, having Pam here did help."

"Did I hear my name?" Pam asked, walking over to join them.

"Hey, Pam. Done saying your goodbyes?"

"Just about. Glad to see you up and around, Sam."

Sam grinned. "And not stuck behind prison bars, right?" He laughed, then coughed. "Guess I have you to thank for that. And for all your help on the dig."

"My pleasure," she said, giving him a hug. "It was one heck of a vacation. But it was all worth it." Pam looked at Jake with a dimpled smile.

"Well, guess I'll go make sure all our gear is stored right," Sam said, making his exit.

"In fact, I think this was just about the best vacation I ever had," Pam said, taking Jake's hand in her own.

Jake squeezed her hand. "You're all checked out of your hotel?"

"Yeah. Even said goodbye to the two Bureau agents assigned to keep an eye on me. I think they were happy they got to stay in a nice hotel for a change."

Jake frowned. "I'm still not thrilled Agent Russell was using us as bait."

"It wasn't quite that bad. It was for our protection, too."

"I'll admit it did work out in my favor, but Peter wasn't much of a threat by that point." After handcuffing Peter, and applying some first aid to his burning eyes, Agent Russell explained how he had kept Jake under surveillance, well aware that Eric wasn't the brains of the operation. Watching with binoculars from Harold and Vera's kitchen, Agent Russell was a bit surprised when Peter arrived. When he saw Peter and Jake disappear into the shed, he decided a closer reconnaissance was in order. The two beagles, however, also crossed the meadow, and after a brief visit with Al and Michelle, decided to check things out for themselves.

"But he did hear enough of Peter's story to show him who was behind it all."

"And that the two cases were related . . ."

"Just like you said they were. Have to admit, you have a knack for cold cases."

"Not sure about that. Twice now you've had to help me out of some pretty tough spots."

"You do have a tendency to get into trouble, I've noticed. Particularly for a mild-mannered egghead," Pam said, grinning.

"Hmm. Any ideas on how I can fix this flaw in my character?"

"I think it's obvious. You'd better keep me close by, Professor Caine, as close as you can. Sort of a bodyguard-slash-girlfriend. Especially if you plan to keep stirring up old crimes. Things heat up fast once you start your snooping."

"Hey, that's not fair. Both times it just worked out that way. You had more than your share to do with it, too."

"Well, maybe I am a jinx, like Heather said."

Jake's retort was drowned out by the arrival of the backhoe. Harold gave them a wave, and then started pushing clumps of frozen dirt back into the exposed units. Jake and Pam hurried away, taking up a position not far from where the first body had been found.

The northwesterly wind, blowing steadily all morning, had picked up and they stood shivering, stamping their feet, as the backhoe maneuvered in the clearing. Harold emptied one load, then drove to the opposite end to gather another. Pam knelt down and picked up a small lump of yellow clay.

"Do you think you'll ever figure out his story? The first bog body, I mean?"

Jake shrugged his shoulders, as the machinery rumbled like thunder across the clearing. "I'll try my best, but archaeology isn't always an exact science. All we can do it try to reconstruct the past based on limited clues. But I'll do my best to make sure his story is told."

STEVEN KUEHN IS A PROFESSIONAL ARCHAEOLOGIST working in the Midwest and has over thirty years of field and laboratory experience dealing with the identification, excavation, analysis, and interpretation of prehistoric and historic archaeological sites. He specializes in the analysis of faunal (animal) remains and has examined bone and shell from sites across North America. After preparing hundreds of technical reports and scholarly articles, the call of mystery fiction grew irresistible and Steve began chronicling the adventures of Professor Jacob Caine, archaeologist and reluctant sleuth. One Jake Caine short story, "Talked to Death," was published online in Mysterical-E. *Sunken Dreams* was the first novel in the Caine series; *Ghost Bog* is his second novel.